HUSH DARLING

A DARK PETER PAN RETELLING

VILLAINS
OF
KASSEL

LYDIA MICHAELS

PLAYLIST

Visit Spotify and listen to the music that inspired Hush Darling as you read!

DEDICATION

This one goes to the women who will never surrender their rights to a self-proclaimed king.

Fuck the patriarchy!
Literacy and human rights for all!

And on that note...
Being entertained by fictitious monsters does not condone monstrous behavior in real life.
Push us too far, and watch Beauty become the beast.

HUSH DARLING
A DARK PETER PAN RETELLING

A Villains of Kassel Novel

By Lydia Michaels

www.LydiaMichaelsBooks.com

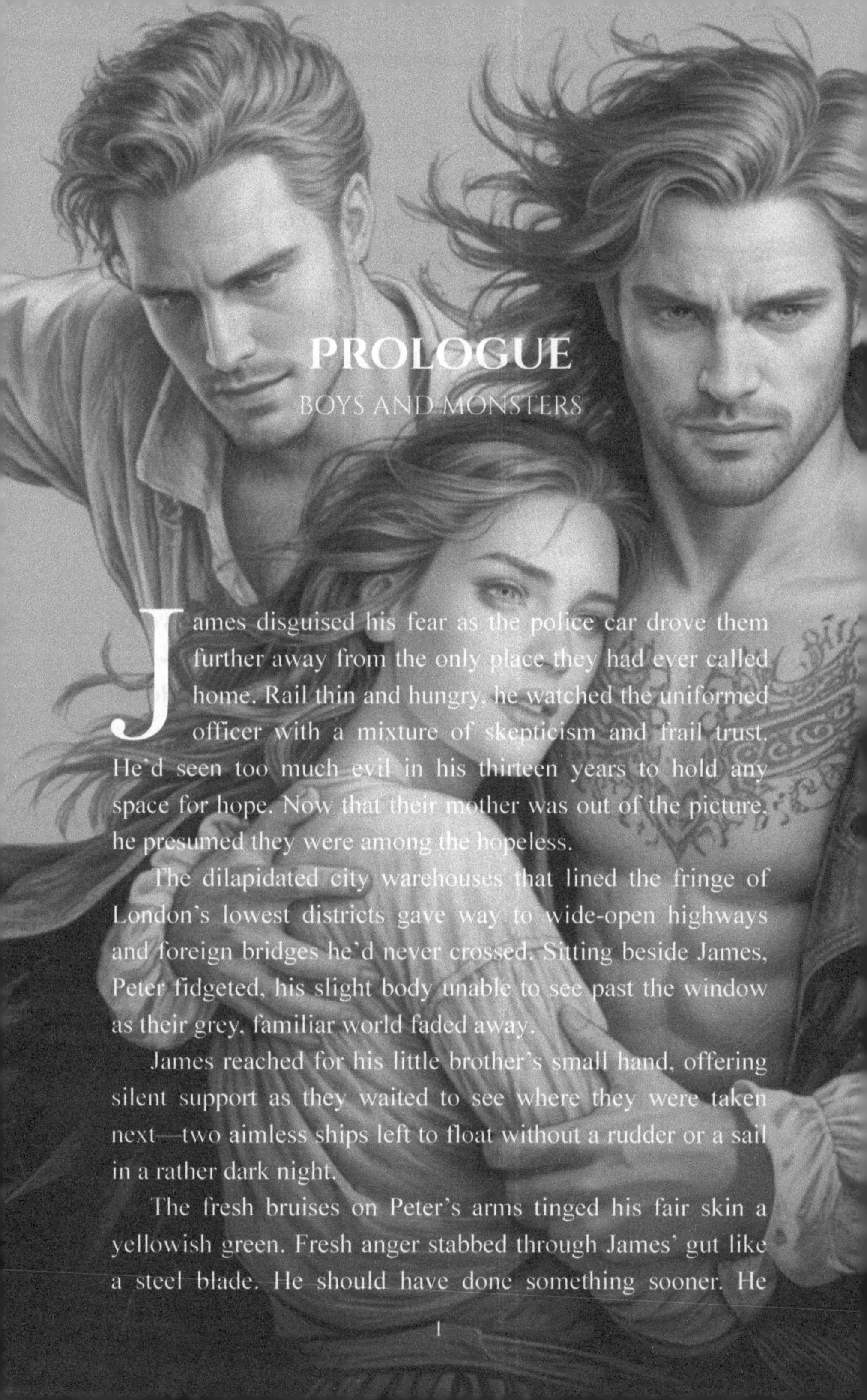

J ames disguised his fear as the police car drove them further away from the only place they had ever called home. Rail thin and hungry, he watched the uniformed officer with a mixture of skepticism and frail trust. He'd seen too much evil in his thirteen years to hold any space for hope. Now that their mother was out of the picture, he presumed they were among the hopeless.

The dilapidated city warehouses that lined the fringe of London's lowest districts gave way to wide-open highways and foreign bridges he'd never crossed. Sitting beside James, Peter fidgeted, his slight body unable to see past the window as their grey, familiar world faded away.

James reached for his little brother's small hand, offering silent support as they waited to see where they were taken next—two aimless ships left to float without a rudder or a sail in a rather dark night.

The fresh bruises on Peter's arms tinged his fair skin a yellowish green. Fresh anger stabbed through James' gut like a steel blade. He should have done something sooner. He should have protected Peter better. He had a duty to protect his brother that went beyond protecting himself.

James had welts, too, but, at the moment, he felt nothing beyond his fury toward the men who hurt Peter. That, and his worry over what would become of them now.

Turning away from the proof of abuse they survived, James glared out the window. His dark eyes reflected in the glass like two fathomless holes leading them into the unknown future. They could only move forward now because they were never going back there again. Their mother was going away for something called neglect, and the men that hurt Peter, well, James could only hope they eventually got what they deserved.

The radio of the squad car chirped as a static voice squawked from the speakers. According to the faceless voice on the other end, they were heading to Saint Mercy's Home for Orphaned Boys.

The officer driving the car had not been the one to rescue them. It was a female who found them. She smelled like roses, and her hair was soft like cotton. She told them they were safe. Then the house was swarming with men in uniforms, each wearing a copper badge and carrying a gun.

James had already forgotten the female agent's face, but he held onto her promise that they would be safe. She said there would be food and clothing and plenty of warm beds for him and Peter. There was a gentleness about her, something the male cops lacked, something James and Peter knew little about but both innately craved.

Peter was too young to understand what was happening but not too old to sense the finality of the day's events. Even at four, he knew enough to fear the unknown. He'd been hysterical when they pulled Mother away and put her in cuffs.

Too young to fully understand, he assumed the men in blue uniforms and copper badges were a threat, so he kicked and screamed when they loaded them into the back of the squad car.

James shut his eyes as the vision replayed. He'd wanted to kick and scream, too, but at thirteen, he was old enough to know that sort of behavior would change nothing. At least now, they would have regular meals, baths, and maybe even stories to help them sleep.

A soft sniffle caught his ear, and he glanced at Peter. His pale blond hair hadn't been washed in weeks, and there was still blood crusted around his nose.

"Hey." James reached across the sprawling bench seat and grabbed his little hand. "We're gonna be okay."

Peter wiped his nose on his threadbare sleeve. "Will Mother be able to find us?"

A cold fist tightened around James' heart. Their mother was the forgetful sort. So forgetful, that she often needed reminding that she had two sons. "Mother's going somewhere else."

"Will we see her again?"

Peter couldn't grasp that their mother had invited those men into the house, that she knew what was happening and did nothing to stop it. James didn't know if that information mattered now. "I don't know."

Peter stretched his dirty neck to peek out the window at the trees rushing by. "Where are they taking us?"

"An orphanage."

He looked up at him, dark circles rimming his big green eyes. "What's an orphanage?"

"It's a place where lost boys live."

That was what they were—lost boys. Lost. James wished

he had a compass for their future, but he only had his instincts.

"When we get there, try not to say too much. Just hold my hand and follow my lead."

Peter nodded, but fear was plain to see on his elfin face. "What if they separate us?"

"I won't let them."

"But…"

"Peter," he squeezed his hand. "They won't separate us. I promise. It's me and you—brothers forever. Understand?" When Peter nodded, James avowed, "Just keep hold of my hand."

He nodded and sniffled. "What if the bad men come?"

"There are no bad men there, Peter. Just boys."

The squad car slowed, and gravel crunched under the tires as they turned onto a long drive barricaded by tall, privet hedges and a towering iron gate.

The officer rolled down the window and pressed a button on a small box. "Sergeant Barrie here to drop off the Hook boys."

A buzz sounded, and the gate slowly creaked open. A giant stone fortress loomed like an impenetrable castle in the distance. Lifeless stone and cold metal bars created baricades of colorless grey behind leafless trees over the bleak and dreary sky. James tried to imagine how lovely it might look in the summers when the gardens were in bloom, but on this cold winter day, such an image was hard to conceive.

The car slowed, and Sergeant Barrie shut off the engine. "Here we are, boys."

Once escorted inside the mammoth stone building, they were instructed to wait on two cold wooden chairs lined up against the wall of a long, silent corridor.

James' heart beat like a slow, ticking clock keeping time, each steady thump echoing like a drop falling into whatever shallow water lined his empty stomach. Peter's feet dangled as he anxiously craned his neck to see into the room where the officer had disappeared.

"Tragic, just tragic," an aged female voice said. "Such innocent… Tarnished. It's a shame how some suffer—and the one at such a young age."

The voices grew nearer, and James sat up straight, ignoring the soreness of his spine and the way his skin pulled at the burns that had yet to fully heal. Placing a warning hand on Peter's leg, he silently urged him to stop fidgeting.

"We should have no problem placing the younger brother. The older ones are a bit more challenging."

James's hand tightened around his brother's as he focused on the whispered discussion about their future. He would not let them separate him from Peter.

"Parents often fear the older children have seen too many monstrosities. They worry how such past negative experiences might impact their future, especially if other children are already living in the home."

"They've suffered a lot, Sister," came the deep, caring voice of Sergeant Barrie. "It would be nice if they could stay together. Brothers need each other."

"Of course." Her tall, thick figure glided from the shadows of the doorway. Cloaked in layers of black, her robes hung like shingles of armor, absorbing any sound of movement as she neared. The only audible tell of her approach came from the heavy rosary beads hanging from her hip, clinking softly like clacking bones.

James sucked in a breath when she glanced over her shoulder and grinned at him. Instead of a smile, he glimpsed a slow, deliberate baring of teeth, yellowed and sharp enough to tear through flesh. She glided like a predator, patient and calm as if biding her time before breaking the illusion of safety.

"We will have them cleaned up and situated in no time. Prayer and a good night's sleep is just what the angels ordered."

Sergeant Barrie glanced back at the boys, his brow creasing with concern. "Perhaps dinner first."

"Of course," the nun nodded.

Her hair was hidden beneath a habit, making her dry, scaley skin all the more noticeable. It looked rigid and rough, like the hide of something that had lived in the dark far too long.

Her beady black eyes were chips of onyx and cold like stone. She took his and Peter's measure quickly, contrasting his value against his younger brother's as if they were a form of currency, and she was a swindler preparing to make a trade.

Didn't Sergeant Barrie see the monster before him? James got the same sick feeling he often felt when his mother brought home dangerous friends.

The reptilian way she appraised him and Peter twisted his stomach in knots. Beneath the black folds of her thick, draped clothing, she could have hidden a hundred weapons. He was certain those gnarled hands that folded as if in prayer hid razor-sharp claws.

She wore no labels or epaulets, only the crucifixion of a dying man. To him, the pendant did not symbolize sacrifice or devotion, only a sign of torment and suffering.

Sergeant Barrie couldn't leave them there. Her authority was apparent, but that did not make her just. James could sense her evil as if the air carried it heavily along the draft, this unrefined lust she concealed for power. She would command impeccable discipline and settle for nothing less.

James swallowed, wondering if he should stand or say something. Perhaps he should take Peter's hand and run. How far would they get? Where would they go? How would they survive?

"We thank you for your time, Officer."

"Sergeant," Sergeant Barrie corrected.

"Sergeant." As she reached out to shake his hand, James glimpsed something else hanging from her belt, tucked deep within the ripples of her black gown. It was thick and leathery, no wider than a ruler.

A chill raced down James' spine as the officer shook her gnarled hand. It was as if he'd just sealed a deal with the devil. "I didn't catch your name."

"Sister Nagina." The name slithered through her slanted teeth.

Peter looked up at him with worry in his emerald eyes. "James, must we live here?"

James frantically tried to think of a way out of their situation. His gut twisted when no alternative solution came.

This was not a happy place. Saint Mercy's Home for Orphaned Boys carried an air of cruelty that bit into the bones like a freezing wind, invisible but life-threatening. Their souls would see no nourishment here.

Sister Nagina looked the type to devour small creatures slowly over time. She'd silently stalk their every move like a crocodile wading at the water's edge, creating a false sense of safety that brought their guard down. Then, at the first sign of weakness, she'd snap.

James had seen her type before, calculating and patient, hungry and vicious. Torment was a game to them.

Sergeant Barrie approached the wall where they were seated and crouched low. "You boys are going to be okay."

James wondered if the lie sounded as unconvincing to the officer as it did to him.

"What about Mommy?" Peter asked, wiping away another tear.

"I'm sure she'll call when she can," Sergeant Barrie promised. Another lie. "I'll make sure she knows how to contact you."

Peter sniffled and leaned into James' shoulder, hugging his arm.

"You're doing God's work, Sergeant Barrie," Sister Nagina said as she glided in like an ominous fog. "Now, you must let us do the same."

The sergeant reluctantly stood and nodded goodbye. "You have my number if anything changes."

"Yes, Sergeant."

They watched silently as the sound of his booted footsteps faded down the dim corridor. Hinges creaked as a cold draft swept through the hall when the officer pulled open the heavy door. The wood moaned, and James flinched when it slammed shut as if the snapping jaws of this place were already dragging them under, far into the depths of the unknown.

"Stand up." Sister Nagina shattered the silence with a hissed command. "Stop that crying," she snapped at Peter.

James scowled and rose to his full height beside his brother, placing a protective hand on his shoulder. Peter wiped his eyes and clung to James, using his body as a shield from the scary nun.

"I want my mommy," Peter whimpered.

Like a shadow stretching over the dark waters of a swamp, still and quiet, she crossed the distance and—*SNAP*—her hand lashed out with the brutal swiftness slapping Peter's face.

"Are you crazy—"

Her hand whipped across James' cheek with equally brutal force, leaving his gaze on the floor and his question clipped. He tasted blood.

"You will not question me. Ever. Is that clear?"

He glared at her through a slow, boiling rage. It was a wonder how anything so ancient could move so quickly. Everything in him wanted to sever that hand from the bone so she could never strike another person again.

"Things will be different here. Eyes on the floor. *Now*."

They stared at the gloomy linoleum tile, the ripples of her gown fanning his periphery like the black banks of a swamp.

"Follow me." She glided down the hall, flowing black fabric waving in her wake as she educated them about the rules of their new home, which felt more like a prison with every passing minute. "You will not speak unless spoken to. Silence is enforced at all times, except for the whispering hour each day at two when you walk the yard—rain or shine. Dawdling will be punished, as will disrespect or possession of contraband. You are expected to be washed up with your beds made each morning before dawn. Breakfast is served at seven, lunch at noon, and supper at six. Food is never to leave the servery."

The scent of stew tinged the air, and James' hollow stomach growled, but the old crocodile kept slithering along, snarling orders.

"You will bathe in the evenings, promptly after supper. Once in your nightshirts, you will wash your day clothes and hang them to dry. Wring them out well. During the winter months, the fabric takes longer to dry, and lazy little boys with wet clothes often catch colds. Illness is not pampered here, as we believe brisk, laborious exercise is the best opponent to sickness. One boy's poor judgment mustn't infect the whole."

She led them up a silent stairwell where the air chilled several degrees cooler. Peter climbed the stairs two steps at a time, earning a cold stare from Sister Nagina as she waited. Peter whimpered at her glare and doubled his speed, accidentally tripping on the last step and falling at her feet.

Her shadow stretched like a looming storm. Violence lurked in the stillness, so James rushed forward to help his brother. Stretching out his hand, he met her beady stare with challenge. She grinned, feeding on their fear the way the predator feeds on prey.

She waved a hand toward a dark room. "Inside."

James hesitated until she poked him forward. The room was frigid with exposed stone walls. Several copper tubs lined up like soldiers.

"Remove your clothes and place them in the rubbish bin. They'll be incinerated in the morning." She handed them a folded nightshirt, the material stiff and itchy. A bar of home-made soap rested on top. "Fill the tubs and wash your bodies, head to toe. Cleanliness is next to godliness."

A pump protruded from the wall, and wooden buckets were available to transfer water. Peter followed him to the wall. They used the pails to fill the tubs, but there was no hot water, and when they removed their clothes, their teeth chattered.

Peter shivered. His bony shoulders shook as his spine protruded, making the bruises on his back all the more prominent. James hushed him before the old nun overheard his whimpering.

"Wash quickly. Then wait on the bench."

James feared what the sleeping quarters might look like if this was the washroom.

She placed an ornate wooden box with gold corners on the table and lifted the lid, blocking the contents from view. From the guts of the box, she pulled a straightedge blade and the sharpest pair of scissors James had ever seen.

"Long hair attracts mites and other unwelcome guests," she said, rounding the bench to stand behind them.

Shivering from their cold baths, they sat on the bench as Sister Nagina cut their hair. Dark hanks of James' brown hair fell to the floor, mixing with the soft, flaxen ringlets of Peter's. His neck and shoulders itched after the haircut, but they were not given anything to brush the pokey hairs away.

Once they were dressed and the tubs were emptied, Sister Nagina led them to the top floor, where the air was coldest. A steady draft seeped through what was likely a broken window, but James could not find the source of the steady current of cold.

She led them to an open dormitory filled with simple beds. The boys all wore the same vacant stare when they looked at James. They kneeled at the side of each bed. Heads shaved just like theirs bent over folded hands. There must have been forty of them, each boy's thin body dressed in the same grey rags James and Peter now wore.

Below the howling moan of the London winds, words murmured like incantations from their lips, fading to silence as danger encroached. Their whispered prayers trembled from their lips in a soft babble too low to translate.

Sister Nagina dutifully inspected each boy's cot with an observant glance as James and Peter followed her to the end of the long room. The other boys observed them, some with curiosity, others with motive.

She pointed to two stripped cots at the end of the long row and faced them. "Make your beds and say your prayers."

James knew no prayers. But he didn't dare admit such a shortcoming. He would learn from watching the others, and he would not stay here long.

She slithered back down the aisle like a cold-blooded reptile into the murk.

Peter's chin trembled as he stared up at James. His mouth opened, and James hooked a finger across his lips, warning him to stay silent.

He showed Peter how to make his bed with the stiff sheet and coarse blanket. He was so exhausted he struggled to think of anything encouraging to say, failing even to remember happier times.

For tonight, James only wanted to dream of places where boys could fly away like mythical creatures on wings, away from the shouting, fighting, and life's painful things. He didn't know any prayers, so he made wishes in his head. He wished to be far from rigid rules and free of this prison for boys. He did not want to stay in a place where children were forbidden to laugh, sing, or play.

By the time the lights went out, James had Peter tucked into his bed. "Just try to think happy thoughts," he told him as he placed a kiss on his head.

"This place is scary, James. I wanna go home."

James didn't know how to explain that this was their home now. "It's only for a little while. I swear, you won't have to stay here long."

"Promise?" Peter held out his little hand, and James grinned. From the moment he taught his brother that a man's handshake was equal to a vow, he clung to that security and used it whenever he wanted guarantees.

James placed his hand in his and squeezed. "I promise."

That night, James dreamed of a place where they could escape. A place where they were never hit, and lost boys were free. He dreamed of wild adventures and long journeys at sea. He dreamed himself powerful, tall, strong, and honorable. He saw a man who could never be bested by monsters again.

It was a magical place he wasn't sure existed. It called to him, stirring a sort of wanderlust in his soul, and when he closed his eyes, he could almost taste the salty sea air on his lips and the freedom promised by such a mammoth ship underfoot.

The clouds would never gather, and the wind would never blow cold. There would be no evil that could beat him because he would be the most powerful man of all.

He did not know if such a Never Land could exist, but he wanted to believe. He wanted to dream himself an untethered force, as free as the wild sea. But as his imagination drifted into a deep slumber, he sensed a siren's kiss pulling him further under. And as his dreams took shame in his mind, a sharp ache formed within his wrist. Instinct tickled up his spine and warned there would be a price for such bliss.

Chapter 1

THE LOST HOPES OF LITTLE GIRLS

Slamming the door, Wendy threw herself onto the bed and wept at the injustice. Tonight was supposed to be *her* night. She waited eighteen long years to garner an invitation to the exclusive gala, and this was her year, but her father had spoiled her plans once again.

She reached for her phone, prepared to text her friends a boiling rant of profanity about how smothering her parents could be, but her screen opened to her social media, and she was bombarded with pictures of her peers dressed for tonight's event.

"Fuck my life." She tossed the phone aside, unable to stomach her friends' joy without being eaten alive by her own jealousy.

The soft wrap of her mother's knuckles preceded the creek of the door. "Wendy, darling, he didn't do it on purpose."

Of course, her mother would defend her father. "He knew how much this night meant to me," Wendy argued, her makeup smearing on the chenille pillowcase.

"Obviously, he didn't, or he would have secured the ticket."

"I told him, Mother! It's all I've talked about for months. He never listens to anything I say!"

Her mother pressed a comforting hand on her back. "Your father's a busy man. He has a lot on his plate."

Wendy sat up, the chiffon sleeve of her ivory gown drooping off her shoulder as a curl spiraled free of her French twist. "He knew what tonight meant to me, and he purposely forgot so I couldn't go. He hates that I'm eighteen now."

Her father was a numbers man, invested in finance and deeply rooted in classical education. He never forgot a date. Nor did he ever overlook an opportunity. This ball would have muddled his control of her future, and he couldn't bear the thought, so he intentionally spoiled her plans by not procuring the correct number of tickets. A calculated lie if she'd ever seen one!

"Father lies when it suits him. If you weren't so enchanted by his charm, you'd see that he's as cunning as a pirate when he wants to be."

Mother scoffed. "Lies? Pirates? Really, Wendy. If you want to be treated like an adult, you must start acting like one. Your father is not out to ruin your life."

"He wants to control everything."

"Enough." Her mother stood, her shimmering sage gown a beautiful taunt that pierced Wendy's heart with envy. "Your father's doing everything he can to secure you a decent engagement."

"You mean he's trying to control my future just like he controls my life now!" How had modern times turned so incredibly old-fashioned where women were concerned? "Did either of you ever think I might want more than a secure marriage and to start a family? What about *my* dreams? What about love?"

"You should be grateful for his guidance. Your father is a wise man who knows a great deal about how the world works."

"If he thinks guiding me toward a man like Peter Pangbourne is wise, then I question his judgment. Not all fortunate men are wealthy in morals, Mother. Peter is far more duplicitous than Father sees."

"The Pangbournes are a good family with strong values, darling. You should be grateful such a prosperous match is even on the table."

She was never escaping this prison. Years after her brothers John and Michael left the nursery, she remained confined by the whimsical, childish trappings—caged in a place designed to keep her innocent.

At eighteen, she was as unchanged as the fixtures in the starlit sky where the constellations never shifted and the masculine planets orbited freely. Girls deserved more than to exist as a backdrop to stars, but decades of advancements in equal rights were somehow being washed away. Scrubbed out by the men who needed to feel superior and rinsed clean by the women who blindly stood by such men. There was a quiet resistance, but it was fading, and every day, Wendy felt less and less in control of her future.

A tear rolled from the corner of her eye as a sense of hopelessness consumed her. Numerous books on the shelves boasted of adventures she'd never know. She was a confined bird, clipped at the wings, with an unsatisfied hunger to explore.

She dreamed of soaring over distant oceans and breathing in the petrichor of foreign soil as rain and mist rolled onto the remote shores. She longed to stand clad in buffalo leather amidst the wildest jungles, to know the exact color of the sunset over the Mojave Desert, and to feel the heat of the Egyptian wind racing through her hair as the sandy heat roughly kissed her skin.

Eighteen years old, and she knew nothing of independent adventures or kisses of any kind. She only knew the constricting confinement of being a girl and all the expectations that suppressed her desires for something wild.

It happened so subtly, the shift from unbound innocence to confinement. With the budding of her breasts came polite correction and refinement her brothers' had never experienced. They knew little of decorum and etiquette, yet their female counterparts suffered such outdated catechisms as if meekness were a rite of passage to the next stage.

But why would any woman seek the approval of a self-proclaimed superior man? Wouldn't that only undermine her independence further?

Every time Wendy was told to cross her legs or sit up straight, a rage burned inside of her. When she was ordered to stop climbing trees and taught to speak in a softer voice, the confinement took her breath away—no oxygen to feed the flame of injustice, and she'd ignorantly conformed until she turned into someone unrecognizable to herself.

Propriety and traditional grooming shaped her in ways that hinted her authentic self was wrong, and that created shame and pressure to conform. Proper society stripped away individuality, stating tenacity was suddenly too forward. They praised familiarity and condemned the alternative, using stigmatized terms like Prima donna, extra, bratty, or diva when all of those things used to mean a woman knew her value and had the courage to expect more.

Regardless of her personal dreams, Wendy slowly started to look like every other young woman in her parents' social circles. Uniform and conventional. They praised her uniqueness as a child, then stifled it as a teen. She never strived for conformity, but she achieved it all the same. Now, as an adult, she wore the constant constriction of values that were not hers.

Why? Because she allowed it to come to this. She stood silently as their traditional ideals cinched tighter and tighter around her life. Little by little, she adapted to the suffocation, making herself smaller, quieter, and less disruptive as she eventually learned how not to breathe. They squeezed out anything unrefined until she didn't know how to exist any other way.

"What is it that men are so afraid of?"

Her mother met her stare in the long mirror. "Pardon?"

"Why are boys permitted to run free and praised for their brave feats while girls are caged like never birds, never given the same chance to fly or stretch beyond their corset strings? Perhaps they're afraid of being outshone? We are the smarter gender, after all."

"Now, you're just being hysterical, dear."

"Right there! Why are women *hysterical,* but men are ballsy when they question the status quo?"

"Trashy language is not going to win any arguments, Wendy. Women might be smarter in some aspects, but so are men. We're made differently."

Wendy groaned and threw herself back on her bed. If she had to listen to one more closed-minded lesson about how boys were boys and girls were girls, she was going to scream. "Women can do anything men can do, Mother."

"Oh, really? Can you pilot a plane?"

"Yes! If I were trained, I could. In school, John always had lower grades than me. I could have destroyed him in flight school, but Father said a pilot wasn't a proper position for a girl!"

Her mother sighed and sidestepped the familiar debate. On some level, Wendy believed she saw the misogyny, but she would never betray her Father, the head of their household, and admit to such notions. It was easier for her to simply agree and conform.

"There are dangers in the real world, Wendy. Women must know how to protect themselves. A good marriage offers a sense of security you'll one day come to appreciate."

"What about passion and love? Aren't they a part of the equation?"

"Conserve your energy for more productive ventures, darling." Her mother tucked the wily curl behind her ear and smiled at her reflection, pleased. "Sink your passions into something rewarding, like charity. Leave the boys to their grandiose ways. Trust me, women are better off avoiding such extremes."

Her future darkened every time her mother showered her dull advice in favor of a quiet life. She might have been content with such a fate, but Wendy would never be one to settle so easily, not without first experiencing both sides.

She craved a rush of adrenaline and could taste the untapped freedom just outside of her latched windows. She'd suffer any hardship to bring that fire inside of her back to life again. She dreamed of uncontainable passion and unpredictable adventures. Such things might cost her every security she knew, but in her heart, she would settle for nothing less.

"I want to be challenged."

"Well, you are rather challenging, dear, so I imagine you'll get your wish."

"You only say that because I'm stubborn, and I know what I want."

"I say that because I know what's possible. Eventually, we all put the fairytale ideals aside."

Wendy planned to do no such thing. She would settle for nothing less than the love of a man who would risk everything to reach her. Her parents knew nothing of such love. They lived in a world of rules and numbers and pragmatic civility.

"You should trust your father's judgment, Wendy. Peter Pangbourne is a handsome young man. Many girls your age would be thrilled to have his attention."

"And many girls do."

Her mother's glare sliced into her from where it reflected in the mirror. "Don't be smart."

Wendy pursed her lips so as not to earn more disapproving looks like that.

What kind of statement was that anyway? *Don't be smart*...

Wendy *was* smart. Smart enough to know Peter was not the kind of man to honor his promises or settle down with one woman.

She wouldn't deny Peter was attractive with his athletic build, sun-kissed tan, and unruly golden curls, but he knew he was handsome, and his arrogance left something to be desired. He'd been texting her on and off since they'd been introduced, but Wendy wasn't gullible enough to believe she was the only one in his call log.

Peter made the impression of a well-mannered, high-society gentleman, but Wendy saw through his façade when he started asking her personal questions. The real Peter Pangbourne had no issue crossing the line of propriety, and it was quite duplicitous of him to have his elders so seamlessly convinced he was a well-mannered man.

His texts not only made Wendy blush but often left her fidgety to the point that her body clenched in strange places. He teased her in a way that made her squirm like bait on a hook. He spoke of mysterious things that left her painfully intrigued, but giving in felt too much like surrendering her choice. She didn't want her parents to decide her future. She wanted the right to be selective and experience a magnitude of things before making her final choice.

"Father only favors Peter because his family is one of the wealthiest in London."

"Wealth is a deserving quality of favor, Wendy." Her mother brushed the wrinkles from her gown. "A wise woman must be financially literate. It's a role we all must play. Without a decent fortune, there would be no property, security, or help within the home. Passion can leave you destitute if you're not careful. Money buys you freedom, so I suggest you marry for wealth. After all, how else would you afford the books you so love? Can't you be content with the adventures in your library?"

Wendy scoffed in her wasted gown. "I've never even waltzed with anyone besides Father. Some experiences need more than paper and ink to be felt, Mother."

"You'll feel all of those things in due time—when you meet the right man and get to know each other."

Would that happen before or after the vows? Wendy rolled her eyes. "That's easy for you to say. You married someone you love."

"True, I love your father very much, but that's not why I married him."

"Then why?"

She dabbed away the gloss at the corner of her mouth as she once more stared in the mirror. "He seemed…sensible."

"Sensible?" Wendy curled her lip. "Was he at least handsome?"

Her mother chuckled in that dulcet bell-like way she so often did. "Your father is *still* handsome."

A soft knock rapped on the door, and John, her eldest brother, stepped in. "Father's ready to leave."

Wendy's vision blurred as she rushed to her brother. "Oh, John, you must give me your ticket. Please! I'll trade you anything!"

"Sorry, sis. I can't. Jenna's already expecting me."

She pursed her lips. Jenna was only seventeen. Why should she attend the gala if Wendy couldn't? She turned back to her mother. "Are you sure Father didn't get Michael a ticket?"

"I'm sure. You know Michael. He's not interested in such things."

"What's taking everyone so long?" Her father appeared behind John. "The limousine is waiting."

Wendy looked away, infuriated by his stubbornness and her tears.

"In a moment, darling." Her mother moved to the dresser. "Wendy, where's your diamond tennis bracelet? I want to borrow it."

Her request was salt in the wound. "Seriously, Mother?"

"Don't be a sourpuss," John said, righting his tie in the mirror as he winked at her.

"All of you, get out of my room!" Wendy snapped.

How dare they mock her feelings?

Outside, Nana barked wildly.

"What in God's name is that dog barking at now?" her father griped, marching to the window to stare through the marbled glass.

"It's too late for deliveries. Something must be out there, George. It's likely just a squirrel or a raccoon."

"It's the driver. He's waiting for us by the gate."

"I'll be ready in a minute." Her mother clipped the diamond bracelet around her ivory-gloved wrist and moved to the window seat. "Where did these leaves come from, Wendy? Did you have the windows open?"

"Why would I have the windows open, Mother?"

Her mother checked the latch, and jealousy twisted in Wendy's stomach as they approached the door. She refused to wish any of them a good night, so she turned her back to the lot of them.

"I just need my stole, George darling, and then I'm ready."

Her father sighed. "John, tell the driver we'll be right there."

They left the nursery without another glance back, and Wendy blinked through the pain of abandonment. Once more, she was forgotten and overlooked.

Deep down, she believed her father did not secure her ticket because he feared she'd embarrass him. He knew she had an unruly side, and he urged her to be more like the refined daughters of his friends. But the longer he held her back, the further she desired to run from his expectations. She wanted to shatter them so he would see, once and for all, that she was her own person.

The click of the front door punctuated their descending footsteps and fading chatter. The house fell into empty silence.

Wendy growled and fell back on her bed. *"Ouch."* Plucking a hairpin from her hair, she scowled and then threw it to the nightstand.

Nana continued to bark even after the limo drove away. She went to the window to see what was out there, but the surrounding mansions were dark, the inhabitants most likely on their way to the ball.

With a sigh, she stepped into the shadows and unzipped her gown, letting it fall into a puddle of wilted chiffon. Slipping out of her undergarments, she pulled on a plain white nightgown and unpinned her hair.

Her eyes narrowed on her reflection as childlike ringlets coiled about her cheeks. Her mind and body were not that of a little girl anymore, yet here she was, dressed the same and ready for bed by eight.

Grinding her molars, she shook out her curls until dark waves fell wildly down her shoulders and back. The dark coal around her eyes had smudged from tears, leaving her blue eyes more prominent than usual. She looked dangerous and slightly unhinged. She liked seeing herself that way and wished others could see this side of her, too.

Her mind once again drifted to Peter Pangbourne. "Let's see what you think of me now, Peter." She reached for her phone, angling the lens upward as she formed a pout with her lips. She snapped a picture and sent it to him.

Her father misjudged him and she should show him just how much. There was something different about Peter. He might dress in designer clothes like the other men of society, but something untamable lingered beneath his surface.

When she first met him, he smelled of grass and wilderness, not the typical scent of a refined gentleman. And once he started texting her in that forward, flirty way, he confirmed that he had a darker side. That was the only side that interested her.

A loud crash broke the silence, and she jolted upright, bolting to her feet. Nana went berserk on the back lawn, barking wildly as Wendy rushed to the door. Cool air teased her ankles, the draft rushing up the stairs from the foyer.

She snatched her robe from the bedpost and rushed downstairs. A chill raced up her spine as she crept along the banister.

"Liza?"

The maid didn't answer.

Perhaps she forgot to latch the door. That would explain such a draft, but what was that crash? Wendy tightened the belt of her robe as another chill raced over her skin.

"Michael?" Perhaps her brother had come by. "Is someone there?"

The fine hairs at the nape of her neck tickled as she crossed the foyer and found the front door gaping open. A sense of unease passed through her as her nightgown fluttered at her ankles with the creeping fog.

"Hello?" She shut the door and jumped when the grandfather clock gonged. The droning clang marked the late hour with a repetitive toll. "Stupid clock."

Nana's bark grew louder. The foolish dog was likely barking at branches rustling in the wind.

"Liza, you left the door unlocked." *Silly maid.* Or perhaps it was her father who forgot to lock the door. "Liza?"

"Gotcha!"

"Ah—Mmph!" A masculine hand clamped over her mouth as the urn in the foyer wobbled and shattered into pieces.

She swung her arms and tried to scream, but the intruder immobilized her. Her eyes widened in utter panic as a thickly muscled arm banded about her waist, lifting her back to his chest.

"I've got you now, Wendy Darling," the masculine voice growled in her ear, and she shrieked, biting into the hand hard enough to provoke a curse from her assailant.

He swept her off her feet before she could break free. Kicking her legs, she clawed at whoever held her. *"Let go of me!"*

His grip only tightened as his dark chuckle tickled her ear, and the scent of wild grass teased her nose. "Hush, little darling, it will all be over soon."

CHAPTER 2

THE SHADOWS OF MEN

Recognition flooded Wendy in a wave of relief and fury. She slammed an elbow into his ribs as hard as she could manage, and he grunted, loosening his hold.

Her feet hit the floor, and she shoved him. "You scared the hell out of me, Peter!"

His mocking chuckle should have aggravated her more, but it somehow softened her fury. "You started it. You should know better than to send a man a picture of yourself looking tousled and freshly fucked."

Her cheeks burned. "That's not what I look like."

"But it is." He reached out a hand and tugged at her unkempt hair. "I just so happened to be nearby when I saw the house was dark. All but your bedroom…"

Flustered, she swatted his hand away from her face and cinched the belt of her robe. "And how do you know which room is mine?"

Rather than answer, he sauntered into her father's study and dropped into the high-back leather chair, kicking his feet up on the desk. "Watch the broken glass." He crossed his legs at the ankle as he lounged back, folding his hands behind his head as if he owned the place.

She tiptoed around the shards. "That vase was an heirloom."

"Oh, no." He said dryly, swiping the gold letter opener off the desk to examine the tip. "How come you didn't go to the party tonight?"

"That silly party? I'd rather save my energy for better things."

He laughed. "Such as?"

She tried to mirror his nonchalance. "Wouldn't you like to know?"

He raised a sharp blond brow with a look of indifference that infuriated her. She detested his lack of concern. Some part of her deeply wanted to matter to him. Maybe not him, but to someone. And she despised the existence of such neediness inside of her, so she concealed it as best she could, turning her attention to the mess on the floor.

Her mother's prized vase was destroyed, and her parents would require an explanation. No one would believe her if she told them Peter Pangbourne had done this.

"I need to find Liza."

"Who's Liza?"

"Our housekeeper."

"She's out back with some guy's arm half up her skirt."

Wendy's eyes bulged. "She is not."

He smirked. "Check for yourself. Why do you think the dog's going nuts?"

Wendy rushed to the window. Sure enough, a couple hid in the shadows of the carriage house. Liza's body pressed to the wall, her leg hooked around some man's hip as the tall figure bucked into her.

Wendy gasped and covered her mouth, turning her back on the erotic image. A million questions raced through her mind. Who was that man groping the maid? Did Liza know him? Did she want his hands on her in such a rough and aggressive way? Liza was only a few years older than Wendy, yet she appeared so…comfortable in the shadows, doing dark deeds. Where did she learn such things?

"Don't look so shocked."

Her eyes met Peter's. "Who is that guy?"

He shrugged and sauntered to the window to get another peek. "If I had to guess, he probably works for the neighbor. The help's always fucking other help."

"Liza has never—"

He drew back the curtain. "*That* is not the body language of an ignorant woman, Wendy."

"Stop that!" She rushed forward and drew the drapes shut. "They'll see us."

Peter laughed. "Dalliance is good for them. When they fuck each other, it keeps them from fucking over us." He flashed a devious smirk. "Who knew you were such a prude?"

"I'm not a prude, I'm…" She was shocked, intrigued, and *very* curious. Crossing her arms, she lifted her chin. "I don't judge."

"You're judging them right now."

"Am not!"

"Look at you. You're completely—"

"Completely *what,* Peter? I'll remind you you're in *my* house. Choose your words carefully."

"Because you're so delicate you might get offended? Please. Call your shock whatever you want, but your innocence is showing. They're just having fun. Haven't you ever slipped into the shadows with a man just for the thrill of it?"

The burn on her cheeks intensified, and he drew back, a knowing understanding flashing in his eyes.

"You haven't? Not even once?"

"That's none of your business!"

That quickly, he lost interest in her personal escapades, which were few and far between, and shrugged with indifference. "You're not gonna tell on the poor girl, are you?"

"I would never!" Though she had initially thought this was something her parents should know, she would hate to see Liza fired. Although she was on the payroll, she was also something Wendy thought of as a confidante and a friend.

Gah! How pathetic to think of the maid as one of her closest friends.

She glanced back at the window, but from her current position, she could only make out the lamplight in the mist. Perhaps that was the luxury of a lower social class—the women seemed to have complete autonomy and the freedom to do as they pleased. Wendy had no idea who Liza answered to when off the clock. For all she knew, the girl lived alone.

If they were friends, Wendy wasn't a very good one. She settled into one of the button-back chairs, feigning nonchalance while every nerve in her body seemed to vibrate with a sense of impending uncertainty.

Seeing Liza had charged the air with carnal energy. Peter glanced around the room. Each time his gaze settled on the spine of a book, or he touched a unique trinket tied to a personal Darling family anecdote, she felt as if he were touching her in secret places.

His cavalier persona filled her with uncertainty. She didn't feel unsafe around him, but she also didn't trust his motives.

Something about his careless demeanor mocked her family's position despite his parents having six times the fortune of hers.

Everything about him screamed wealth, yet he always appeared somehow tousled and half put together, as though he threw his clothes on in a rush. Which made her wonder why she assumed his clothes were off in the first place.

Drawing in a slow, deep breath, she tried to trace his earthy scent. Did she sense a touch of women's perfume?

She wished he would say something, but he seemed to forget she was there. He pulled a book down from the shelf and paged through the chapters. Dropping into a wingback chair, his long legs landed in a sloppy tangle as if he were bored and forced to wait there.

She tried to think of something clever to say but worried she might be a disturbance. What did men and women talk about on dates? She was utterly clueless but knew enough to know that she was not impressing him. Did she even want to impress him? She certainly didn't want him to leave with the impression that she was an immature child.

In his silence, the house faintly creaked as it settled. The lingering trail of her mother's lavender perfume tinged the air, and the soft prattle of rain tickled the dry leaves that covered the earth. It was as though time had frozen, and the muffled sounds of London's typically noisy streets were miles away.

Peter threw down the book he held and sprung to his feet as if catapulted from the wing-back chair and prepared to rush off to his next adventure.

"Wine?" she blurted, strangely compelled to keep him there.

He stilled and shrugged. "Sure."

Breezing past her, he helped himself to her father's collection. Uncorking the crystal decanter at the bar, he sniffed it. That was her mother's personal favorite. Wendy swallowed, hoping he didn't take enough for her parents to notice.

Liquid trickled into a glass, breaking the silence as the dry scent of flowers and fruit filled the air. He poured with the familiarity of someone who had indulged many times before.

Walking a glass across the room, he slid the long stem into her hand. "For you."

"Thanks." She watched his fingers and mimicked his hold of the cup.

Funny how each room could hold such a different feeling in one house. While the nursery was a familiar place of safety and innocence, her father's study was the opposite. She typically only came in here when her father gave her a lecture.

Peter returned to her father's chair—a throne of authority in this house—and raised his glass. "Drink."

She sipped, and a warm, calm bloomed in her chest. The flavor was rather pleasant, softening her posture when it hit her belly. Who knew wine could have such an immediate effect on a person's tension? No wonder her mother enjoyed her evening glass so much.

Peter studied her, sipping his wine in a silent challenge, and she matched him swallow for swallow. They played this game for several minutes, and by the time her glass was half empty, her worries seemed small and foolish—little laughable wisps of nothing. So she giggled.

"Something funny?"

The wine had placed an unbreakable bubble of amusement in her throat. "Not particularly." She smiled and slouched back in her chair, studying him with undisguised interest.

While she might not want to marry him, there was something undeniably fascinating about Peter Pangbourne. Perhaps it was his duality. Her father didn't see the side of him she thought of as his shadowed self, a side of him that intrigued her far more than the façade he adorned in proper company.

When she finished her glass, she decided she liked wine very much. She also decided to unravel the mystery that was Peter Pangbourne.

Lifting her glass, she said, "I think I'd like some more."

He carried the decanter from the bar. Once wine filled her cup again, he left it on the surface of her father's desk. How would she replace the stolen contents before her parents returned? The worry disappeared as quickly as it arrived.

Instead of returning to the chair, he casually leaned against the edge of the desk, stretching his legs directly across from her.

She looked up as she sipped her wine, drawn to this darker, reckless side of him. Gentlemen bored her as much as twittering debutantes, but trespassers and thieves… They held an edge of intrigue.

Was that what Peter was at heart? Wicked and immoral? How far would he go to break the rules of society, and how much was he willing to fall out of favor? Perhaps he could help her after all.

"Your lips are red." His eyes creased in the corners as he watched her over the rim of his glass with that dark emerald stare.

Her fingers rushed to her mouth, and she flushed. Where was that sense of numbness coming from? Her fingers? Her face? She laughed. "I feel a bit like I'm floating on a cloud." The wine seemed to filter reality as if this were all a dream and the consequence wasn't real.

"You're drunk." He set down his glass.

"After one glass?" Was that even possible?

"I don't mind a lightweight." He leaned over her, pressing his hands into the arms of the chair. "I wonder, does your mouth taste sweet like grapes now?"

Her heart skipped a beat as she swept her tongue over her lips. "I think yes."

"I bet your lips are warm, too, like fresh fruit on the vine." He stood only a breath away. "Or maybe they're bitter like tart poison?"

She scowled. "Why would my lips be bitter?"

"Maybe petulance has soured you." The side of his smile kicked up. "There's something rigid inside of you, something that doesn't know how to bend."

She scoffed. "I'm not petulant."

"You're snippy. That's the exact definition of petulance."

"Are you suggesting I have a stick up my ass?"

"I'd bet my entire fortune nothing's ever been near your ass." His gaze briefly dropped to her chest, then returned to her eyes. "You care too much about what other people think. Stuck between society's expectations and your desires…It's why you're so tense. You're like a taut rope in a tug-of-war with no give."

"You think I'm prissy," she whispered, a pinch of shame nipping through the numbness.

"I *know* you're prissy, but that's not the problem."

"You think I have a problem?" Her brows drew together.

"A big problem."

Should she be frightened? The wine had muddled her thinking, and she was a bit confused. "W-what is it?"

"I think, little darling, you're wound too tight. You need someone to give it to you, just like that guy's giving it to your housekeeper right now—hard and rough enough to rattle your teeth." He laughed. "But by the look of shock on your face, I bet you've never even been kissed. At least not properly."

Cold dread crawled through her. Was her naiveté that transparent?

Her gaze dropped, but he caught her chin, forcing her to keep looking at him. "It's true then." He cocked his head, a small divot forming between his blond brows. "Is it because you don't like men?"

"No. I like...men."

She didn't want to confess her innocence was the result of captivity, that she had the autonomy of a child, always accounted for, and never allowed to roam free. He would laugh and make fun of her if he knew the extent of her parents' control.

"Then why has no one kissed you?"

"There hasn't really been the opportunity—"

"Oh, please." He released her and paced to the desk. "If a woman wants to be kissed, she is kissed. You obviously don't want such things."

She sat up. "But I do!"

"Then why has no one kissed you yet?" He was back to leaning over her again, his quick movements leaving her dizzy.

What excuse could she offer? The truth was, she lived the sheltered life of a child. Perhaps it was better to be seen as a priss. "No one has impressed me enough to earn *my* kisses. Did you ever think of that?"

He grinned. "That was my first thought."

Relieved, she sighed.

But then he was in front of her again, leaning closer as he whispered, "Do I meet your high standards, Ms. Darling?"

Her back pressed into the chair, and her heart raced. Did

he meet her standards? She wasn't sure they were all that high when it came to kissing. It was only a kiss, and she hated not knowing what such simple things felt like. But she was hardly going to throw herself at him. He'd enjoy that too much.

"I'm still deciding," she said, tipping up her chin.

He gave her space, so she set down her once again empty glass and straightened her mother's sewing box on the table, hoping to relieve the fidgety energy that bounced inside of her. When she accidentally knocked an antique thimble onto the floor, it plunked softly onto the carpet and then rolled noisily onto the planked floor.

"Shoot."

"I've got it." Peter scooped the thimble up like a handful of jacks and tossed it casually in the air. He held open his palm, and she stared up at him as if it were a trap. "Take it."

Her lungs tightened as she held his stare. Touching him felt like consenting to something unknown, so she held her palm open below his. The slight weight dropped into her hand, and she closed her fist and then frowned in confusion when something sharp poked her. She opened her fist and found not a thimble but an acorn in her palm.

"How…?"

He tossed the thimble in the air, flashing an arrogant grin as he caught it with the dexterity of a magician. "Things aren't always as they seem."

A strange shiver rushed through her as if marking this moment in time with a stitch. She felt the shift in her soul as if her decision in the next few seconds would change the trajectory of her entire life.

"Why did you come here, Peter?"

"Because there's something different about you. I knew it

the first time I met you. You're not like the others. You try to be, but you're not very good at it."

She scowled. "What does that mean?"

"Trust me, it's a compliment." Her breath hitched as he shifted closer without noticeably moving. "Don't be scared," he whispered, delicately tucking a wisp of hair behind her ear. His warm breath mingled with hers as his head slowly tipped—

"Wait!" She ducked under his arm and jumped to her feet.

"What's wrong?"

She shut the door, pressing her back to the wood and ensuring they had privacy. But when his green eyes settled on her, something twisted in her chest.

This was wrong. Not because it was improper but because it was Peter. A strange sense of deja vu flooded her as if she'd been here before. Perhaps it was the wine, but something unsettled her stomach and made her doubt everything she was about to do.

"I…"

"You don't have to fear me, Wendy. We're more alike than you realize."

How did he know what she was like? She was overthinking. The kiss needed to happen. It was time. So what if Peter was the first man to kiss her? Kisses were meaningless in the grand scheme of things.

She was putting too much thought into this. If she didn't get out of her head it was never going to happen. "Liza could come back at any moment."

He sauntered across the room with the confidence of a wild jungle cat. "It would be rather hypocritical of her to tattle on you, don't you think?"

Why did she shut the door? Closing herself in with him

felt like a mistake. But as long as they were behind closed doors, no one would know what they'd done, and that—strangely—felt right. Something inside of her demanded this moment stay a secret.

That peculiar sense of wrongness called to her, but she still wasn't sure Peter was the right man. Her inexperience and curiosity scrambled her instincts. She wanted to be kissed. The end. It was time.

"Just a kiss." She sensed he wanted more, but those secret parts of herself were not for him.

"That's all I need." The walls closed in around her as his long shadow blocked the filtered moonlight. The heat of his body warmed her front. "I'm very confident I could surpass your standards once you let down your guard."

She could not shake the need for caution.

His hand pressed into the door, just beside her head, and her shoulders drew back, but there was nowhere for her to go. He had her pinned. "Tell me you want it."

"I don't know what I want," she whispered, her voice barely audible. She only understood this great desire for more.

His hand pressed to her stomach, forcing her spine flat against the door. "What do you feel here—where a woman's desire grows?"

She felt lots of things. Fear, curiosity, wanderlust, and things she had no name for. Her pulse skipped wildly as shivers danced across her skin. Fate seemed to pull her in toward something unknown.

She leaned in and whispered, "I feel too many things at once."

"Good. That's how it should be—confusing and exciting—terrifying and exhilarating."

The sash of her robe loosened, and cool air needled the

thin material of her nightgown as a reminder of impropriety. Despite Peter's boyish playfulness, he possessed the unmistakable entitlement of a man, and she could not underestimate how dangerous he could be.

His warm fingers curled ever so slightly around her ribs, and her nipples tightened. Painfully aware of her unbound breasts, a mere inch above his touch, she tried not to breathe.

"Show me you're not a priss," he challenged, closing the distance and sliding his hand higher.

Warm lips pressed into hers, firm then soft and coaxing. Adrenaline spiked in her blood, and her nerves tingled as his tongue swept into her mouth. Her eyes stayed wide as he moaned, then he pulled away before she even had a chance to enjoy what was happening.

Disoriented, she frowned.

"Just as I thought," he said, tasting his lower lip.

"What is it?"

He sucked his lip and frowned. "You taste like innocence."

Her heart stopped as mortification drowned her. She ruined it. Why would she think she could impress a man when she had no experience?

Then his gaze met hers, exhilarating promise hiding in the jade pools of his stare. He wasn't mocking her at all. "I can help you, Wendy. I can teach you. I could show every kind of kiss."

"There are others?"

A wicked grin curled his mouth. "There are many." He leaned close, a deep chuckle tickling her ear as he caught her earlobe between his lips and nibbled. "There's necking."

Shivers chased up her neck, racing down her spine until

her bare toes curled against the wood floor. How could her ears feel so much?

His lips trailed over her racing pulse, and her breasts heaved with every nervous breath. His hand dragged upward, cupping her possessively.

"Then there's suckling." His thumb slowly treaded over the sharp tip of her nipple.

She should stop him. She knew better than to let him touch her so freely, but she wanted to know everything. She was sick of feeling ignorant. As a woman, she would need to know such things. But when his touch trailed lower, she whimpered.

"Peter…"

He slipped his hand between her legs, only the thin silk of her nightgown separating them. "Then there's the sort of French kiss, the kind that makes a woman pray to God. It starts *here.*" His hand turned to cup her intimately. "That's how stars are born. They're all just little jewels of light that pierced the sky when a female's pleasure passed by."

She couldn't imagine anything so poetic created by a man's touch.

"But I'm not sure you're ready for all that." He abruptly withdrew his hand and stepped back, leaving her disoriented.

Once again, she distrusted him. Tightening the lapels of her robe, she frowned with disapproval. "Very funny."

He glanced over his shoulder. "Funny? Hm. I wasn't trying to be funny." He lifted his wine and drank with indifference.

Her eyes narrowed. Was she a game to him? Was this some sort of ploy meant to confuse her to the point that she'd consent to anything? "Why are you here, Peter?"

"I was nearby when I got your text." He pulled out his

phone and swiped his thumb over the screen. "Very nice." He flashed the image to her, and she looked down, regretting ever sending such a photo.

"How did you know I was home?"

"I saw your light on."

She frowned. "How did you know which window was mine?"

"The trellis isn't hard to climb. To be honest, your father should be more careful. Anyone could break in and snatch you. Imagine how devastated he'd be, losing his only daughter. What bargaining chip would he have then?"

Bargaining chip? Was that how he saw her? But more importantly…"You looked in my window?"

He smirked. "Last I saw you, you were arguing with your father. He keeps a pretty tight leash on you."

Her mouth opened to argue, but she silenced the lie. He was right.

"Do you want to escape?"

"And go where?"

"Anywhere. We can have an epic adventure. Have you ever been to the Never Lands?"

The Never Lands were one of many provinces in the Isles of Kassel. Exclusive to the most elite visitors, summoned by invitation only. Kassel was said to be a hedonistic playground for the wealthy, but it was also rumored to be extremely dangerous to outsiders. Money was power, and with extreme power, laws ceased to exist.

"Of course, I've never been to such a place."

The most corrupt villains often took the form of idols. Rich and famous celebrities and billionaires played a role in public and on screen, but in private, they lived much different lives. People—of any class—could not be trusted to act honorably when privacy was guaranteed. However, modern technology exposed some of their dirty little secrets, and little by little, the world was learning how devoid of morals the men and women of Kassel could be.

"Don't look so scandalized. The media makes it seem far worse than it actually is."

"You've been there?"

A montage of images played through her mind as she thought about all the stories she'd read on the internet about sex parties and women disappearing. Did Peter know about such things? Was he involved in crimes?

"Of course, I've been there. How else would I invite you?"

This went far beyond her family's status.

"More than once?"

"More times than I can count."

Who was he? The Grimm brothers, two of the wealthiest men on the planet, oversaw the Isles of Kassel the way kings once ruled realms. They were said to decide who had the right to visit their islands.

"Do you know the Grimms?"

He flashed a devious smirk. "Perhaps."

The sprawling coast of the islands boasted impenetrable wilderness. The Isles of Kassel split into a peninsula of scattered private properties. One could only reach the islands by sea or aircraft, but the territory was tightly protected, and outsiders only caught glimpses by satellite.

Peter stepped forward. "You're intrigued."

She met his stare. Who wouldn't be? "Are you really friends with the Grimms?"

"I know Jay more than Will." He shrugged. "They like to

live an elusive life. I wouldn't say they have friends, just people of interest."

The Grimm brothers were two of the most powerful, calculating men alive, rumored to have done some twisted things on their private Isles. But they were so elusive they were never caught or found guilty of any crimes. They were untouchable.

Politicians needed their money. Wealthy men wanted their connections. Fortune-hungry women would sell their souls for their company. And women like herself knew better than to ever involve themselves with such formidable men.

Was Peter one of them? Had she underestimated his wealth and position? The Pangbournes were notably affluent, but she never assumed they might reach the degree of the families associated with the Isles of Kassel.

"What do you say, Wendy? Do you want an adventure?"

"You can't be serious," she said, calling his bluff.

"You don't believe me," he said with a snide little snicker.

She crossed her arms and dared him to prove her wrong. "I guess I don't."

"Lucky for you, I love a challenge." He caught her hand and tugged her forward, then stopped. "Wait a sec." He rubbed his jaw. "I'm not sure you're up for such an extreme journey. Kassel's not for the meek."

She scowled. "I'm far from meek."

"I should hope not! I'd hate to get you there and then have you start complaining that you want to go home."

"I wouldn't—"

"I think you would. You seem like a bit of a powder puff."

She stiffened. "I'll have you know, my life is a long list of risks and gambles I've yet to take! Just because I haven't been to many places doesn't mean I won't eventually see everything there is to see."

"As a wife?" He looked doubtful.

"I'm not married yet."

"But you will be soon. Your father's making sure of it."

What the hell was her father saying to people? "My father doesn't control me."

Laughter burst past his lips. "Then why have you lived such a sheltered life, Ms. Darling?"

She lifted her chin. "Just because the men in my life severely underestimate me does not mean I'm some helpless waif!"

"How do they underestimate you?"

"In every way possible! They think I'm weaker, too sensitive, too fragile. They can't conceive that I might have dreams outside of marrying a future bureaucrat!"

"Do you?"

"Of course I do! My father doesn't know the real me."

"And who might that be?"

At that moment, she realized he'd baited her. He found a nerve and struck the chord hard enough to get a real reaction, which left her feeling vulnerable and exposed more than anything else.

"I…I don't know." Peter was not a safe person to confess her doubts to. "I only know I'm meant for more than childbearing domesticity."

He grinned as if her admission pleased him, and a sense of intimacy tightened between them, shifting the energy in the air much like it shifts before someone shares an incriminating secret.

"I think there's something feral in you." He studied her for a long moment, not in the playful way he had before, but with deeper investment as if just realizing her hidden value. "That must be terrible for you, getting paired off with men based on nothing more than their bank accounts."

"Security is important." She sounded like her mother.

"Security is for graveyards. Life is important. Living is how we know we're still alive."

"Well, money gives you freedom."

He glanced out the window. "The maid has a hell of a lot more freedom than you and nowhere near your fortune. Money is an illusion of safety. We're all one crisis away from bankruptcy—moral or otherwise. You shouldn't let finance control your future so much."

He was right. "If I knew another way, I'd take it."

"There are plenty of ways. You could walk out that door right now—"

"And do what?"

"Anything you want! You're an adult. Nothing's stopping you."

But something was stopping her. The fear of being cut off, of facing scarcity. The fear of disappointing her parents, shaming them, not living up to their expectations… It all weighed on her to the point that she felt anchored to this time and place, forced to be exactly who they told her to be.

"Do you want to feel alive, Wendy?"

Her breath caught in her chest as he lifted her chin and seemed to look deep within her soul. It was the question of all questions because the seclusion of her current life was killing her. More than anything, she feared becoming dead inside if something didn't change soon.

This time, she couldn't lie. "Yes, I want to feel alive."

He leaned close, teasing his lips to the corner of her mouth, then trailing his nose along her cheekbone as he whispered, "You can forget them all. Just turn off the pressure and responsibility you feel toward them, and there will be no guilt. You'll be amazed how quickly you forget them. Just say the word, and we'll fly away."

Consent danced on her tongue, caged only by her teeth. The desire he mentioned earlier burned in her belly like a glowing ember. Would she ever have such a chance again?

"I don't know…"

He laced his fingers with hers. "Say yes. Later can wait. They can all wait. Only you can make this time count the way it should." He stared into her eyes. "Think of how delicious it will be to do something reckless and totally selfish for a change."

If she left with him, her fate would be in his hands. Could she trust him? What *exactly* was the cost of her passage from this repressive cage into the Isles of Kassel? She suspected it was far steeper than a kiss.

"Will you take me to the Never Lands?"

Backing her into the bookcase, he cupped the back of her neck and kissed her with far more aggression than he had before. Her hands pressed into his chest, but she soon softened and closed her eyes.

"That's it," he whispered, hiking up her robe and nightgown until his warm hand dragged along the back of her thigh, much like the strange man outside had groped Liza. "Prove you're not the helpless little girl they think you are. You're Wendy Moira Angela Darling."

She broke the kiss. "How do you know my full name?"

He reached over her shoulder and tapped her emblazoned name on the plaque. "*Prima Ballerina.* Impressive."

She flushed with embarrassment. Peter was in his mid-twenties, so such awards probably looked juvenile and foolish to him.

"You're mocking me."

"Not at all." He glanced at the line of trophies. "I find these pieces of your past charming. What a perfect little life you've led."

He liked teasing her, but she wasn't sure they were friends. "Can I trust you?"

"Absolutely not. But nothing worth having comes without risk." He jerked her into his grip. "What's it going to be? Singing to the stars by midnight or playing with sewing boxes while sipping tea, waiting for your dull husband to arrive?"

She scowled at such a nasty taunt. "I drank merlot tonight."

"What a wildling you are!" He looked satirically scandalized.

Her eyes narrowed. "Well, then perhaps you should show me where the rest of the wildlings are so I can be corrupted properly."

A wicked grin curled his lips. "That's all you needed to say."

CHAPTER 3

HAPPY THOUGHTS

"Why are you scowling?"

Wendy turned her attention from the private jet to where Peter stood on the tarmac. "This isn't exactly what I had in mind." She'd hardly had a chance to grab her slippers when Peter rushed her out of the house.

"Adventure's all about spontaneity. Stop sulking." Peter loped up the stairs to the jet, leaving her standing in nothing more than a nightgown and robe.

She could not believe she was boarding a plane this way. He was not her favorite person at the moment.

Already aboard the jet, Peter popped his head out the door and shouted, "You coming, or are you already chickening out?"

"Says the fully dressed man…" she grumbled, hiking up her robe to climb the steps to the jet.

Wendy had never been much for air travel, and once she was seated, her true fears emerged in the form of cold sweat and fidgety hands. She checked again to make sure the buckle was fastened tightly.

"Nervous?"

Why was it so difficult to admit her insecurities to him? "I, um, get a little motion sick when I fly."

He eyed her dewy skin and smirked. "That's bullshit. If you're afraid, just say you're afraid."

"I'm uncomfortable."

"If uncomfortable means afraid."

She growled and snapped, "Well, it's not an illogical fear. We're essentially hurtling through the sky at thirty-five thousand feet in a tin can."

He dramatically clutched his chest. "I'll have you know I spent thirty million dollars on this *tin* can. That's roughly a thousand dollars of security for every foot you'll be away from the ground."

She supposed that counted for something. She tugged the seat belt strap as tight as it could fit and glanced out the window. Unfortunately, her tension remained.

The jet's engine rattled to life, vibrating the floor. When Peter touched her thigh, she flinched.

"Relax. Stop focusing on all the things that could go wrong and think happy thoughts."

Forcing her shoulders back, she stared forward. She needed to overcome these silly fears, or they would hold her back in life. She had big plans for adventure, and that meant getting a grip. But, honestly, maybe she was more of a sea traveling adventurer.

"Do you want something to help you relax?"

She scowled at him. "Of course not. I'm not *that* afraid."

He shrugged, indifferent to whether she accepted his offer

or not. Maybe he took something, which was how he was so calm and careless about everything.

She gasped when the jet taxied into position for takeoff. There would be no going back once they were in the air.

But she didn't want to go back. She wanted to escape her boring life and do something daring. She could not let the fear of the unknown cripple her.

The engine got louder. "Oh, God…"

As they picked up speed, the force of their acceleration pressed through her chest and her body anchored into the chair.

Happy thoughts…

Happy thoughts.

Happy thoughts!

"Away we go," Peter practically sang as she closed her eyes to focus on her breathing.

The plane leveled out, and she exhaled. Peeking through one eye, she saw stars and clouds against the night sky. They were doing it. She was going to the Never Lands with Peter Pangbourne. Her grip on the armrests loosened, her body a mixture of nervous excitement and terrified exhilaration.

"Take a look at that skyline." He pointed toward the dark window where London's lights glowed below.

There was something intimate about sharing that view. Their vibrant, pulsing city was alive with light yet so calm and still from this distance.

Thinking of her family at the Club XXVII gala tonight, she smirked. Her envy was gone. This was far better than some stuffy party. Even John and Michael had never been to the Isles of Kassel.

In a few hours she would be able to claim that she's seen more than both her brothers! How rebelliously marvelous!

Her belly swooped at the realization that her family would return home before her and find her bed empty. She should have left a note, but there hadn't been time. Peter rushed her out the door so quickly she was lucky to have put on shoes. She could always text her parents once they landed. They needed to realize she was an adult, and if they couldn't come to that conclusion naturally, she'd force them to see.

Although she wasn't breaking any laws, they would be furious with her decision. Her father would see her rebelliousness as deliberate disobedience. He never explicitly said, "Don't go to the Isles of Kassel," but she was pretty sure the Never Lands were on the list of forbidden places she wasn't meant to visit.

She hid a smile, exhilarated by her defiance. This was precisely the wake-up call they needed if they were ever going to see her as a free-thinking adult.

The moon beamed as they passed the twinkling stars. She recognized the dome of Saint Paul's Cathedral, and London Bridge looked tiny from such a height, as did Big Ben. They reached full height over the River Thames, and she sat back, much calmer than she'd been at takeoff.

"Beautiful, isn't it?"

"It is—oh." He was looking at her, not the view.

They were alone in the cabin, and in the silence, she could hear his breathing and hers. Realizing her actions not only sent a message to her parents, she considered what this might imply to Peter, and the gravity of her choices settled in.

Shit.

Was this what people meant when they accused women of using men for their money? She didn't want his money, only his access to the unknown, but perhaps that was the same thing.

Did she care?

At the moment, no.

Later would come. But for now, she reveled in the excitement of spontaneity and ignored all thoughts of consequence.

Weightless. Aimless. Helpless. Truly reckless. She laughed, still able to taste the sweetness of her mother's wine on her lips.

Peter's nearness stretched around her until his proximity was all she could feel, yet no part of his body touched hers. Her heart raced at such a surreal predicament. She was taking a fantastical journey with a man who was essentially still a stranger. She was at his mercy. Was she insane for doing this?

The thought made her laugh.

"What's funny?"

"This." Was it not obvious? "I'm on a private jet with a man I hardly know, in my nightgown, flying off to the Never Lands." She covered her face and laughed some more. If only he knew how utterly boring her day-to-day life was. "Pinch me. I must be dreaming."

He slid his hand to her inner thigh and pinched.

She squeaked, slamming her hands over his. "Hey."

"You asked me to."

"I didn't mean literally."

Her gaze dropped to his trapped hand, and a boundless sense of possibility ripped through her. The moment was too dreamlike to be real. Too infinite. Too vast. And somehow, it *was* real. Where was the hovering sense of impending doom? It was as if consequence could not reach her here, with him.

Testing the strange sense of surrealness, she relaxed her posture and met his gaze. Their stares locked. The corners of his green eyes creased as the silk of her gown slowly lifted. She should shove his hand away but she didn't.

"You're already braver than you were." He gently repositioned her hands at her sides.

She swallowed as his fingers trailed lightly over her bare flesh. "This part never scared me."

He raised a brow. "Is that so?"

She feared her ignorance being exposed, but not his touch. Meeting his stare, she held eye contact with him as he gradually nudged her thighs apart with bold intention. It was up to her. If she wanted him to keep going, she would have to open for him.

Emboldened by the challenge in his eyes, her legs fell open, and her eyes shut. When his fingers traced over her panties, she sucked in a breath and tipped her head back. He teased over the damp spot of arousal, making the fabric wetter and drawing a shy gasp from her throat.

Sensations jolted in places she'd never felt before. His fingers slipped beneath the material, gliding purposefully along her skin. Then he pressed inside.

"Wait." She gripped his wrist before his finger could fully penetrate her.

He chuckled, delving beyond where any man had touched before, only to pause at her notable panic. "You *are* innocent, aren't you?" His voice darkened into a low whisper, full of intrigue. "Relax." He pried her grip loose and set her hand back on the armrest. "I won't hurt you. I just want to check something."

Her breath hitched as he slid a finger inside of her and teased the place of resistance that validated her virginity. Mortified, she snapped her knees together, trapping his hand. Her brow pinched with uncertainty, and she bit her lip.

"It's true then. Part of me actually thought it was an act."

He thought she was faking ignorance? "Why would you think that?"

He lifted a shoulder. "Women do all sorts of things to get my attention. I never had a thing for virgins…But I also never had my finger inside of one. I'm starting to see the intrigue."

Her breath hitched as he ever so slightly swirled his finger inside of her.

What if he told people about this? She didn't want to be the center of gossip or remembered for being a virgin. She feared others learning such secret things about her. But what if he told them? What if he said she was the type of girl to let a stranger finger her on a plane?

"What's it going to be, Ms. Darling? Shall I show you how to sing to the stars?"

Her lips parted, but her words disappeared as the cabin jostled.

His hand vanished from between her thighs, leaving her bereft and oddly aware of the hollowness where his touch had been. More turbulence shook the plane, and her body tensed.

"What was that?"

"Relax."

"Pardon me, folks," the captain's voice squawked over the speakers. "We've hit a pocket of turbulence. There's a small storm up ahead, but we should pass it quickly. Please keep your seatbelts fastened for your safety until I announce otherwise."

"*What?* We're flying through a storm?" Her calm vanished.

Peter let out a crowing laugh. "We're in the clouds, Wendy. Storms are perfectly normal up here."

Lightning flashed in the distance, outlining the billows of clouds ahead. The stunning view of vastness left her feeling small and helpless. When the cabin shook, her nerves sparked. Each jostling rattle wound her tension tighter until she was a coil spring about to pop.

"It's only air. There's nothing to fear up here. We're all alone."

"That doesn't help me. Is that lightning?" A bright bolt webbed the sky.

Her dreamlike state shifted to a nightmare as the plane tossed about. They dropped several feet through the air, and she cried out in fear, unable to hide her panic.

"Just shut it out."

"I should have shut you out!" She reached for her phone, but the pocket of her robe was empty. She checked her other pocket. "Oh, my God. I left my phone at home."

Regret swamped her as she pictured her parents' worrying. Then there would be the absolute devastation of learning she was aboard a plane that crashed once the story splattered all over the news. Was she even recorded in the flight log? What if she just became a missing person, a lost girl who was never found?

"Hey." He removed his safety belt.

"What are you doing? The turbulence——"

"I'm fine." He fully faced her as the plane shuddered about and gripped her shoulders. "You're fine. We're fine. It's just wind."

Panting, she searched his stare for reassurance but found no anchor there. They were just words, not actual guarantees. He was a stranger. His confidence could not protect her anymore than——

His lips sealed to hers, and she squeaked.

Pushing at his chest, she tried to shove him back, but he tightened his grip, forcing her to accept the kiss. His hand closed over hers, pressing her palm against his chest. "Feel my heartbeat. Nice and steady."

"Peter—"

"Hush." His tongue slid into her mouth, distracting her from the sense of danger and sending her thoughts to a different place. When he pulled away, the turbulence had slowed, and the plane hardly jostled.

"There," he said, as if proving he'd been right all along and there was nothing to worry about.

Her eyes narrowed. "Well, you don't have to look so smug about it."

The captain's voice returned. "We're past the storm now, folks. Feel free to remove your safety belts and move about the cabin."

Her mercurial mood swings between euphoric enthusiasm and terrifying dread gave her whiplash. Any more excitement, and she'd exhaust herself before they landed.

They traveled in silence for a stretch. Peter didn't attempt to touch her again, which was for the best. She just wanted to land safely on the ground.

When they reached the coast, the jet circled the Isles of Kassel, and she stared in awe at what only a few people in the world could claim to have seen.

Several small, interconnected islands dotted the dark sea. She wished it was daylight because, at the moment, it looked a bit ominous and wild.

"Which are the Never Lands?"

Peter pointed to a small grove of an island where illuminated mansions twinkled through the canopies of palm trees. "There."

Lush everglades curved wildly about the landscape in an undisrupted sign of organic life. She'd expected it to be more occupied and populated by buildings, but the Never Lands were mostly made of trees and jungles.

All the isles appeared darker than expected. Where were the people? This wasn't at all as she imagined and her stomach pinched with unease.

"Where's your family's house?"

"Who said anything about family? The Never Lands are mine."

The overhead bell chimed. "This is your captain speaking. We're preparing to land. Please fasten your seatbelts, and we'll have you on the ground shortly."

Wendy straightened her clothes, eager to get off the plane but nervous about what might come next. Peter glanced at her and chuckled.

She glared at him, unsure what was so funny. "Why are you laughing?"

He smirked. "No reason. Tonight should be fun—once we loosen you up."

"*We?*"

"Yeah, me and the Lost Boys."

Her expression fell. Who were the Lost Boys?

CHAPTER 4

LOST BOYS

The jet descended with great precision onto a small tarmac. The Never Lands might look unoccupied and peaceful from above, but they were pulsing with hidden verve below. The air was alive with unseen inhabitants, and the bass could be heard in the distance as if the wild woods sheltered a hidden nightclub.

Aside from the small airport and tower, nature grew wildly, unrestricted by whatever manmade obstacles encroached on the land. Ivy and vines climbed and twirled about the street signs and pavement as if the groundkeepers couldn't cut the overgrowth back fast enough.

Branches dangled from footbridges, stretching from the canopies of lush, towering trees. Wildflowers bloomed in bright colors that challenged the shade of the night sky. The air was thick and humid, causing ringlets to curl about her face as she followed Peter toward a dim path that led to the woods.

He pressed a hand to her back. "Shall we?"

She looked around but saw nothing but trees and the dotted line of hanging lanterns. "Is there a car?"

His smile stretched. "Why would we need a car? We're here." He led her onto the grass in a direction that felt inherently wrong.

Insects trilled from hidden crevices. Tiny creatures skittered below the underbrush. The earthy scent of damp soil tickled her nose, but there was also the intoxicatingly sweet fragrance of exotic flowers, some in colors too vibrant to name.

"Thirsty?" Peter offered a flask.

She took it and sniffed the fruity contents, knowing enough to assume the sweet smell likely masked something potent and dangerous. She hesitated, not because she was afraid, but because she wanted nothing to dull her senses or her wits.

"No, thank you."

"Such a scaredy cat."

She frowned and then snatched the flask. "I'm just not a fan of fruity drinks." She took a tiny sip and sputtered. One drop was enough to steal her breath. "What is that?"

"We call it nectar."

"That is *not* nectar." She cleared her throat. Only grain alcohol could burn like that.

Nightbirds cawed, and the hum of insects amplified as they trekked a path between the dense trees. Branches rustled as unseen animals launched about. The nearby trickle of a stream caught her ear, but it was too dark to see beyond a few feet. The deeper into the jungle they traveled, the louder the rush of water grew. Perhaps there were waterfalls nearby.

Her heel sank into the spongy ground, capturing her slipper in the mud and pulling it off her foot. "Oh!"

Peter caught her arm as she hopped on one foot. He crowed with laughter when her other shoe also got stuck in the mud.

"Oh, no!" Clinging to his shoulders, she lost her balance, and her bare foot sank into a soggy clump of mud.

"Well, they weren't the most sensible shoes for exploring."

"They're slippers! I would have worn appropriate footwear if you had given me a moment to dress, but you rushed me out the door!"

"Women are notoriously late. This isn't a fashion show. Besides, we both know you don't own a pair of hiking boots. Look how distressed you get over a little mud. You haven't hiked a day in your life."

She was getting tired of his assumptions. "You're a jerk." Bunching up her robe and nightgown, she glared at him, her feet fully submerged in the slimy mud now.

"Are you finished having a fit over your precious slippers?"

"Asks the fully dressed man wearing close-toed shoes."

He shrugged and crouched. "I don't mind the mud." He removed his shoes and cuffed his designer pants to stand barefoot with her. "Happy?" He tossed his shoes into the shadows.

"Yes." She glanced at the woods. "Are you leaving your shoes there?"

"Shoes are useless here. Nobody wears them. You'll see. This is a *less is more* sort of place." He proceeded down the path, leaving her to follow.

"Ugh." She winced as mud squished through her toes. "I probably should have updated my vaccinations before coming here." How was she to know such an elite place would be so savage?

"Did you say something?" Peter yelled from up ahead.

"No." Every step squished more mud between her toes and made her wince.

"Just follow me, princess. I'll get you there!" His voice echoed through the trees.

Wendy wrinkled her nose and shadowed him down the dark path. "I'm on a vacation with a lunatic."

Mist hung low in the air, clinging closely to the gnarled roots of trees that appeared centuries old. The forest was a mixture of danger and discovery that left her in a constant state of awe. The tangy essence of fruit on the breeze sweetened every breath. She couldn't wait to see this untamed land in daylight and hoped they would have a little time to explore its secrets before returning to London in the morning.

Peter loped back to walk beside her, studying her expectantly. "Is it not the most exotic place you've ever seen?"

Their arrival invigorated him to an almost intoxicated point. Or perhaps he'd had too much nectar from the flask. The way he pranced beside her with his hands in his pockets and a wide grin stretched across his elfin face made him boyish and childlike.

"I hope to see it in daylight."

"Oh, you will! And then at sunset, and under a full moon when everything is aglow with blue light, and by sea, and from the trees, and on the backs of wild beasts, and from the cliffs of the wildlings—"

"Peter," she laughed at his hyper enthusiasm. "I have to go back to London eventually. I can't stay here."

He frowned. "But you wanted an adventure."

"And I'm on one, but I have responsibilities at home. My family will expect me to return."

He cocked his head. "But you wanted to escape."

"I have a family, Peter—"

"A family that suppresses your right to live."

"That's a little extreme."

"Is it? When was the last time you wrapped your legs around something for the sheer joy of it?"

She scowled at him. "You know perfectly well that I've never wrapped my legs around anything."

"Not even a tree swing?"

She gaped at him. He totally set her up for that. "I didn't realize you were talking about the trees."

He laughed. "That's okay. You don't strike me as much of a swinger anyway. But I am!" He rushed into the woods, leaving her on the trail in the dark.

Only shadows and the trill of insects surrounded her. "Peter?"

His crowing voice echoed from deep within the woods, and then a large creature flew from the trees, swooping low to the ground. Wendy ducked as the bird nearly buzzed her head in a flash of green and gold. But it was not a bird. It was Peter, swinging from a vine that must have been a hundred feet long.

"Come on, Wendy, swing with me!" he yelled, winding back and forth like a pendulum.

He was insane. "I don't swing!"

"Where's your sense of adventure?" He swooped by again, losing momentum as gravity slowed him to a twirling dangle. "Are you afraid of heights?"

"No, but I'm in a nightgown with muddy feet, and I'd much rather reach the house than climb trees." He was lucky he didn't break his neck. The vine was nothing more than a tangle of leaves and branches. "Can we please keep moving?"

"All I hear is priss, priss, priss, priss, priss, priss, priss."

She ground her molars. "Look, I'm not in the mood for juvenile games." She slapped her ankle when a mosquito bit it. "Could you please go back to acting like an adult and take me to your house?"

Dangling ten feet overhead, his foot held in a loose knot where the vine looped. He laughed at her. "Ms. Darling, you sound rather irritable."

"Mr. Pangbourne, that's because I am irritated," she said between clenched teeth.

"Is it because we got interrupted by the turbulence?"

She scoffed. "No, it's because my tour guide is a reckless man-child."

"I could finish what we started on the plane. Maybe that would improve your mood."

She gaped at him. "I can't believe you just said that." Unsure where she was going, she stomped off.

"What? I was being generous!"

She growled and kept walking toward the steady beat that pounded in the distance. It was not a sound of nature but the sound of human life. Perhaps someone there could help her. Peter claimed the Never Lands were his, but he also mentioned lost boys. There were clearly others on the island. At the moment, she could easily trade her escort for someone less annoying.

A twig snapped behind her, and she turned, startled to find Peter at her back.

"Did I scare you?"

"No. And what is this obsession you have with my fear."

He shrugged. "Girls are always in distress."

"Hardly. We have much more fortitude and courage than society realizes."

"There's a spider in your hair."

She swatted wildly only to realize he was teasing her when he laughed. Composing herself, she glared at him. "You're a child."

He smirked. "You only say that because adults forget how to have fun. It's like some sort of amnesia. You might already have it."

"It's called responsibility."

"More like indentured slavery if you ask me."

"Well, I didn't."

"Half the rules are unnecessary. People are too afraid of chaos."

Typically, she'd agree with him, but with each muddy step and stinging mosquito bite, the thought of her secluded bedroom grew more and more attractive.

Speaking of chaos, he'd removed his jacket and tie, and a storm of confusion whirled inside of her.

He rolled his sleeves, exposing the strength of his forearms. His tanned skin and muscular physique were undeniably attractive, but his cavalier behavior was a total turn-off. Unfortunately, he wore unruly well. And his unpolished, bad boy appearance confused her all the more.

"What are you looking at?"

Realizing she was staring, she dropped her gaze and asked, "Do you hear that music?"

"That's just the Lost Boys."

"And who are the Lost Boys again?"

"My friends."

She self-consciously looked down at her clothes. "How many are there?"

He quietly counted on his fingers. "Six. Seven if you count Belle."

"Who's Belle?"

"She's the only girl in the group. I can't very well call her a Lost Boy."

"What are the others' names?"

"In the Never Lands, our names are whatever we choose. You can be whoever you want to be here."

He wove about the woods as if dribbling an invisible soccer ball. Every few seconds, he'd leap over a tree root or ollie off a trunk, careless enough to defy gravity. His energy seemed endless.

"Well, what do you call them?"

"First, they call me Pan—short for Pangbourne. Then there's Tate, Nibbs, Bayne, Cass, and the twins, Thayer and Tristan."

"They all live with you?"

"God, no! Although they rarely leave." He frowned. "I don't actually know if they have homes. They're always just…around. Like homeless nomads."

"You don't know if your friends have homes? Didn't you ever ask or try to visit them?"

He shrugged. "I guess I never took interest." He doubled his pace. "But they'll go nuts when they see you!"

The louder the music pounded in the jungle, the stranger this journey seemed. Peter was prancing from tree to tree like a squirrel on cocaine while she grew increasingly concerned about the people she was about to meet in nothing more than her pajamas.

This sort of uncertainty is exactly what she deserved after such an impetuous decision to run off with a stranger. How had she ever believed herself safe with him?

Something slithered through the underbrush and hissed from the shadows. She stilled. "Did you hear that?"

"Hear what?"

"I don't know. It sounded…slimy."

"It was probably just a Never Snake."

Her eyes widened. Did she even want to know what a Never Snake was?

"Or could be a Never Spider. They make a lot of noise when they're full grown."

With that disturbing information, she rushed forward to walk next to him again. There was so much nature surrounding them the ground seemed to breathe, in and out, as if alive. "How much further?"

"We're here."

The pulse of beating drums thumped as laughter erupted from the other side of the trees. Water splashed, and male voices hooted like a fraternity.

She'd gladly trade her jungle surroundings for a frat house.

Peter cupped a hand by his mouth and crowed. The sound echoed back in what she presumed were the Lost Boys' voices.

Leaves rustled, and a tiny female burst from the foliage. The woman had pixie blonde hair and perfectly toned flesh. She squealed and hurled herself at Peter's chest, wrapping her legs about his hips.

"You're back!" She wreathed her arms around his neck and kissed him deeply.

Eyes wide, Wendy cleared her throat.

The woman's elven features narrowed on Wendy as she slid down Peter's body to stand on the ground. She wore a bohemian-style sarong that showed off her hips. Her torso was bare, and her green crop-top barely covered her breasts.

Peter caught her arm. "Easy, Belle. She's with me."

The tiny woman took Wendy's measure. Was this the sort of petite figure Peter was attracted to? Wendy generally liked her body, but this woman's waistline was smaller than her thigh. As her gaze traveled upward, her insecurities doubled.

Belle curled her lip and jammed a fist into her side, returning her attention to Peter. "Who is she?"

"This is Wendy Bird—she's still a fledgling."

Wendy drew back at the nickname. "Excuse me?"

Peter laughed. "You know, because you hate to fly, and you've never really left the nest." He waved a hand at the other woman. "Wendy Bird, meet Talia Bellfrey, but we just call her Belle."

"It's nice to meet you, Belle." She held out her hand. "And you can just call me Wendy."

Ignoring her outstretched hand, Belle looked up at Peter. "Why is she here?"

"Because I wanted her."

"Oh, really?" Belle's pixie features caught the moonlight as she crossed her arms over her chest. "Wanted her for what?"

"Whatever I feel like."

Wendy tried to clarify. "Well, actually—"

"No one asked you." Belle marched angrily through the hedges, disappearing in the direction of the music.

Wendy turned to Peter, completely baffled by his friend's reaction to her. "Are you two a thing?"

"What do you mean?"

"I mean, she was all over you, and that wasn't what anyone would call a warm welcome."

"That's her problem. Sometimes, people get possessive for no reason. It's annoying."

That might be true, but Wendy needed to understand what she was walking into. "Are you sleeping with her?"

"How could I be sleeping with her when I'm standing right here with you?"

He was purposely being obtuse. "You know what I mean, Peter! Have you had sex with her?"

"Oh. Yeah. We all have."

"I beg your pardon."

He waved away her scandalized expression. "Stop being such a prude. I told you, we don't like rules in the Never Lands."

Wendy's stomach soured. It was a mistake coming here. She no longer found his duplicity cute and worried she might be at the mercy of a madman.

Her parents were likely home by now or about to return home. Would they visit her room? How long would it take for them to realize she was gone? Perhaps she could get home before they noticed she was missing.

"Come on, slowpoke." Peter led her through a copse of trees where gnarled roots rose from the earth and coiled about.

Wendy kept her gaze on the ground so as not to trip. Splashing and uproarious laughter erupted when Peter lifted a curtain of vines and waved her forward. A mansion made almost entirely of glass walls presented a storefront display of a luxurious home. Music blared, and men launched from balconies into an in-ground swimming pool below.

The moment Wendy stepped off the muddy forest floor onto the smooth stone, all movement ceased.

"Peter's back!" They yodeled like maniacs and charged, but they didn't run to Peter, they ran to her.

She screamed as they lifted her off her feet and hoisted her overhead, spiriting her away like a tribal sacrifice. "Peter, help!"

Her voice was lost amongst the shouting as they jostled her like a sack of potatoes. Stars bounced overhead, then the support gave way, and she went soaring through the air. All sound silenced as she broke the surface of the water and sank like a stone.

Cold water engulfed her screams as bubbles erupted from her mouth. Survival instincts kicked in as her toes slid along the floor of the pool. She propelled herself upward, her arms flapping wildly as her lungs burned. Her eyes bulged.

She was going to die.

Panicked, she whirled her arms but couldn't reach the surface. Blurred faces stared down at her, not one wobbly figure coming to her aid. Her lungs convulsed, the pain forcing her to shut her eyes. Then, she was being yanked upward.

The moment they broke the surface, she gasped and choked, rolling to her side and hacking against the pavement. Hanks of wet hair clung to her face like seaweed as she spit out gulps of water from her convulsing lungs.

"Wendy, can you breathe?"

A heavy hand walloped her back, and water gushed from her mouth. She sputtered and coughed, swatting him away.

"Can't you swim?"

A gasping, painful inhalation was all she could manage to answer. Never before had she felt so close to death.

Peter's fury erupted when he turned on his friends. "What the hell were you thinking? *This* is how you greet a guest I bring you?"

"We didn't know she couldn't swim!"

"Why would you greet anyone like that?" Peter stormed with great anger. "Answer me!"

"Belle told us to. She said you brought a woman who thinks she's a bird, and you wanted to see if she could really fly. We thought it was your idea, Peter."

Peter's eyes burned a deep emerald green as he turned his rage on the others. "Is that true? Did you cause this, Belle?"

The men stepped back, exposing the arrogant female as she lifted her chin in defiance. Wendy stopped sputtering to hear what she had to say, but no excuse or apology came.

Belle crossed her arms and glared at Peter. "So what if I did? Who is she to you anyway?"

Water dripped from Wendy's drenched clothing as she stood, shivering. "What I am, or am not, to Peter makes no difference. I'm a human be—"

"I wasn't talking to you, bitch."

Wendy drew back, never as enraged as she was at that moment. "Who the hell do you—"

"Fuck off."

"All right, that's enough!" Peter shouted. "Belle, apologize."

Wendy's nightgown and robe clung to her body, exposing every curve as she panted and scowled at the little viper. It was clear that no apology was coming from the little terrorist.

The Lost Boys sidled behind Peter, showing their alliance. Wendy shivered and waited for Peter to do something. There had to be a consequence.

But when Belle refused to apologize, he only turned and yelled at the boys, "Use your heads! There are other ways to get a beautiful woman wet, you imbeciles!"

Her chattering jaw fell open. He was making a joke of the matter? She nearly died!

The men laughed as if paid to do so. Wendy understood then that Peter wasn't their equal. He was their leader.

She hardened her brow and stepped forward, making it clear that this was a serious situation. Arms crossed her chest, she shivered and looked up at him like a wet rat. "Peter," she used his name the way her mother sometimes called out her father, making a statement by only speaking one word.

He read the look in Wendy's eyes and understood that jokes would not resolve this level of nastiness and all humor left his expression. The air chilled as he turned his authority back to Belle. "Talia Bellfrey, I hereby banish you from the Never Lands."

A collective gasp hissed behind Peter.

"Peter," Belle rasped in utter shock. "You don't—"

He held up a silencing hand. "This is my home, and Wendy is my guest. You betrayed me."

Malice blazed in her cruel stare as she glared at Wendy, vengeance radiating from her tiny form. Belle sprung, lunging at Wendy.

Peter yanked her back and shook her roughly. "Still, you disobey me? Get out of here, and don't come back!"

He flung her away with such disgust that Wendy almost felt sorry for the girl. "Peter, maybe we just need to cool—"

"Leave!" Peter barked, ignoring Wendy's voice. He glared at Belle. "I can't even look at you!"

Her green eyes flooded with unshed tears, and then she turned and bolted into the woods. A mixture of regret and anger welled inside Wendy as she shivered and dripped onto the pavement.

Peter turned and shouted at the men, "I want you to prepare a room for Wendy. This will be your punishment. Choose the best room and fill it with every comfort you can find. It's the least you can do after greeting her like barbarians."

Wendy shivered, wishing someone would get her a towel.

When the Lost Boys only nodded, Peter shouted, "*Move!*"

They scattered into the enormous glass home, and Peter snatched a towel from a lounge chair. Wendy's teeth chattered as he wrapped it around her trembling shoulders and pulled her close.

"You're freezing." The heat of his chest was too warm to reject, so she nestled closer to him. He hooked a finger under her trembling chin and lifted her face. "I think you're in shock. Fair warning, I'm not above taking advantage of your vulnerable state."

Leading her to one of the lounge chairs, he pulled her onto his lap. Despite the tropic-like humidity and the press of his warm body, she couldn't stop shivering.

"You'll never get warm in sopping wet clothes. We should take these off."

Perhaps she *was* in shock because she didn't object when he peeled off her robe. Her nipples stabbed through the transparent silk of her nightgown, and Peter lifted a brow. "I can see every inch of you, Ms. Darling."

She moved to cover her breasts, but he caught her wrist.

"Don't." Leaning forward, he closed his mouth over the turgid tip of her breast and bit gently through the wet fabric.

"Peter—"

"Let me."

He had no authority over her, yet she obeyed. He pushed her arms down and stared at her body as if he owned her, pulling the thin strap off her shoulder and peeling the material away from her chest to expose her nipple fully.

"That's better."

He reached forward but stilled when the sliding door opened. Wendy jerked the towel over her chest.

"Room's ready," one of the men called.

Irritated by the disruption, Peter stood and held out a hand. "Come. Once we get to your room, we can get you out of that wet gown."

CHAPTER 5

MOONLIGHT REFLECTIONS

Once again, Peter's mercurial moods were giving her whiplash. Since arriving in the Never Lands, he'd acted like a hyper teenage boy, lost his temper, banished Belle, and groped her. Wendy had no clue which version was the real Peter. Perhaps they all were.

As they entered the house, she shivered under the central air pumping through the vents. The house smelled of freshly washed linens, furniture polish, and something deliciously masculine with a touch of earthiness.

The men anxiously awaited. "Which room?" Peter asked, his tone impatiently curt.

The twins pointed to the left, and Peter took her arm, hauling her that way. Her bare feet slapped noisily on the porcelain tile as she rushed to keep up.

The nervous one who spoke up at the pool apprehensively rubbed what she suspected was a lucky rabbit's foot. "I'm sorry we threw you in the pool, miss Wendy. We were only playing. If we knew you couldn't swim—"

"Tate!" Peter snapped, and the man silenced.

Shocked by Peter's rudeness, she yanked her arm free and touched Tate's hand that rubbed the rabbit's foot. "It's okay, Tate. It was a misunderstanding, that's all."

He looked instantly relieved, then bashful as he smiled. "You forgive us, then?"

"Enough." Before she could answer, Peter tugged her into the room.

"Peter, stop." She yanked her arm free again. "What's gotten into you? We were in the middle of a conversation."

"A boring conversation." He dove onto the tower of ruffled pillows. "Oh, look. A bed."

Turning back to the Lost Boys, she thanked them, "The room is lovely. Thank you."

"You like it?"

"I picked out the pillows!"

"I found the blanket!"

"I picked the flowers!"

"I swept the floor and got rid of that—*umph*." One of the men elbowed Tate in the ribs. "I mean, there was nothing gross in here whatsoever. It was totally clean when we started."

She figured it was better she didn't know what biohazards or creatures they removed. "Well, it's perfect now."

They turned their attention to Peter, fishing for more praise that did not come.

Peter lounged on the bed, appearing bored and disinterested in what the rest of them were doing. She didn't understand their dynamic. Why fawn over someone who paid them no mind and scolded them like children? Who made him their leader?

"Perhaps now is a good time to learn your names. I'm Wendy. And I know you're Tate."

Tate grinned and nodded happily, twin dimples winking in his round cheeks.

She moved down the line to the bare-chested one wearing a necklace of entwined antlers. "And you are?"

"I'm Nibbs," he said cheerfully, liveliness buzzing from his impressive physique as something fearless and reckless danced in his blue eyes.

"A pleasure to meet you, Nibbs." She turned to the tall one. He leaned against the wall, radiating arrogance. "And you are?"

"They call me Bayne." Something untrustworthy flashed in his eyes. "The Never Lands can be a dangerous place for a woman. It would be wise to watch your back."

So far, he seemed the only true danger she'd stumbled across. "Thank you for the warning. I will."

Peter slipped his arm around her, and Bayne's jaw ticked. As Peter nuzzled her neck, his eyes narrowed on her another degree.

Not needing another enemy, Wendy shouldered out of Peter's grip. But Bayne continued to glare at her. Was he jealous? She didn't quite understand the dynamic between these men yet. There was a sense of hero worship but also an extreme sense of territorialism.

"How long is she staying?" Bayne asked, clearly put out by her presence.

Peter scowled at his rude friend. "As long as I want her to stay."

The other man stormed off in a huff.

"Ignore him," Nibbs said, rolling his eyes. "If Bayne's not the center of attention, he's in crisis."

How sad that a grown man could be that reliant on his friend's attentiveness. His narcissism and neediness were obviously caused by deep-seated insecurities, and while he tried to appear powerful, his dramatic exit only left the impression of bratty self-doubt. She pitied him.

"I'm Cassian," the burly one said as he stepped forward. "Friends call me Cass." A wide smile flashed beneath his fuzzy beard, giving the impression of a big teddy bear.

"Lovely to meet you, Cass."

"I stashed some of my extra flannels in that bottom drawer there. They're long, so they'll probably fit like a dress on a little thing like you."

She appreciated his thoughtfulness. "Thank you."

"My Pleasure. I also put some extra blankets on the shelf in the closet. It can get cold at night, especially when the seasons change."

"Oh, I only plan on staying one night, but thank you."

"Only one night?" Tate looked alarmed.

"What's the benefit to one lousy night?" one of the twins asked.

"Why rush home?" Peter asked as if her plans were news to him. "The Lost Boys made you a good room. Don't you like it?"

"Of course I do, but, Peter, I have responsibilities. This was only supposed to be a short trip."

"I never said that."

Stunned that he thought it could be anything else, she gaped at him. "Well, I'm saying it."

He waved away her words and lounged on the bed. A damp spot formed under his wet clothes. "People always say they need to do *this* or *that* when, in reality, they don't *need* to do anything. If something needs to be done, someone will do it."

"I don't want someone else to do everything for me. I like

having responsibilities. People are counting on me." It was a matter of integrity. Her eyes narrowed at the sprawling wet spot. "You're getting my covers wet."

"So? You're not going to sleep for hours."

Maybe she would need the blankets Cass left after all.

She turned her back on him. "You must be Tristan and Thayer." The twins stood side by side like a mirror image of each other and beamed under her attention.

"That's us," they said at the same time. "We did good, didn't we, Pete?"

They showed more interest in impressing Peter than meeting her, but there was something innocent and sweet about their hero worship.

"Yeah, yeah, the room's great. Whatever," Peter said, once more waving away their need for praise. Then he jumped off the bed and corralled them toward the door. "Everyone out. Wendy's cold, and I need to warm her up."

The Lost Boys laughed as if understanding exactly how Peter planned to accomplish the task. "Let us know if you need a hand," the twins called.

Wendy gaped, and Peter shut the door. "Let's get you out of those wet clothes."

"Hold on." She held up a hand and glanced at the connecting bathroom. "I think I want to shower."

"Great." He peeled off his wet shirt, exposing washboard abs and a tan chest sculpted with muscle.

As soon as he unsnapped his damp pants, she clarified, "Alone."

He paused from stripping. "What fun would that be?"

"It's not about fun. It's about avoiding hypothermia." She opened the bedroom door. "So, if you'll excuse me…"

"Seriously?"

"Seriously. But can you wash my nightgown so it's dry tonight?" She could wear one of Cass's flannels when she got out. And maybe she could make a late supper for the Lost Boys as a thank-you for setting up her room.

"Gonna have to take it off if you want me to wash it."

"Well, yes." She eyed the door, but he didn't budge. "Fine. Turn around."

He turned, and she quickly peeled off the wet nightgown, careful to keep her body covered with the towel. She flung the sopping wet fabric over his shoulder.

"There."

He turned and faced her with a smirk. "The boys did a nice job placing that mirror there."

Her eyes darted to the wall where Peter had been staring, and she scoffed. "Jerk!"

He laughed and kissed the tips of his fingers as he opened the door. "Lovely tits and a juicy ass. Enjoy your shower, darling."

She slammed the door at his back and groaned, her face burning. "It's like living with a fifteen-year-old."

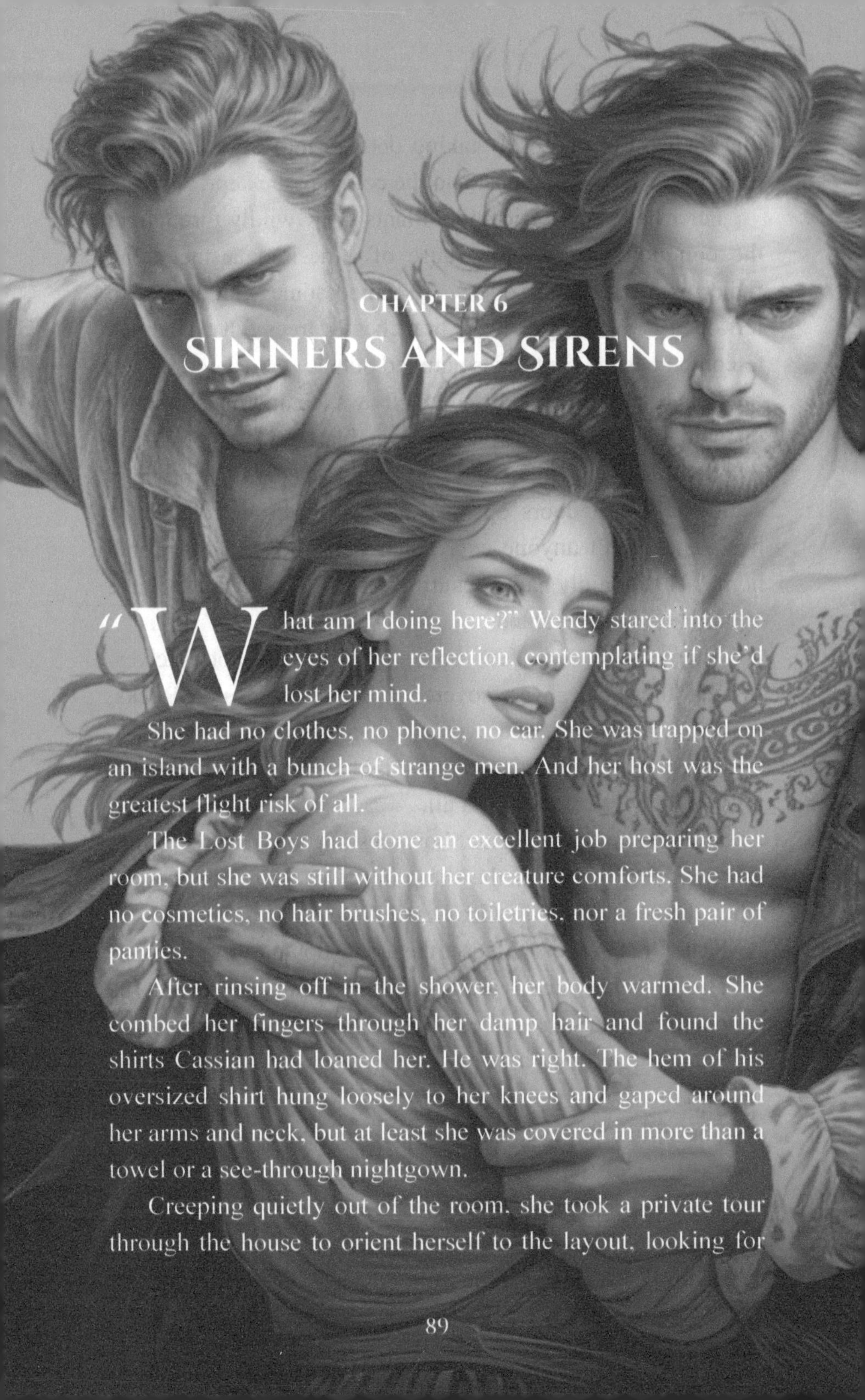

CHAPTER 6

SINNERS AND SIRENS

"What am I doing here?" Wendy stared into the eyes of her reflection, contemplating if she'd lost her mind.

She had no clothes, no phone, no car. She was trapped on an island with a bunch of strange men. And her host was the greatest flight risk of all.

The Lost Boys had done an excellent job preparing her room, but she was still without her creature comforts. She had no cosmetics, no hair brushes, no toiletries, nor a fresh pair of panties.

After rinsing off in the shower, her body warmed. She combed her fingers through her damp hair and found the shirts Cassian had loaned her. He was right. The hem of his oversized shirt hung loosely to her knees and gaped around her arms and neck, but at least she was covered in more than a towel or a see-through nightgown.

Creeping quietly out of the room, she took a private tour through the house to orient herself to the layout, looking for the kitchen but purposely taking detours into other rooms to get a better idea of her host and the company he kept.

Peter had an eclectic style. Plants grew wildly throughout the common areas, not because of a desired aesthetic but rather as a result of laziness. It seemed some windows were left open for so long that the branches of trees felt welcomed to come in as the central air pumped out.

Leaves hung over ledges like elbows leaning on a bar after one too many cocktails—casual yet blatantly wasteful. She recalled how her father would yell when she and her brothers accidentally left doors open, accidentally letting cold air or heat out. Didn't anyone ever teach Peter how to care for a home? He certainly had a beautiful one, but he seemed to take all this luxury for granted.

There were very few books but lots of bookshelves. Instead, the shelves were covered in eclectic treasures. Rocks, fossils, dried leaves, and even a few pelts pinched her heart. Primitive, hand-crafted weapons laid about like children's toys, but they weren't toys at all.

She examined a rustic bow resting on a windowsill. Grazing her finger over the sharp tip of an arrow, she gasped when the needle-like tip sliced easily into her skin.

"They're savages." She set the arrow down.

Birds, bears, and various mounted things with horns watched her through soulless eyes as she snooped about the house. Did they hunt all of these creatures in the jungles she trekked through to get here?

She didn't understand why men needed to kill beautiful things to feel powerful. While they made for beautiful trophies, it seemed a rather savage and cruel way to boost one's ego. Perhaps it was the volume of death surrounding her that disturbed her most. Buckskin couches, fur rugs, mounted heads, towering bears, and stuffed birds created a steady reminder that these men might appear sweet, but they were very dangerous to those they considered prey.

Abandoning the den, Wendy went to find the kitchen—for real this time. Turning the corner, she came up short and gasped. Her heart jolted to the pit of her stomach as she came face to face with a crocodile hanging from an invisible fishing line, frozen in time and posed as if diving through water.

The exquisite preservation of such a monstrous beast stole her breath. It was so lifelike her hand trembled as she reached out to touch its scaly, cold flesh. But she needed to feel it to prove it was real. She might never have the chance to stand so close to a crocodile again—at least, she certainly hoped she wouldn't.

Jagged teeth and dragon-like scales gave the creature the essence of a prehistoric killer. It hung mid-lunge, jaws pried open in a grotesque pose of aggression. Wendy instinctively became more watchful as she approached. Those razor-sharp fangs appeared set to devour her. She tipped her head, finding a deformed reflection of herself in its onyx eyes, eyes that were forever glaring.

The beast was an enormous fossil of fury. Touching its dried, dull flesh felt as reckless as it did courageous. This was the cracked hide of an ancient predator, grown by the nutrition it found by devouring smaller living things.

When they were young, such monsters were unfathomable. Mother told them stories in the nursery about many horrific creatures. Those myths of menacing villains would leave her awake for hours, but no beast—not crocodile or bear—was ever as terrifying as the lawless, immoral men in those stories.

Long after her mother would tuck them in and say good-night, Wendy would stare at the murky shadows of her childhood room, her heart pounding in her little chest as the house creaked and settled. John and Michael would fall sound asleep while she waited in fear for one of the depraved villains to show up and steal her away.

It was never the monsters she dreaded. It was always the evil men. Some part of her feared they would inevitably find her and punish her for enjoying such wicked stories so much.

She didn't know why she loved the darkness of those tales. She only knew that there was something exhilarating in the fear that made her feel alive the way nothing else could.

Closing her arms, she held herself tightly, waiting for the familiar chill to pass. Just like when she was little, her heart raced like an ever-ticking time bomb set to go off as she stared up at that croc, wondering what sort of man could kill such a thing.

It was three times her height, and while she logically understood it was dead, she couldn't dismiss its right to her fear, nor could she dismiss the hinting desire that she liked the rush of adrenaline pumping through her veins. There was something delicious about her proximity. Standing close to something so dangerous made her feel alive. Could closeness with the hunter do the same?

She slowly traced a finger over the sharp tips of the croc's rigid teeth. They were unnaturally polished, gleaming in the dim hall light.

"You don't scare me," she whispered, amused by the thought of Peter taking time to brush the monster's teeth.

Drawn into its hollow, insatiable gaze, she sensed the promise that a villainous soul never dies. This creature was hung here intentionally for a reason. This was no harmless exhibit. It was a dark echo of time meant to warn and remind guests that their host held a great deal of power.

Perhaps Peter also wanted to remind himself of that fact. Maybe this creature combatted his insecurities with affirming beliefs every time he passed it, a reminder of just how formidable he was.

Angling her head, she examined its thick, webbed claws. "Did you at least get a few swipes in before he finished you?"

"Do you always talk to dead animals?"

Wendy jolted to her full height and spun around. Bayne watched her from a darkened doorway, his untrustworthy eyes sharp and as soulless as the crocodile's. "How long were you standing there?"

"Long enough." He pushed off the door frame and sauntered closer. "It was one of Peter's first kills when we arrived."

"We?" She didn't realize he had accompanied Peter for so long. Maybe, like the crocodile, he was just another scary relic they kept around as a reminder of power.

Bayne moved like a snake in captivity, slithering about his cage as if he knew every corner by heart.

"I'm Peter's oldest friend," he said, purposely implying his rank so there was no misunderstanding her place in this chaos.

Oldest, but far from closest, she thought.

Wendy straightened her spine, less intimidated by reptilian men now that she looked into the eyes of a real crocodile. For whatever reason, Bayne seemed threatened by her presence. She didn't trust him. And she didn't play games with people she didn't trust.

"I was looking for the kitchen."

He pointed to the far end of the hall. "Second door to the right, straight on 'til you hit granite."

"Right. Thanks." She left him in the hall and headed in that direction.

The kitchen was a treasure trove of luxurious appliances. She hadn't expected to find anything in the cupboards beyond junk food, but there were abundant ingredients and fresh produce. Someone had taken the time to stock the shelves well, which made her wonder if servants were hiding somewhere.

She nosed through the fridge, drawing inspiration for her menu from the available ingredients.

"How was your shower?" Peter's deep voice startled her from behind and she turned her back to the cabinets.

"For tall men, you sure walk silently."

Peter grinned. "You learn to move silently from hunting. Part of the fun is waiting out your prey to arrive."

Was she the prey?

His jade stare traced over her bare legs, then returned to her face. She tucked a strand of damp hair behind her ear.

"How was your shower?"

"Delightful. Thank you."

He once again glanced down at Cass's shirt she wore, and his easy expression faded. "Help yourself to whatever you find in there." He stole a green apple from the basket on the counter.

"Thanks. I didn't expect to find the kitchen so well supplied."

He bit into the apple and shrugged. "The servants take care of that."

Relieved at the confirmation that there were servants, her

mind tucked that information away for later. Perhaps she could rely on them for a ride back to the airport.

Wendy gathered ingredients and decided to make her famous chicken and dumpling soup. It was her father's favorite, so she assumed the Lost Boys would like it too.

As soon as the celery, carrots, and onion started to sizzle, the men sniffed their way into the kitchen to find out what smelled so delicious. Like a pack of hungry dogs, they lingered by the stove, silently begging for scraps.

She put them to work, tasking each one with the simple jobs of a sous chef. "Salt?" she called as she pinched the thyme off the thin branch and sprinkled rosemary into the broth.

"Right here," Nibbs offered, rushing forward with a wooden salt cellar. He leaned over the large pot and breathed in the steam. "That smells divine."

Cass crowded her back and looked over her shoulder at the raw contents. "How do you turn that into a stew?" She could smell the earthiness of his clothes and something undeniably tempting on his skin.

She stirred the ingredients with a long wooden spoon. "With a little heat and the right ingredients, you can make just about anything." She handed off the wooden spoon and directed Cass to keep stirring so she could get some space from all that potent male energy.

Moving to the island, she measured out some dry ingredients.

"What's that?" the twins asked as she dumped flour into a deep bowl.

"This will be the dumplings."

Peter watched but didn't share the Lost Boys' curiosity. They were very helpful and responded well when she acknowledged their efforts with gratitude. "Who wants to set the table?"

"I will!" Cass, Tate, and the twins all volunteered at once.

Wendy handed off plates, spoons, napkins, and glasses so they could all contribute.

Peter wore an expression of boredom as he waited for the soup to finish cooking, and Bayne kept to the shadows, always watching with that calculating stare from the outside looking in.

There was something unnatural about him as if his upbringing embedded a sense of distrust, and he didn't know how to form relationships. Yet somehow, he stuck by Peter all these years.

"How did you all meet?" she asked, casually disguising her interest as she kneaded the dumplings.

"We were prisoners," Peter said as he chomped on the scraps left on the cutting board.

"Prisoners? Of what?"

"A wretched beast who locked us in frigid cells where we had no choice but to serve the evil that trapped us."

Was he joking? She thought he was, but the others lowered their gazes. She couldn't tell if they did so to hide smirks or out of some form of respect.

"I escaped first." Peter proclaimed, slamming down the cleaver to cut off the green leaves of a carrot. "Then Bayne. Then the others."

She frowned. He spoke as if telling a bedtime story, but there was a solemness in the air that hinted at the truth.

Peter hopped off the stool and came to stand behind her, holding the carrot to her throat like a blade. "We were never captured again. From then on, we made the rules."

"We take the prisoners," Tate said, nodding in agreement.

"Like pirates," Nibbs nodded.

Wendy cleared her throat and gently pushed away Peter's hand. "Pirates?"

"Aye," one of the twins said. "We take what we want and want for nothing."

"You could be a pirate, too," Peter told her. "We could call you something wicked, like Red-Handed Wendy—the innocent bird who escaped her cage and never got caught."

She gave him an unimpressed side glance. "For a bird, I'm not the best when it comes to flying."

"You'll learn."

Nibbs perked up. "We can teach you to swim, too! We can teach you anything you want to know. There are no rules here, except for one."

"And what is that?"

"Peter's in charge," they all said at once.

She looked at each face, noting the resolute loyalty in their eyes. How did Peter become such a high-ranking leader among a group of seemingly equal friends? And how much of what they said was actually true?

"It's time to clean the chicken from the bone," she said, putting the crew to work.

Peter might be their leader, but they followed her orders easily, coming to work around the island and helping in any way they could. All but two.

Peter observed the Lost Boys, and Bayne observed Peter. Always on the outside. Always apart from the rest.

Of all the boys, Cass and Tate were her favorites. They were sweet, helpful, and eager to please. She was learning their personalities quickly. She bet Cass was a cuddler because he liked to touch everything and often put his hands on her shoulders in an open show of affection. She liked how he made her feel at ease.

Tate was the ultimate people-pleaser. The mere thought of disappointing others made him anxious, so he always asked what he could do next.

Nibbs was also helpful but in a much more flirtatious way. He'd reach for a spoon and casually touch her hip or playfully dot flour on her nose. The more she permitted, the further he pressed his luck, once even whipping a tea towel at her behind, but Peter stopped that with a quick reprimand.

"Enough," Peter said, snatching the towel from Nibbs and tossing it aside.

He stepped behind Wendy, sheltering her body with his. Possessive arms slid beneath hers as he rested his chin on her shoulder in an unmistakable claim. The others instantly backed off.

She could have shouldered him away. She could have purposely given the other men more to do. But there was something pleasant about his territorial claim. No one had ever touched her so possessively, and while she wasn't sure about her feelings for Peter, she was becoming more certain she wanted a man who would unflinchingly claim her as his own.

Preparing dinner was a bit like playing house. A hierarchy naturally formed, one where Peter played the role of father and Wendy was the mother. The Lost Boys deferred to Peter's authority as much as they craved her nurturing praise.

That fantasy shattered, however, the moment Peter swept a hand under her shirt to grab a handful of flesh.

"Peter." She caught his wrist and gave him a warning stare. Surely, he didn't think to touch her with the Lost Boys present.

Peter met her glare with a grin and stepped forward, pressing the hard bulge of his arousal into her stomach. Her breath caught, and she arched back against the counter. He needed to stop.

"What are you doing?"

He leaned closer. "Whatever I want."

She looked back at the Lost Boys, who watched them with unblinking eyes. Not a single one looked concerned for her safety. Or—if they were concerned—none appeared willing to interfere because that would mean going against Peter.

She could have pushed him away, but she didn't. Slow and possessive, he dragged his other hand under her damp hair and caught the back of her neck. Something inside of her caught fire under his possessive hold. The alarming thought that liked being a prisoner, liked knowing that someone else was responsible for whatever happened next, caught her off-guard.

"Peter, the boys are watching." She could feel their hungry stares egging him on.

"So?"

"So—" The moment she opened her mouth, he closed the distance and sealed his lips to hers. Her resistance softened. Soon enough, she seemed to have no willpower at all.

He lifted her to the cool granite countertop, wedging his hips between her knees. Her legs naturally wrapped around him, her ankles locking at his back as he ground into her. Deep, slow kisses cast a spell as liquid fire burned low in her belly. His hands roamed down her back, trailed up her spine, and tangled in her hair. Only when she felt him loosening his belt did reality set back in.

"Peter." She nudged him.

The twins were grinning, and Tate was flushed. Cassian's

broad shoulders moved with every heavy breath while Nibbs bit his lip. Bayne was the only one who glared but they all made her uncomfortable.

"Peter, we have to stop."

"No, we don't."

Her face flushed as she clumsily made eye contact with Tate. "Yes, we do." This time, she shoved him back with more firmness and quickly scooted off the counter, carefully keeping her gaze down until her embarrassment abated. "The soup's about—*Hey!*"

The room turned upside down as she was scooped off her feet and thrown over Peter's shoulder. "The soup can wait."

He carried her through the house to a room she hadn't seen yet. A door slammed behind them, and he tossed her onto a plush bed of deep green blankets and soft, velvet pillows. He grabbed her ankle and tugged her to the edge, causing her shirt to rise to her ribs.

"Peter, wait."

His shirt came off, and he was on top of her once more, kissing her in an attempt to confuse or silence her objections.

"Peter—"

"Shhh."

She shoved an arm into his neck and turned her face away. "Peter, wait."

"Why?" He unzipped his pants.

"Hold on!" She scrambled back the moment she felt the heat and weight of his arousal against her bare thigh. "P-put that away."

He frowned and sat back, stroking himself almost perfor-matively. "Why?"

"Because we're moving too fast."

"Who says?"

"I do, for one."

He rolled his eyes. "I thought you wanted to have fun."

"I do. But that doesn't mean I'm going to have sex with you."

He laughed dryly as if stunned. "Wendy, I thought I made it clear that I intend to fuck you."

The crude shift in his language diminished her arousal, and she scowled. "Well, you don't always get what you want."

He laughed again. "Uh, yeah, I do."

"Not with me."

He paused as if this were the first time he heard the word no. "Seriously?"

"Seriously." She shoved down her shirt. "I'm not sleeping with you."

She wasn't sure when her mind had changed, but sometime in the course of the last few hours, it became abundantly clear that Peter was the *love 'em and leave 'em* kind of guy. She didn't need a betrothal, but she certainly needed to feel like more than an impulse that would likely be forgotten the moment he finished.

He rolled his eyes as if his judgment could further cave her will. That sort of manipulation might work with other women, but for her, it only further detracted from his attractiveness. She crossed her arms over her chest and met his challenging stare with an unbudging one of her own.

He climbed off the bed and put on his shirt. "Whatever."

Uncertainty nipped at her courage when he opened the door. "Where are you going?"

"Out. If you're not going to fuck me, I'll find someone who will."

Her jaw went slack, and he left her in the empty room. Her shock might have made her cry if she weren't so furious.

He was going out to fuck another woman? While she was still here?

She should be grateful she was learning who he really was before things went too far, but somehow, his rejection still caused an ache in her chest. What if she was making an enemy of an ally she needed? She was still at his mercy and reliant on his cooperation to get home.

She scowled, her inner turmoil jerking her thoughts about in an infuriating manner. What sort of gentleman behaved in such a way to his guest? Peter was no gentleman at all. He was a scoundrel and a spoiled whore.

Her resistance hardened like armor as she climbed off the bed. "Think you can bully me?" she grumbled, smoothing out her hair. "Let's see you find someone else while I'm here. I think you're all talk, Mr. Pangbourne."

Straightening her shoulders, she went to find the Lost Boys. Peter had a jealous side, and if he wanted to play games, she could play too.

CHAPTER 7

ALL CHILDREN, EXCEPT ONE, GROW UP

Wendy was still in a temper when she returned to the kitchen. Lifting the metal lid off the soup, she set it down noisily, enunciating her mood. "Cassian, taste this."

Cass rushed over to the stove, happy to be of assistance.

She held out the spoon, cupping her hand underneath. "Careful. It's hot."

"I can handle some heat." He took a bite and closed his eyes. "Mmm…" He swallowed. "I can't remember the last time I tasted anything so delicious."

She smiled, and her frustration faded. There was no rule saying her enjoyment on this trip needed to rely on Peter and his horny, mercurial moods. "Did your mother cook?"

"My mother?" Cassian frowned. "I don't remember my mother."

"Oh." His answer surprised her, and she didn't want to trespass on a touchy subject.

"None of us do," the twins said. "We were orphans."

Her pity seemed misplaced, as they were all grown men

now. But it was sad to think that not a single one of them had the love of a mother growing up. "Is that where you all met? An orphanage?"

Cassian, Tate, Nibbs, and the twins nodded. She had no idea where Peter and Bayne had gone.

Was that what they meant earlier when they said they escaped? Did they remember the orphanage as a prison? Her heart pinched as she pictured them each as little boys. And if Peter was the first to escape, did that mean he was adopted by the Pangbournes and not their biological son? So many realizations filled her with an urge to nurture and take care of all of them.

"Who's ready for soup?" They all perked up. "Bring your bowls to the stove."

They lined up with their bowls as she ladled out the contents. She didn't bother to call Peter, figuring he'd find his way back eventually.

The kitchen grew quiet as the men ate, the silence only broken by the occasional groan of satisfaction. The deep grunts and moans became so animated she blushed as they started to sound almost sexual.

Peter showed up just as everyone finished having thirds. She was glad she made such a large pot, because these boys could eat!

Showered and dressed in fresh clothes, Peter carried an air of untouchable confidence, making it clear he was still disappointed in her decision not to fuck him. Bayne followed him around like a salivating lapdog, desperate for every scrap of attention he could get.

As much as she'd looked forward to experiencing all the Never Lands had to offer, she now wished she'd never come at all. "If there's a way I can get in touch with the pilot—"

"He's gone," Peter said, lifting the lid off the pot and peeking inside at the little soup that remained.

"When will he be back?"

He shrugged and grabbed a bowl. "When I call him."

She ground her teeth. "Peter, I have to go home eventually."

"And eventually you will." He sat at the table as if put out by her tedious chatter. "I would have never brought you here if I'd known you'd be this high maintenance."

Her lips firmed. "I am not high maintenance!"

"Sure you are."

She growled in frustration and brushed past him, purposefully bumping his shoulder so the soup spilled off his spoon. The Lost Boys drifted out of the kitchen, and she washed the dishes in stewing silence as Peter ate.

When she got to her guest room, her nightgown was lying on the bed, freshly laundered and pristine. Her robe was also there.

She stripped out of Cassian's shirt and changed into her own clothes. If Peter wanted to go out, he was going to take her with him. "Let's see how smooth your game is then," she grumbled.

When she returned to the kitchen, her steps staggered to a halt. The counters were spotless and the food had all been put away. She didn't know who did this, but she was grateful for their help.

The Lost Boys appeared, looking especially handsome in their night clothes. They collectively smelled divine, and she realized the lot of them would have no problem getting laid with or without her presence.

"Wow, don't you all look dapper." Hair was styled, jaws

were shaved—save Cassian's—and clothes were pressed. It was quite the transformation.

Nibbs studied his reflection in the toaster. "Gotta look our best for a lagoon party."

"A lagoon party?" That sounded fancy. She looked down at her nightgown and robe, wondering if she should stay back after all.

"What's the matter?" Tate asked, noticing her concern.

"I'm in pajamas."

"So?"

"I can't go to a party this way."

"Yes, you can," Thayer argued.

When she twisted her lips, the boys crowded around. "Maybe lose the robe?" Nibbs suggested, already stripping the silk covering away.

If the party was at a lagoon they would be outside in the heat, so she didn't need the layers. Maybe her nightgown could pass for a dress. "I feel silly and underdressed."

They stared at her chest where her unbound breasts pressed against the thin silk.

"Nah," Thayer said, swallowing tightly. "You look good."

Tristan nodded, agreeing with his brother as his stare remained trained on her nipples.

"Very hot," Cass agreed.

"Sexy," Nibbs added, licking his lips.

"That's enough." She turned around and moved her robe to the back of a chair. "I left my shoes in the forest."

"It's a lagoon party. No one wears shoes," Tate explained.

Nibbs laughed. "Half the people don't even wear clothes."

"What?" Her eyes widened. "What kind of party is this?"

"The fun kind." Peter appeared, stuffing something into his pocket. "Let's go. We're leaving."

They filtered out the back door, and she shivered under the night air. It was much colder than it had been when they arrived. "Maybe I should bring my robe after all. But then I'll really look like I'm in my pajamas." At least now, her night-gown might pass as a dress.

"I have an idea," Cassian said, rushing back inside the house as the others walked ahead. A moment later, he returned with a dark maroon coat. "You can wear this."

He swept the long duster jacket over her shoulders, and she slid her arms into the silk-lined sleeves. Wool ruffles spilled from the cuffs like waves, and brass buttons trailed along the lapels as if mapping out a hidden treasure. The trim was fine leather with long tails and beautiful detail stitched into the worn wool. It was a high-quality couture coat.

"Where did you get this?"

She sniffed the collar and closed her eyes at the dark, mysterious scent hidden there. Whoever wore this coat before wore it with authority. The masculine energy coming from the weight and detail spoke volumes about its true owner.

"We stole it."

"You *stole* it?"

"Yeah, but don't worry. It's yours now."

"Who did you steal it from?" She needed to know who the owner was. Desperately, she craved a name to put to this hypnotic scent.

Cassian grinned and leaned forward. "It belonged to a pirate. Peter snuck onto his ship in the still of the night and stole it right out of the captain's private chambers."

"A pirate?" She grinned, intrigued by a tale of danger.

"They call him Black Jack. Peter swears he's always lingering off the coast, spying on him, but he can't figure out why. He's a dangerous man, so stay alert and tell us if you see anything."

She envisioned a towering man with dark features and limitless authority. "Did Peter get caught when he stole the coat?"

"No, but I'm sure old Jack was furious when he woke up and realized it was stolen from his private chambers. Crooks don't like it when they're the ones getting robbed. But Peter's always gotten a kick out of taunting those who think they're better than him."

"How do you know he was a crook?"

"All pirates are criminals. They steal whatever they want and live lawlessly. But Black Jack is the greatest sea devil of all."

That may be true, but Peter also stole. Did that make him a pirate, too? His friends shamelessly admitted to living without rules. All but one. Perhaps that made Peter the captain of their little crew.

"Well, regardless of who the coat's true owner is, thank you. I love it." And now she felt dressed enough to attend a party.

"You're welcome. We better catch up to the others before Peter gets angry."

She couldn't care less about Peter's happiness at the moment. He was the one who left her behind, after all.

The lagoon was located on the banks of Peter's island. It wasn't a far walk, but a muddy one. Due to the jungle's humidity, surfaces were constantly wet with dew, making everything slippery. Wendy was grateful when they finally reached the sand.

The lagoon was a small grotto that opened to an endless

sea. The water sparkled under the moonlight, each little ripple glinting like diamonds dancing beneath the night sky.

Sensual music and wild revelry echoed off the jetties and from the hidden caves. While there were plenty of men present, it was mostly feminine voices Wendy heard. She suddenly felt shy and uncertain by the number of strangers who apparently were all familiar with each other—familiar enough to kiss and touch and—*oh my*.

Her eyes widened at the couple railing away in the stark openness of the beach. Okay, this was *that* sort of party. She took Cassian's arm so she wasn't standing alone.

Capriciousness carried on the breeze. The Lost Boys were gone, as was Peter. "Where are the others?"

Cassian shrugged. "We don't need them." His arm tightened around her. "They're probably getting drinks, or dancing, or swimming, or maybe already fucking."

She gaped up at him, and he laughed.

"What did you think we meant when we said lagoon party?"

"Not that."

He chuckled. "You'll have fun, especially if this is your first time."

He had no idea how literal the term 'first time' truly was for her.

The air came alive with something sinful. Crystal-blue water shimmered as it lapped at the banks where pale pebbles and pink shells glittered atop the white sand. The tranquil setting seemed at odds with the throbbing music and gyrating bodies dancing around the grotto.

Beautiful women lounged on the larger rocks like jewels on display. They wore tightly fitted dresses, elegantly detailed sarongs, and glittering bikini tops. All of them were in impeccable shape, with figures that could make a supermodel jealous.

Fragrant, tropical flowers grew wildly among the dunes. The salt air rolled off the sea, disrupting the naturally fruit-scented breeze of the Never Lands, hinting at something ominous unfolding.

She searched the horizon but only saw darkness. Soft splashing mingled with low moans along the banks of the lagoon as techno music pulsed from the grotto. Wendy preferred the outskirts of the party, but Cassian pulled her closer.

"I'll catch up in a minute," she said, slipping from his grip.

He hesitated only a second before loping off toward the others.

Wendy scanned the lagoon as palms waved overhead. What was she doing there?

A woman laughed, the ethereal sound singing through the breeze like a haunting melody that stole everyone's attention, including hers. And there was Peter, lying amongst a school of women petting and fawning over him.

Wendy's lips firmed into a flat line. He was certainly making progress on his goals.

"Oh, Peter, you're so muscular," one woman purred, stroking his bare chest where his shirt had been unbuttoned.

Her gaze went to the water where others swam naked, no doubt performing dark deeds beneath the surface. Didn't the cold bother them?

While the sand still held a bit of warmth from the sun, the wind was cool. She had no plans of going near the water, so she kept a safe distance and stayed hidden in the shadows of the trees.

Despite the serene nature of this place, an ominous shroud hung in the air. The idyllic, dreamlike mood boasted of fantasies, but there was also a lurking sense of danger. Though the lagoon mimicked a careless place of temptation and seduction, an undercurrent of peril waded in the undertow.

The mysterious women reminded her of sirens, the kind that tempted the sailors to their deaths at sea. From the melodic way they spoke to the captivating way they lured the men closer, they enchanted everyone who came near enough to get swept away by the current of lust and desire.

Then she noticed the familiar figure of another woman hiding in the shadows, much like herself. Belle was scowling at Peter as he lounged amongst the sirens while they poured him wine and massaged his body.

Wendy quietly approached Belle, wondering if their exclusion somehow created an alliance. "Is it always like this?"

Belle glanced at her dismissively, her scowl returning to Peter. "Yes."

Wendy followed her gaze, feeling forgotten by Peter but not as betrayed as his little outcasted friend. She didn't know or care to know their history, but she personally lost interest in being more than his acquaintance after seeing how quickly he jumped from female to female. No wonder the woman was angry.

She glanced back at Belle, taking pity on her. "Are you in love with him?"

"Only a fool would love Peter."

Maybe she was a fool then because she appeared deeply bothered by the sight of him with other women, and she'd tried to drown Wendy for merely showing up tonight.

What was it about Peter that made him so captivating?

Women not only loved him, but men also craved his attention. Perhaps it was that his attention never lasted longer than a few minutes, and its rareness made it all the more valuable.

Wendy didn't love Peter, but she certainly allowed him liberties she'd never allowed anyone else. At the hint of regret, she turned her focus to other things.

"You aren't friends with those women?"

"Who? The mermaids?" Belle curled her lip. "Fuck those bitches. They'll sweetly drown you all the while acting like they're doing you a favor."

"Like you tried to drown me?"

Belle met her stare. "I wasn't pretending to be sweet. At least with me, you know where you stand."

Speechless, Wendy could only blink. They were all bitches.

"You're all wasting your time anyway."

Wendy frowned, not liking the idea of being grouped in with those women. "What do you mean?"

"Everyone knows Peter's future's promised to someone else."

"Who?" Her father certainly knew no such thing. Neither did she for that matter.

"He's betrothed to Lyra Wilde."

Wendy's eyes widened. "Peter's engaged?" Her stare jerked to the cluster of women fondling him. One had her hand in his pants while another kissed him. "That…whore."

"He'll never go through with the wedding. Peter sees marriage as a debt. And Peter hates feeling indebted."

Wait until Father learns this, she thought. That should shatter any lingering illusions about Peter being an upstanding gentleman.

"How does his fiancée feel about him kissing other women?

"She has no control over him. Peter's his own person. He's wild like the woods, and he does what he wants."

"Well, eventually, he'll grow up. All men have to."

"Not Peter."

One of the sirens straddled Peter's lap. Belle scoffed in disgust and walked away, leaving Wendy, once more, abandoned and alone.

Frustrated by the spectacle he was putting on, Wendy marched over to her self-involved host, disrupting him before a true Roman orgy began. "Peter."

He didn't hear her. His face was hidden by a curtain of hair belonging to the woman currently making out with him. She cleared her throat.

The moans stopped, and several sharp, glistening eyes turned on her like vipers in a basket. Their thick, feathered lashes batted indifferently as their full lips pursed over what were most likely mouthfuls of fangs. Their cold hostility didn't deter her.

"Peter," she snapped with enough firmness to get his attention.

Up close, the women were more frightening than pretty. The one that had been kissing Peter had long, jet-black nails.

"Who are you?" the clawed one asked, taking her measure with a quick, unimpressed glance.

"I'm Wendy." She looked at Peter, but he only grinned, folding his arms behind his head as if to say, *I warned you.*

Her fury from earlier could not compare to what she felt now.

He just laid there like a spread of overpriced caviar that started to smell. She wanted to leave but didn't know the way back to the house. It was clear Peter would be no help. He was only worried about himself.

"You're despicable."

Turning her back on him, she searched the lagoon for the Lost Boys. One of them would surely help her get home.

The beach was now overcome with naked bodies, and in the moonlight, many of the figures looked the same. She spotted the twins sharing a woman whose moans echoed through the night, then saw Nibbs thrusting wildly into a busty woman spread out along the jetty. Her stare bolted back to the twins as they pleasured the woman with their mouths, one at her breasts, the other feasting between her thighs.

Her horrified gaze darted back to Peter, and he laughed.

"You'll have to pardon Wendy," he told the females surrounding him. "She's a bit of a prude."

The women snickered, whispering behind their claws and hissing judgments through their sharp fangs. The magic of this ethereal place entirely faded as she understood she was on her own. Peter was only interested in fucking her, and it was now abundantly clear that they were not friends.

Irritated, she stormed off in a rage but couldn't escape the sounds of slapping flesh, catlike cries, and masculine moans.

How could Peter bring her here only to forget she existed? He was intentionally being cruel to punish her for not having sex with him, selfishly thinking only of himself. The longer she watched the debauchery unfold from the shadows, the more her bitterness grew.

She was just about to risk getting lost in the jungle when a commotion broke out between Peter and his Mediterranean harem. Wendy perked up, trying to see what was happening.

Peter was on his feet, frantically adjusting his clothes, as he rushed toward a copse of trees on the other side of the grotto.

The women called him back, but he ignored their pleas. What was he rushing off to?

Understanding dawned when Wendy spotted a dusky beauty scowling from the shadows. Ah, was this the fiancée?

Raking his fingers through his mussed hair, Peter approached the woman. He spoke, but they were too far away for Wendy to hear their words. Peter reached for the woman's hand, but she flung his touch away. Inwardly, Wendy smirked. Served him right.

There were no tells of affection between them, but Peter still tried to reason with her. It seemed strange that anyone would have that sort of hold over him, even if it were weak at best. But this woman showed no desperation for his attention. She appeared only to want his respect.

The outsider held her shoulders back, her body language boasting of confidence as Peter peppered her with excuses. When she heard enough, she slapped his face, the resounding whack loud enough to still the nearby onlookers.

"Filthy *cockslut*!" his fiancée snapped, and Peter's hands balled into tight fists at his sides as everyone stared, holding their collective breaths.

The perilous energy vibrated across the lagoon. Peter had a temper, but would he use it on the woman he was promised to marry? He had been the one in the wrong, after all. It was a train wreck, and the lagoon bystanders couldn't look away, but Wendy had seen enough.

Chancing that she might get lost, she traced her steps back to the dunes and headed toward the forest. She hardly made it to the trees before Peter caught up with her.

"Wendy, wait!"

Oh, now they were friends. "Leave me alone, Peter."

"You can't leave."

"I can, and I am."

He caught her arm. "You don't know the way."

Apparently, his little tussle with The Future Missus had concluded. She glanced over his shoulder, and the dusky beauty was gone.

"Why didn't you tell me you were engaged?"

He waved away her words. "Because I'm never getting married. Marriage doesn't interest me."

That much was clear. "I want to go home."

"Well, we aren't heading back to the house for at least—"

"Not your house, Peter. I want to go *home,* to *my* house."

He laughed as if confused. "Why? You haven't even done anything fun yet."

"Is this what fun is to you? Having sex with random strangers at a lagoon?"

"Yes." His crowing laughter mocked her, and she frowned.

"Well, it's not fun to me."

"Maybe it would be if you loosened up a little."

She had the urge to slap him so his other cheek matched the one wearing the red handprint of his fiancée. "Grow up, Peter."

"I am grown up."

"No, you're not. You're just an entitled little boy trapped in the body of a man, terrified that people won't like you anymore if you stop spoiling them with lavish gifts. Maybe if you thought about someone other than yourself for a change, you'd have real friends. Instead, you just have an entourage of people reliant on you, much like I'm reliant on you to get home. Their loyalty isn't earned. It's bought. And the sad part is—since you brag so often about being a master of avoidance when it comes to real responsibility—I don't even think you're the one footing the bill."

His smile faded to a cold scowl. Apparently, she hit a precious, privileged nerve. "The house is that way."

He pointed past the dunes into the shadows where night creatures chattered and hissed.

When she looked back, he was stomping back to the party where he wouldn't have his worth as a man challenged. A tear of frustration tripped past her lashes, and she batted it away. No way would she allow some privileged man-child to make her cry.

"You okay?"

Startled, Wendy gasped and pivoted. Cass watched her from the shadows of a nearby tree. How long had he been there?

"Me?" She cleared her throat and wiped her cheeks, hiding the fact that he'd startled her. "I'm fine."

He pushed off the tree trunk and slowly came closer. "No, you're not. Girls don't cry when they're fine."

"You're right. They cry when they're angry."

At that, he lifted a brow. "I've never heard anyone talk to Peter that way." He grinned. "You're pretty badass, Wendy Bird."

"Please don't call me that. And Peter was being a jerk. He deserved everything I said."

Cassian nodded. "He's had it easy since getting adopted. None of us went to wealthy families except Peter."

Calling the Pangbournes wealthy seemed like an understatement. "Having money doesn't entitle someone to treat others like crap."

"No, his privilege makes it easy. No one ever calls him out the way you did. And if they do, Peter cuts them off."

She sighed. How was she ever getting home?

"Don't worry. He'll do the right thing eventually. Image is important to the Pangbournes. He's just gotta blow off some steam first."

Wendy crossed her arms and shivered. She'd only apologize if he took her home. Until then, she wouldn't trust him. He was already back among the women, having his ego and other things stroked.

She sighed, and Cassian held out his arms for a hug. "Bring it in."

Wendy hesitated, then closed the distance. He wrapped her in a tight bear hug and held her for several heartbeats.

"He doesn't mean the stuff he says."

She pulled back from his warmth and looked into his eyes. "Don't make excuses for him."

"I'm not. Peter's complicated. We all are. That's what happens when you grow up in an orphanage. Survival makes you selfish. The twins lost their parents in a fire. Nibbs lost his in a car accident. With my mom, it was drugs. But Peter… He was abused for a long time before they rescued him. Unfortunately, the orphanage wasn't the sanctuary many thought."

"They were that cruel?"

He nodded. "Peter never knew it could be different until he was adopted. And once he realized some adults were actually nice, he never wanted to think about the nasty ones again."

"Did the rest of you ever get adopted?"

"No, we ran away. We found Peter, and he helped us hide until we came of age. Then we didn't have to run anymore."

"Hide where?"

He grinned as if to say some secrets were meant to go to the grave.

She now understood that there was more to the story. Perhaps there was love to their loyalty after all. "I shouldn't have said those things to him."

"Don't sweat it. Peter never stays angry for long. He prefers to think happy thoughts."

That made sense now that she understood his background better. "It's nice that you all have each other. In a way, you're like brothers."

Something flashed in his eyes. "Peter doesn't like when we call ourselves that."

"Why?"

"Because he had a brother once. It's a touchy subject."

"Oh." She wanted to know what happened to his brother. Had he been at the orphanage, too?

Before she could form a question, Cassian asked, "What do you say we try to have some fun?"

She glanced out at the lagoon. "I'm not sure I know how to have fun like this." Perhaps she was a prude.

He laughed. "You've just gotta loosen up."

"I don't know how."

"Well, for starters, you need a drink. Here."

He handed her his cup, and she sniffed the contents. "What is it?"

"We call it seawater. But this..." He withdrew a small capsule from his pocket. "*This* is pixie dust."

She examined the pill, which looked as harmless as an aspirin. "What's it do?"

"It fills your head with happy thoughts and makes you fly."

"So, it's drugs?"

He chuckled. "Don't act so scandalized. You're not driving anywhere. It's going to be a long night. Might as well make the best of it."

"Have you done it before?"

"Yeah, plenty of times."

She debated. She'd never done drugs before, but maybe that was her problem. "Will it help me loosen up?"

"Absolutely."

She wasn't sure what to do. "I don't know."

"How about if I promise to stay sober and watch over you? I'll make sure you behave."

She wondered if she could trust him. "You won't drink?"

"Not a drop." When she still hesitated, he said, "Look, it only lasts a couple of hours. I promise to watch over you the whole time."

Wendy chewed her lip. Maybe this was exactly what she needed—a little push to knock her inhibitions down. "Okay."

He grinned and snapped the capsule in half, dumping the powdered contents into the seawater. "Bottoms up, darling."

CHAPTER 8

FAITH, TRUST, AND PIXIE DUST

The silver powder shimmered with an unnatural gleam, floating on the surface of her beverage like a small galaxy of stars. She swirled it into the seawater with her finger and took a sip.

"Ugh." She grimaced at the bitter, metallic taste. "It's like licking the edge of a blade."

"Just get it down."

She hoped this wasn't a mistake. Keeping her eyes on Cassian, she guzzled the sour contents, swallow after bitter swallow, and gasped when it was finally empty.

"Gross. How long before it—"

Her words cut off as the world shifted. Waves thrummed in the distance as shadows formed in the swells.

"Whoa. Everything's moving."

Cass caught her arm as she wobbled. "Is it hitting you already?"

Colors melted, bleeding together in hues so bright they vibrated. "The beach is breathing."

Cassian's laughter echoed as if a million miles away, but only as loud as a whisper. "Let's find a place to sit down."

He led her toward a cabana bed. Various groping couples groaned along the way, and she stared at the way they touched each other. "Are they all doing this? Is that why they're so free?"

Cassian's mouth moved as he answered, but she could only hear the vibrating colors and moans of people having sex. She smiled at him as her skin began to hum, every nerve in her body a live wire unraveling like silk from a spool.

"I feel amazing," she confessed, swaying from his muscular arm.

"Oh, boy. Maybe I should have given you half a dose."

"No, silly," she laughed, falling onto an empty cabana bed. "I feel incredible—as if I'm floating on air and made of mist."

He lounged beside her, resting on his elbow as he stared into her eyes.

The air thickened around her like velvet and honey, and she licked the sweetness off her lips. "Do you taste that?"

"Taste what?"

She stared up at the stars. "My lips."

"Really?"

He shifted closer, and she looked at him. He was very close. "You gave me a shirt."

"I did." He dragged his finger over her hip. "But I like this better."

"Mmm. Do you?" She reached for his cheek, leaning into his warmth. "Your face is so fuzzy, like a teddy bear."

He caught her hand. "Careful, darling. Bears don't like to be teased."

"I'm not teasing."

"Are you sure?"

She searched his eyes and nodded. "You won't hurt me."

"Of course not. My only goal is to make you feel good."

She moaned. "I feel pretty good at the moment." She continued to stroke his cheek. "Everything's so sensual and alive."

"I can make it feel even better if you want."

She closed her eyes and hummed peacefully as the darkness came alive. The air sang, and colors danced. "I hear everything."

He brushed a wisp of hair away from her face. "What do you hear?"

"The universe is singing to me." She seemed as weightless as a music note and softer than a whisper. "I know I'm here, but it's like I'm also there."

He traced his fingers down her arm, leaving a trail of goosebumps on her skin. "Where's that, darling?" He had such a deep, comforting voice.

"It's like I'm in the stars. I can see everything."

When she closed her eyes, the Never Lands spread out beneath her like a map. She was soaring without moving. Every heartbeat was a lifetime that only lasted a second, yet she saw everything in the blink of an eye.

"Is this what he meant when he said women could sing to the stars?"

"Not quite." His breath teased her cheek. "Do you want me to show you how to sing like that?"

She peeked at him through her lashes. "Maybe?" She wasn't sure if Cassian was any safer than the rest of them, but her curiosity was undeniable. She truly wanted to know what everyone else seemed to know. Taking his large hand, she pulled him closer. "Touch me, Cassian."

He trailed his fingers slowly along her jaw and down to her collarbone. She sighed and arched into his touch, and her nipples tightened against the silk of her nightgown, shivering when his hand trailed between her breasts.

"Should I stop?"

"Why would you stop? It feels wonderful."

He cupped her breast possessively. "Even this?"

"Especially that." There was something about the aggressiveness of his hold that tightened the loose knots inside of her, bringing her to full attention.

"You like it a little rough, don't you?"

"I don't know. Maybe." She kept her eyes closed.

"I think you do." He nuzzled her throat with his lips, the crinkle of his beard abrading her soft skin. "Have you ever been held down and fucked?"

Her breath hitched as his mouth sealed to hers—

"What the fuck do you think you're doing?"

Cassian's touch disappeared, jolting Wendy out of the sensual haze. Peter stood at the foot of the cabana bed scowling at his friend.

"Did I say you could touch her?"

"Peter, relax. We were only having fun."

Wendy blinked in confusion. Was that a knife in Peter's hand? "You think I brought her here for you."

"No. But she was upset. I was—"

"I saw what you were doing."

Rolling to her stomach, Wendy slithered to the edge of the cushion and stumbled onto the sand, laughing when she landed in a heap.

"What the fuck did you give her? She can barely walk."

"I can walk!" She held up a finger, needing a moment to find her bearings.

"Peter, I only gave her a little pixie dust—"

"You fucking drugged her?"

"Not without her consent!" Cassian shouted, holding up his hands defensively. "Peter, I swear—"

"You're a dead man." Peter charged, toppling Cassian to the sand, and others swarmed around them.

Wendy could only laugh. "Don't be such a prude, Peter." No one seemed to hear her over all the fighting.

The pixie dust made it impossible to get upset. She turned her gaze to the sea as something caught her eye. A dark shape materialized out of the night like a phantom rising from the black. It sliced through the water with silent, lethal grace, and she wondered if she was hallucinating.

On her feet, she stumbled toward the cliffs. Shadows against shadows, the midnight waves parted as the enormous hull of a ship plunged toward the lagoon like the blade of a sword.

This was not a yacht or an ordinary cruise ship. This was a relic made of warped wood and iron. Black sails rippled silently, undetected by the others who watched the fight.

The air shifted as she wobbled to the cliff's edge. Something wicked and forbidden radiated from the ship's bones as if she were the one luring it in. Emboldened, she leaned over the edge where the tide had receded, and rocks protruded from the surf like jagged, black teeth.

Pale moonlight glinted against the ship's prow, revealing a gilded figurehead—half-woman, half-beast. She glanced back, too far away from the others to call the ship to attention. Could no one else see it? Maybe it wasn't real.

Wind beat at the tails of her coat, lifting them like sails as she blocked the mist from her eyes and squinted. The black ship glided closer, lanterns swinging from the rigging, and her pulse quickened. A tall figure stood at the front, holding a long telescope to his eye, staring directly at her. She swore he was looking into her soul.

"Black Jack," she whispered, her words swallowed by the raging surf below.

The shadowed figure turned and spoke to the men at his back. Time seemed to snap forward, and everything moved quickly. He called to his crew, but she couldn't hear him over the crashing waves. How had she wandered so far away from the others? Should she go back and warn them?

Time stretched and spiraled. Rooted to the banks of the cliff, the cold ocean wind cut into her as the thick wool coat flapped wildly at her back. She held out her arms, wondering if she could fly.

"*Pirates!*" someone yelled, breaking her haze.

Everyone started to scream as rowboats approached the banks and pistols shot into the air.

Wendy staggered back from the cliff, startled by how close she'd come to falling as danger erupted on the beaches to her back. Someone was supposed to be watching her. But as she looked back at the lagoon, black figures swarmed the banks, and she knew she was on her own.

Were they pirates? They had to be after something. People didn't simply storm beaches and terrorize civilians for no reason. Or did they? This was the Never Lands. One never knew what to expect here.

She should help. Or at least hide. Hiding was probably best. Pivoting toward the dunes, she slammed into the rock-hard chest of none other than Satan himself.

He snatched her arms in an unbreakable grip and bared a lecherous grin. "Gotcha now, little one."

Then Wendy could only hear her own screams.

CHAPTER 9

BLACK WATERS

Wendy's blood-curdling scream ripped through the night as she stared into the sinister eyes of a pock-marked face covered in tattoos. Beyond the labyrinth of black ink, hung dreadlocks as thick as snakes.

His hand covered her mouth as a gun clicked by her ear. "One more scream like that, and it'll be your last, understand?"

She nodded frantically, her heart racing so fast she could barely speak. Eyes wild, she spotted the silhouette of distant figures falling to the ground. This was no hallucination. Masked men infested the beaches, and no one was coming to help her.

The frightening man jerked her around to face the water. His powerful hands trapped her arms at her back in an unbreakable grip as he fastened her wrists in coarse rope. It was so surreal she hardly protested, her mind lost in a drugged haze and her instincts traveling too slowly to her brain.

"Time to go." The wind knocked out of her lungs as she was hoisted onto his shoulder. Before she knew what was happening, they were soaring off the cliff and flying toward the jagged rocks below.

"I can't swim!"

"Then you better hope I don't let go."

A shot echoed through the air just as frigid water closed around her. His shoulder lodged under her ribs, shoving the air from her lungs, then she broke the surface as he pushed her upward.

"*Help—mph!*" Tossed roughly into a small rowboat, she winced as pain shot through her bound arms and skull.

"What did I say about screaming?"

She tried to scramble back, but there was nowhere to go on the small boat and her tethered arms made it impossible to escape. He grabbed her by the silk of her nightgown and yanked her forward. Darkness blinded her as a burlap sack was shoved over her head, making it hard to breathe.

Panting frantically, she tried to sit up only to get shoved back down.

"Stay put." The tiny craft wobbled wildly, and she feared they might capsize.

The clatter of oars sliding through the holds met the lapping water. Where was he taking her? In only a short minute, the screams of the lagoon were distant whispers, and her panicked breathing and the pounding of her heart became all she could hear.

When he grabbed her again, she kicked, the heel of her bare foot connecting with something that felt like a jaw.

"Little bitch!"

He roughly yanked her off the floor of the boat, and she screamed, kicking wildly. Then, she was shoved forward with no way to catch her fall. Her foot tripped over something, and she stumbled. Once more, the frigid water pulled her under as true fear set in. He yanked her to the surface by her bound arms.

"See what you've done!"

The wet sack over her head made it impossible to breathe, and he yanked it off her head.

"Please!" she sputtered. "I can't swim!" She didn't stand a chance of surviving the water with her arms tied.

"Are you going to behave?"

"Yes, I'll be good." Ice filled her veins as she shivered and begged for mercy. "Please, don't put me in the water again."

"Quiet!" he snapped, rowing them further out to sea. Soon, the sloshing of the water became all she could hear until he finally said, "We're here."

She looked up as a black wall blocked her view of the sky. They were at the ship.

Her teeth chattered. "What happens now?"

"You shut your mouth and do exactly as I say." He yanked her forward, banding a thick arm under her waist as he carried her like a rag doll.

Their craft wobbled precariously, and the blood rushed to her head as she feared falling into the water again. He climbed up a rope ladder with one arm as he held her in the other, and soon, the water was two stories below.

She was tossed onto another hard surface, and pain radiated up her arms. "Asshole!"

Several men chuckled as they crowded around her, and her courage evaporated. They grinned down at her with missing teeth and dreadful scars. It was then she understood some fates were worse than drowning.

The weathered wood whined as the ship rocked, and the tall mast loomed overhead as ripples of black sails whipped overhead.

"What a pretty little thing she is." The men crowded closer, leering and blocking out her view of the night sky.

"Capitan's gonna like her."

"What's your name, princess?"

The pungent odor of their unwashed clothes stole her breath. Gunpowder misted the air like fog, reminding her how dangerous these men were. She worried for Peter and the Lost Boys.

"Please," she begged, awkwardly scooting back as much as she could with her arms tied. "My family has money. They can pay you. I promise they'll reward you if you keep me safe."

"It ain't your money he's after."

"That's enough gawking, boys." The terrifying man with the dreadlocks reached for her once more.

"No!" she shouted in protest. *"Please!"* But none of the other men came to her aid.

Terrified of where he might be taking her and what he planned to do, Wendy bit into his arm until she tasted blood.

He yanked her head back by the hair and growled, "Bitch!" His teeth were filed into points and covered in silver.

She spit at him, and he flinched and dropped her to her feet, but still kept hold of her arms.

"I'll see that you pay for that," he threatened, wrestling her toward a door that appeared to lead below deck.

"She sure hates you, Jukes," one man snickered as the others watched complacently.

She dragged her feet, scraping her heels along the splintered planks. *"Help!"* Her flailing was of no use when he hoisted her onto his shoulder again, this time knocking the wind out of her so hard she nearly vomited.

His heavy footfalls stomped along the black planks, taking

her deeper and deeper into the bowels of the ship. The sound of the sea disappeared as they entered a cramped hall that led to a dimly lit stairwell.

She completely lost her sense of direction by the end of the labyrinth. Then he threw her down once more. This time, she landed on an ornate carpet, but it still hurt like hell.

"Bastard!"

He sneered. "I'm far worse than a bastard, princess."

He lit a candle, and she blinked at her elaborate quarters, startled by such opulence. Fine furnishings, books, and maps filled the dim space. In the corner, a chest brimmed with gold and strings of jewels. The musty scent of old wood and a faint whiff of rum tinged the air, but also something else. Something rich and threatening. Something…familiar.

"Who are you people?"

"Your worst nightmare." He tossed a pile of rusted chains on the floor.

"Please—"

"Begging won't save you." He yanked her to her knees and roughly tugged the ropes.

The moment her arms were free, she sprung to her feet, but he was faster.

Her face hit the floor before she took a single step, and she whimpered when he pinned her beneath his indomitable weight.

Breath hot on her cheek, he snarled, "Next time you try something like that, I'll break your arm. Nod if you understand."

She closed her eyes, swallowing back another whimper, and nodded.

"Sit up and hold out your arms."

She did as he said, terrified he'd hurt her again. Her

clothes were sopping wet, and the long coat had become impossibly heavy. She looked at the chains and hesitated.

Flipping back his black coat, he flashed the butt of a pistol holstered at his hip. "Do I need my gun?"

Swallowing back a sob, she reluctantly extended her arms. The heavy, metal cuffs closed around her wrists with a click, and she dropped her weighted hands to her lap.

He moved to the other side of the room, where the chain hooked to an iron latch on the wall. She studied her surroundings, categorizing what items might cause the greatest threat to her safety. An antique bed with deep red drapes and a velvet canopy dominated the shadows. The moment she set eyes on the bed, it became harder to breathe.

He turned the crank on the wall and the slack of the chains tightened. Her eyes widened in horror. What sort of person kept chains like this?

Once the limp of the chain hung neatly overhead, giving her only enough freedom to rest her arms, he carried a wooden bucket to the carpet and dropped it by her side.

"W-what's that?"

"Your privy."

How long did he plan to keep her chained up like this? "I think there's been some kind of a mistake."

"There's no mistake." He withdrew his pistol, checked the chamber, then returned it to the holster at his hip. "The boss will be down shortly."

He wasn't the boss?

He opened the door.

"Wait. Please!" But he ignored her, and the door locked behind him. "You can't just leave me here! *I'm British!*"

CHAPTER 10

THE DEVIL IN RED

Wendy lay on the floor, her cheek cold with tears as she rested her face against the carpet. She decided some time ago that she was better not thinking right now because when her mind worried about what might happen to her, she went into a full-blown panic attack.

Time was hazy. Whatever drugs were in her system had worn off, and there was nothing left to dull the fear. She was going to die here, or worse. She was sure of it.

These men were not interested in negotiating, and their brutality had been more than proven. But she knew it could still get far worse.

She ached for the familiarity of her safe little nursery and would give anything to have that sort of security back. A cage shared with monsters was far worse than any gilded cage her parents locked her in.

What an absolute fool she was. She could have avoided all this if she only knew how unhinged Peter Pangbourne was.

She blamed him for bringing her here but also held herself accountable for stupidly trusting a stranger.

What was taking so long?

As much as she dreaded the future, she wanted to know what was coming next. That brute, Jukes, said the boss would be down shortly, but that had to be at least an hour ago.

In the unmoving silence, she studied her surroundings. Despite the lawlessness of this ship, there existed undertones of order, however tyrannical. These pirates were not of the Never Lands or any land. They belonged only to themselves and to the sea. A thought that terrified her, especially as someone who couldn't swim.

Wendy had always been enchanted by danger, but the truth was, she wasn't cut out for a world without consequences. She liked order and achievable objectives. Those things didn't seem to exist here.

How was she going to escape this place? The deck had been strewn with ropes and barrels, plenty of places to hide, but they were at sea, and leaving the ship promised a watery death. Besides, the men outnumbered her at least ten to one.

The ship's rocking turned her stomach as muffled voices passed in the hall. Fear confined her as much as the chains holding her. Soon, something would happen. She didn't know what, but she sensed it coming closer.

Rolling to her back, she grew still and listened. Minutes passed, perhaps hours. Every now and then, she'd hear masculine voices holler. What happened to everyone at the lagoon? Were they dead? Was anyone left to save her?

Heavy footfalls approached, and her heart jolted into a rapid gallop. She forced herself to stand up despite how frozen and stiff her bones were. This was it. She could not lay helpless on the ground, awaiting her sentence. Whatever was coming for her, she would be prepared. Balling her hands into fists, she rose to her full height, ready to fight.

The metal lock on the door clicked, and the chains rattled as she stepped back. The air left her lungs in a whoosh. Nothing could have prepared her for the man who stepped inside.

Tall and broad, with hair blacker than a raven's wing, he entered the room and locked the door. His authority was palpable. He was obviously the owner of the ship, perhaps by deed or law, but more so by his presence. When he finally looked at her, she felt him in her stomach.

One glance at her oppositional stance and he chuckled. "A little, wet mouse." Flicking an invisible fleck of lint from his cuff, he closed the distance slowly. "Don't strain yourself. Resistance, at this point, is futile."

His low voice carved through the air between them, deep enough to leave scars. She stayed standing no matter how much she trembled.

"What's your name, little mouse?"

"W—Wendy."

"Wendy, what? When someone asks your name, give it to them in its entirety."

"W-Wendy Moira Angela D-Darling."

He glanced over his shoulder and raised a dark brow. He had the lean muscle and graceful confidence of a wild jungle cat. "Do you typically speak with a stammer, Wendy Moira Angela Darling?"

"No."

He moved as though the air bent for him, as if everything in his path was under his command. Dragging a chair across the floor, the scraping sound rubbing her nerves raw, he let it wobble into place beside her. "Sit."

She glanced at the chair, reluctant to give him the upper hand.

"When I give a command, you obey."

Shaking like a leaf, she met his hard stare with challenge, refusing to follow his orders.

"Very well." He swept his boot behind her ankle, tripping her off her feet. She fell into the chair. "I don't repeat myself."

She cowered under his hard stare, the heavy chains jangling as she situated her arms. He moved to the hearth and lit a fire, and she closed her eyes, grateful for the anticipated warmth.

After lighting several long candles about the cabin, he pulled another chair to the carpet and turned it to face her but didn't sit. At the sideboard, he poured two glasses of blood-red wine.

"What brings you to the Never Lands, Wendy Moira Angela Darling?"

Her heart thundered wildly in her chest. "I came here with a friend."

"Peter?"

"Yes." She was surprised he knew Peter's name.

"Are you sure he was only a friend?"

She'd been asking herself that same question all night. "I... thought he was a friend."

"Speak clearly."

"I am."

"No, you're not."

"I don't know what you want me to say."

"Was he your lover?"

Stunned by his bluntness, she shook her head.

"Are you lying? I despise liars, Ms. Darling."

Her chin quivered. What if the truth got her punished? She didn't know what he wanted to hear.

"I'm telling the truth."

He wore danger the way one wears a perfectly tailored suit. Leaning forward, he dragged a knuckle up her cheek, slowly swiping away a tear, his watchful eyes missing nothing. "Convince me to trust you."

She closed her eyes, staving off more tears. "I don't know how."

He caught her chin, forcing her to meet his stare. His sculpted features appeared hard as stone, a complete contradiction to the fullness of his sensual lips.

"You do know. Convince me."

When he spoke, his voice sent shivers down her spine. His dark hair framed his face in shadows, and his gothic clothing spoke of wealth and elegance, black-on-black, with the slightest silver detail on the wrist.

He was older, perhaps in his mid-thirties. And despite the danger radiating from every square inch of him, there was something devastatingly beautiful about his cruel face.

"I'm waiting."

"I don't—"

He grabbed her by the jaw again and snarled, "Don't play naive with me. You're a female. There are a myriad of tools at your disposal. Show me why I should trust you."

Flinging her face away, he sat back and watched her expectantly.

Did he assume she'd use her body to persuade him? What else could he mean? She was running out of time. If she didn't do something, he was going to threaten her again.

Her voice was small, shrinking under the pressure of his dark stare. "I don't know how to persuade you."

"Perhaps you should get on your knees and try."

"You want me to beg?"

"That's a start. But I expect it will take much more than begging to get me to trust you."

"I… I've never been with anyone that way before."

His eyes narrowed, and he cocked his head. "How old are you?"

"Eighteen."

"Then you're old enough for a lover."

"But I haven't…that is… I don't…" There were ways to prove her innocence, but she hoped it didn't come to that.

He held up a silencing hand. "Do you shake from fear or cold?"

Her teeth chattered from the chill in her bones, but she trembled out of pure fear. "My clothes are soaking wet, and I've been on the cold floor for hours."

He arched a brow. "That doesn't answer my question. But it does bring about another one. Are they *your* clothes?"

She glanced at her sleeves and stilled. Was this Black Jack, the true owner of the stolen coat she wore?

True terror gripped her as she feared being punished for another man's crimes. "Not the coat."

"I assumed not." He grinned as if her answer pleased him.

Hopefully, that was enough to win his trust. She tested the theory. "Are you going to hurt me?" As his piercing emerald gaze drilled into her, she continued to tremble.

He had a wicked smile and mouth made for sin. "Such a bold question for a quivering little mouse, but we mustn't spoil the surprise." He stood and pressed the wine glass to her lips. She tried to reach for it, but he pushed her cuffed hands away. "Sip. It will warm you faster than the fire can."

She extended her neck, and he tipped the glass. The dry

bouquet chased away the taste of saltwater and tears. When she pulled back, he cupped the back of her head, holding her lips to the wine as it poured down her throat.

"More."

"*Mmp*—" she moaned in distress as he tipped the glass against her mouth, forcing her to keep drinking.

"That's it. Keep going."

Her eyes widened, wondering if he'd poisoned the wine. She swallowed and swallowed, her stomach uneasy from her rough journey and sloshing uncomfortably. Her brows pinched as she looked up at him, fearful she might be sick.

"Swallow all of it," he said, tipping the glass so much that a trickle spilled past her lips, down her chin, and onto her chest. "Good girl."

Her head was fuzzy, and the room spun when he finally pulled the empty goblet away.

"You take direction well."

Her skin remained cold, but the wine had warmed her insides.

"Now, tell me again, was Peter your lover?"

"No."

"And why is that?"

"Because I've never had one."

"Which makes you what?"

Her cheeks heated. He was going to make her say it. "A virgin."

"A virgin," he repeated thoughtfully, rubbing his hand along the black stubble of his defined jaw. "I think more wine."

He swapped the empty glass for the full one, and she leaned back in the chair. "Please. I can't drink anymore."

"Don't be silly." He stood, once more cupping the back of her head and looking down at her. "Open."

"Please—"

His hand knotted in her hair as he growled, "Open. Your. Mouth."

Terrified of what he might do if she disobeyed him, she parted her lips. He pressed the glass to her mouth, and wine flooded her throat. Gulp after gulp, she tried to get it down, but it was too much. Choking, she sputtered and turned her face away.

He jerked her head back. "Did I say you could stop?"

"I can't—"

"No?" He dumped the contents over her mouth, letting the wine spill down her neck and chest. "Now, look what you've done."

"I didn't do anything!" She started to cry, but her tears earned her no mercy.

Gripping her jaw, he forced her to look up at him. "When I tell you to open your mouth, you open it. When I tell you to shut your mouth, you shut it. Is that unclear in any way?"

"No, sir."

He released her with a thrust of his hand. "You've made a mess of yourself."

She glanced down at her chest. The silk of her nightgown was soaked in red, and one of her straps had snapped, leaving her partially exposed

He refilled the goblet with wine and paced the carpet. "I'll ask again. Was he your lover?"

"No," she sobbed. "I told you the truth the first time!"

He gripped her by the shoulders, pinning her to the back of the chair. "Are you raising your voice at me?"

"No. I'm sorry."

"I suppose there's only one way to find out if you're telling me the truth." He shoved her nightgown to her hips, and she locked her knees. "Open your legs."

She froze, refusing to accept that this was her only choice.

He caught her by the throat. "That was a command, not a request."

When she still didn't move, his touch gentled, and he trailed his fingers over her throat. Jolted by such extreme polarity, she started to cry.

"Let me explain what happens to those who disobey me on my ship. First, they're punished. Then, they're taken to the lower deck, where they're locked up in the dark. Their rations are less than everyone else's, but there are plenty of rats, plenty of ways to keep from starving if one has the constitution to survive. Sometimes, my crew wanders off. They're not the most moral of men. That far below-deck sound doesn't always carry either." He met her stare. "Now, let's try this again. Open your legs."

Wendy closed her eyes and forced her thighs to part, but even then, they only separated a mere inch. His investigation was deliberate and impersonal.

She gasped as his finger wedged inside of her.

"Stay still." His gaze focused on the wall past her shoulder, his face close enough that she was tempted to bite him.

She whimpered at the bizarre sensation of having a stranger feel inside of her, and then the intrusion was gone.

"You told the truth." He returned to his chair. "You're a virgin."

Her jaw hardened. "I have no reason to lie."

He sat back and studied her. "If you're so innocent, why were you at a lagoon party?"

"I was a guest. Technically, I wasn't even invited. This entire night has been a long line of mistakes."

"There are no mistakes."

There was something untamed prowling beneath his polished exterior, something uncontrollable that warned her that laws didn't apply to him. If this was some sort of ransom, she might be able to help him get what he wanted without endangering herself further.

"Why did you bring me here?"

"Do I look like someone who explains himself?"

"No," she admitted. "But if I knew what you wanted, I could possibly make things less difficult. I do as I'm told—most of the time."

"Only most of the time?" He leaned an arm over the back of the chair and arched a brow. "Tell me about a time when you did something you shouldn't have."

"I came here."

"Something else. Something before today. Something you've never told anyone."

Her mind blanked. "I can't think of anything."

"Try." He swirled the wine in his glass. The scent alone was enough to intimidate her. "Has it come to you?"

Paralyzed by fear, she begged, "Please. I'll be sick if you make me drink more."

"I'm losing my patience."

"I'm trying to think—"

"Three…"

"I don't have any secrets!"

"Two…"

"Please!"

"One. Time's up. Open—"

"I cheated on my senior project!"

He stilled, then tsked. "Wendy Moira Angela Darling."

"Please don't make me drink any more wine. I'll tell you anything you want to know."

"How did you cheat?"

"I paid a boy on my street to write my essay for me."

"What was the topic of the paper?"

"I forget."

"No, you don't." He lifted the wine.

"It was something about ethics!"

He laughed. "You cheated on a paper about ethics?"

"I know how that sounds, but I was—"

"Did you pass?"

She looked down, ashamed. "I got an A—the highest grade in the class."

"What an immoral little liar you are. What other unethical things have you done?"

"I'm truly not that interesting. My parents are extremely strict."

"Which only tells me you have a craving for acting out. Tell me all the ways you've disobeyed Mumsy and Daddy."

She shook her head. "I came here. They think I'm in my bed right now, but I snuck out."

"And how did that happen?"

"Peter came to get me."

"Why would he do that? You said you're not lovers, and you seem unsure if he's even your friend. What did you promise him?"

"Nothing."

"Don't lie to me. You did something to provoke his interest."

She lowered her gaze, ashamed of what they would find as the last text on her phone. "I sent a picture of myself."

"What kind of picture?"

"The immoral kind."

"Be more specific. Show me what you were doing in the picture."

She closed her eyes and swallowed. Leaning forward, she plumped up her breasts like she had for the selfie. When she opened her eyes again, his expression was unreadable.

"So, you're not completely innocent." He sipped the wine and studied her. "Are you attracted to Peter?"

"No."

"Were you?" He held her stare.

She debated what would get her in more trouble, the truth or the lie. "Yes, at one time I found him attractive, but my feelings have changed."

"So you've said. But what of his feelings? Does he still want you?"

"Peter wants everyone—"

"Does he want to fuck *you*? Answer the question."

She swallowed. "Yes."

"Good." He set down the glass of wine. "You're not leaving here a virgin."

"*What*—"

"This can happen in one of two ways. One will have pain, the other will not."

Terrified of not only this man but all the men above deck, she panicked. "You can't force me."

"Don't assume to tell me what I can and cannot do, Ms. Darling. The depravity of my childhood alone would bring you to tears. But I have no intention of forcing you. As I said, there are two options. The sooner you make up your mind, the faster it will be done and over with. Option one, you surrender. Option two, you take time to think things over."

It had to be a trap. "I want the time."

"Of course, you do," he said all too easily. "I'll call for Jukes and he'll escort you below deck where you can contemplate your options and take all the time you need."

"Wait. Below deck with the rats?" Unable to accept that this was her reality, she closed her eyes. If the outcome was inevitable, what was the point in suffering below deck? At least up here, there was a fire to keep her warm. It wasn't a complicated choice, but it wasn't that simple either. He was a stranger and a terrifying one. But he was still a lot better than Jukes or the others in his crew.

He once again lifted her chin and forced her to meet his dark stare. "It can be as easy as cheating on a paper. Simply tell yourself you've made a choice and decide to live with it."

"Please," she whispered softly, unsure of what else she could say. "My family can pay you—"

"I'm not interested in your family's money. I'm only interested in the one thing Peter wants but cannot have."

"Why?"

"That's not your concern."

Her vision blurred as she felt the walls closing in. She'd give anything to be back in her bedroom, safely tucked beneath the covers of her small bed.

"Tears will not save your virtue any more than begging will. You must choose. Do you consent?"

She couldn't bring herself to say the words, so she silently nodded.

"Very good." He went to the door and removed a key from his pocket. "You'll have a light supper and a bath."

She'd expected him to start tearing away her clothes the moment she agreed, not feed and bathe her. "You won't hurt me?"

He cocked his head, studying her for a long moment. "Not all pain is unpleasant, little darling."

"I'll give you what you want. Just please don't hurt me."

He tsked. "Such a pretty little beggar you are." He crossed the room and crouched before her. "Careful what you promise. I'm not an easy man to please."

She believed him. "I won't fight you. I promise."

His full lips slowly twisted into a smile as his gaze dropped to her chest, where the wine had stained. He openly appraised her body in a way no man ever had.

"You're quite a temptation. I see why Peter wanted you." He traced his knuckle softly down her cheek. When his black stare found hers, dark promise reflected back. "What if your pain is exactly what I want? What if I won't be truly satisfied until I possess you in such a way that you're left broken for all other men? What then, little darling?"

She sucked in a jagged breath, fighting back her tears as he trailed a finger down her chest.

"Will you still surrender then?"

She nodded, understanding that denying him would only lead to her suffering.

"That's a good girl."

"*Ah*—" She looked up at him in shock. He pinched the tip of her nipple so tight that fresh tears sprung to her eyes.

"Yes, eyes on me. Let the pain in." His grip tightened another degree, and her breath hitched. "You can cry if it helps."

She gasped, but for some reason, his permission dried up her tears. Pressing her trembling lips into a firm line, she held his stare defiantly. Her body adjusted to the pain, and she was soon able to push it away.

"How very brave you are, little mouse."

He released her breast, and she sucked in a sharp breath, doubling forward when the blood flooded back into the tip of her nipple. The absence of his touch burned in ways she couldn't explain, and some part of her wanted his touch back.

He stood. "Say thank you."

"What?"

"You heard me."

She swallowed, unsure if she'd ever met such a tyrant. "Th-thank you."

He yanked her hair back, tipping her head so she looked up at him. "Now, say it without the stammer."

"Thank you."

"Good girl." He cupped her breast possessively. "You'll thank me every time I touch you. Understand?"

"Yes." He released her. "Thank you."

He paused at the door and grinned, pleased by how quickly she learned. "Very good, little mouse. Your bath will be here soon. Any trouble and all promises go out to sea."

CHAPTER 11

THE DANCE OF THE DEPRAVED

Wendy's heart pounded as the steady creak of the ship's hull whispered through the dim cabin, each forceful beat shaking her to the core. Over the salt air, she smelled the sweet scent of pipe smoke. She tried not to panic as she waited for her bath and what might be her last meal.

Her nose pressed to the leather lapel of her jacket, the buttery scent of broken-in leather a strange comfort to her wild mind. The same smell hung in the air whenever the captain came close.

The door opened, and two crew members entered, carrying a broad copper tub. She curled her shoulders inward and crossed her legs, sheltering her body from view as much as possible. They moved as if commanded not to look at her, setting the tub in the center of the room facing the hearth. A third and fourth man entered, each carrying buckets of steaming water.

They filled the tub, taking trips to collect more water until soft tendrils of steam curled into the air. Her body ached to submerge in that balmy heat, but she feared bathing in the presence of men.

She couldn't recall another time she suffered so many deeply conflicting desires. But she had a sense that this would not be the last. If this was her fortune in life, her future was about to become impossibly challenging. Nothing in her background remotely prepared her for what was coming.

The men left the captain's quarters—save one. The lingering crew member looked different from the others. His moth-eaten clothes were higher quality, but dulled from sun and time. Still, she recognized the shadow of a gentleman in his stare.

He did not leer or approach her in a threatening manner. On the contrary, he moved with measured dignity, eyes downcast as he fetched a cloth and revealed a heavy, ornate key.

"I'll spare you the indignity of bathing while bound." His voice, though polite, carried a hint of roughness as if worn from years at sea.

Was he going to unchain her? Was that allowed? She only slightly flinched when he lifted her wrist. His gaze remained focused on the cuffs and never strayed.

The moment the heavy metal fell to the floor, she pulled her hands protectively to her chest, rubbing the chafed skin.

"I'll turn my back while you slip into the tub, Miss." He set the towel on her lap and looked away.

She rose on stiff legs. "Thank you."

How strange to thank those who held her captive, yet she was inexplicably overwhelmed at the moment with gratitude for the bath and his regard for her modesty.

She moved to the tub before removing her coat and nightgown. The man kept his back turned, as promised, giving her the necessary time to test the temperature of the water and strip out of her clothes. She draped the coat over the back of a chair and paused before setting it beside the captain's. Her brow furrowed as she noticed the same intricate stitching in the lapels, confirming that this was indeed Black Jack.

"Where did the captain buy his coat?"

The man cleared his throat but didn't turn. "The crew makes them, miss."

"Where did they learn the design?" The intricate work had to come from a skilled seamstress on the islands.

"The designs are the captain's."

Leaning forward, she sniffed the collar, finding the same soothing scent clinging to the soft leather. What did it say about her that she liked how her captor smelled? She wasn't sure she wanted to know.

Her nightgown was in tatters, so there was no point hanging it up. Letting it fall to the floor, she stepped over the lip of the tub and submerged her body in the warm water, clumsily sloshing the water over the sides.

The man kept his gaze averted but settled into the empty chair. "The water is warm enough for you, miss?"

Why was he being so nice to her? "Yes, thank you."

He didn't break the silence for a long time, and her sense of peace slowly transformed into unease. What if he was one of the last people she ever spoke to?

"Will you tell me your name?"

"Name's Gideon Star."

She didn't know what to say next. She wouldn't lie and say it was nice to meet him, so she asked, "Do you like the captain?"

"Never gave it much thought. A crew obeys their captain. Whether one likes him or not is irrelevant."

Curling her shoulders inward, she pushed the water over her skin. "But do you like him?"

He was quiet for a long moment. "Well enough, I suppose."

She looked about the lavish quarters, wondering if part of the captain craved a different life. She glanced over her shoulder, but the man wasn't watching her. She sensed humanity in him. If she ignored his purpose here and the worn appearance of his clothes, she could imagine him as one of her father's peers.

"You weren't always a pirate, were you?"

He stood and cleared the table, never letting his gaze stray toward the tub. "No, I once owned property and inherited a small fortune, but that was a very long time ago, and fortunes come and go."

Although he moved about the chambers, he never dared to look at her. She watched him as he spread a cloth across the table, smoothing the creases with care.

"You lost your fortune."

"The one I had at that time, yes. It only takes a few poor choices to change a man's entire world."

"Or a few wise ones."

"Touché." He set out a new bottle of wine and clean glasses. "That's something Hook might say."

"Hook?"

"The captain," he explained. "Captain James Hook. He's an exacting man, but not a cruel one. Not unless he has to be."

"They don't call him Black Jack?"

Gideon stilled from polishing the silver cutlery. The fine pieces glinted in the flickering lamplight as he carefully inspected each one before laying it down. "Those who value their lives don't."

What if this wasn't the pirate the Lost Boys spoke of?

She considered the matching coats. It had to be the same person. Peter had told her that people went by any name they wanted in the Never Lands. Perhaps Captain James Hook went by two names, and his enemies called him Black Jack.

Gideon set the table with fine bone china adorned with delicate gilded edges. Even the goblets appeared to be crystal. Why such opulence?

She looked at the candlelight. The ambiance confused her. The captain said she would have a light snack, but Gideon appeared to be setting a scene for a luxurious feast for two.

Was this a practiced act? His men seemed to know the dance so well.

"Does he make a habit of feeding the women he kidnaps?"

"I'm afraid we're not in the habit of kidnapping women." He looked back, finally meeting her eyes as if to show his sincerity as he softly warned, "Careful, dear. There are ears everywhere."

What did that mean? When he said nothing more, she reached for the washcloth and crude lump of soap.

The sharp scent of bergamot filled the air as she silently washed her body. It was another scent she smelled on the captain, and she strangely liked it when it should have made her sick.

Gideon arranged a small vase of flowers. Nothing about this situation was normal.

Did they know what the captain planned to do to her?

She flushed at the memory of him shoving his finger inside of her. How mortifying and dehumanizing. Yet, here she was, preparing herself for more. There was definitely something wrong with her.

"The captain's not without his compassion," he said as if sensing her worry.

She thought of the sultan who married a new Arabian wife every night, only to order her death by the following dawn. It wasn't until one particular woman held his interest that the murders stopped.

"What does the captain like?" If she wanted to survive, she would have to play the game.

"He values loyalty above all else. Cross him, and it will be the last thing you ever do."

Her shiver of fear only galvanized her determination. "You said his name is James?"

"Aye, but I wouldn't call him that if I were you. Best to stick to Sir or Captain."

Using his name could create a sense of intimacy. If she treated him like a respectable gentleman, he might meet her with similar respect.

The elegant table created a romantic scene that mocked the true nature of her predicament. She sensed him preparing to leave and panicked at the moving of time.

"Is there anything else you can tell me, Gideon?" She purposely used his name to establish a sense of trust. She needed whatever help she could get.

"Do as he says and don't complain. That's my advice." He moved to the door. "I'll lock the door but leave the chains off. Prove yourself trustworthy, and he'll be pleased. Try anything conniving, and he'll see that you're punished. Don't make me regret my kindness, miss."

He had been kind, but she was a captive. She didn't know if she would keep her word. Still, she nodded anyway. "Thank you."

"Stay safe, miss." He bowed and backed out of the room, the heavy latch turning and locking from the other side.

As lovely as the warm water felt, she couldn't waste time sitting there passively waiting for the future to unfold. Climbing out of the bath, she wrapped her body in the towel. Her heart thundered as she scanned the room.

She rushed to the table and snatched up a silver knife when footsteps approached. The cold metal was heavy in her hand, and she spun just as the door opened.

Captain James Hook stilled at the threshold, his dark gaze dropping to the knife in her hand. "So you've chosen violence."

The heavy silver clattered to the floor in shameful surrender. "No."

He shut the door, apparently unthreatened by her access to the sharp cutlery. "I assume your bath was pleasant?"

She recalled his earlier orders about gratitude. "Yes. Thank you...James."

He paused from removing his boots and looked at her. "Careful, darling. No one calls me by my first name."

"I'm sorry, sir."

"That's better." He slid his leather boots off and tossed them aside.

Power pulsed in the air as something dark and ominous slithered through her insides. She stepped back as he looked at her with unapologetic hunger. Only a towel concealed her body from his view, but he seemed to have a good enough imagination to picture what she hid underneath.

The longer he stared, the tighter her insides coiled. She lifted her gaze and straightened her spine, refusing to show that he intimidated her.

A low chuckle spilled past his lips. "So brave, yet so timid."

He crossed the room, which had warmed from the fire. It also helped that she was no longer chilled to the bone.

Hooking a finger under the material, he tugged, and the towel fell away. "That's better," he said, amused. "Courage is a tempting look on you."

Hopelessness choked her. This was it. There was no way out. His dark stare stripped away all lingering pretense, and she lifted her chin, proving she wouldn't cower.

It was a strange paradox. He was a lethal man, but also a beautiful one. It wasn't fair that evil could be so pretty. She needed to remember who and what he was, a vile criminal set on ruining her. How strange that she would inevitably thank him for it.

She shivered and pressed her lips in a flat line. When her arm moved to cover her breasts, he gently tucked it back at her side.

"No, no. I want to see my prize."

Never before had she stood nude before someone, let alone a man. Every breath was visible, and her chest burned with humiliated outrage. If she made an enemy of him, she'd never survive. She needed to calm her emotions and lead with logic.

"What are you thinking, darling?"

She was thinking that, despite him being her adversary, some twisted part of her could do this. She needed to please him, not torment him. He ultimately had control, and if she made this difficult for him, he would make it far worse for her.

Like a Chinese handcuff, the more she tried to force her exoneration, the more trapped she'd become. True freedom rested in captivity. And she had years of experience when it came to confinement.

If she cooperated and did as she was told, he'd start to trust her. Trust was the key to escape. The sooner she earned his trust, the faster she'd break free.

Forcing herself to abide his command, she relaxed her arms at her back and straightened her spine. "I'm just waiting for you... James."

He closed the distance in two long strides. That quickly, the look in his eyes shifted from amused to dangerous. She cowered, but he caught her by the arm in an unbreakable grip.

"I'm not a game you get to play, little girl."

Her bravado vanished, and she sucked in a breath as his hand tightened. "You're hurting me."

"Something I warned you about, but it seems you have a problem with listening." His grip tightened another degree. "Let me make this crystal clear. I'm in control, not you."

"J-James, please—"

He shook her hard enough to rattle her teeth. "What did I say about using my first name?"

"I'm willingly surrendering to you. I'll give you whatever you want. But you're hurting me."

He flung her away and turned. "You will address me with respect."

"Okay. I'm sorry, sir."

His eyes narrowed. "Put something on."

He wanted her dressed? "I have nothing. My nightgown is—"

He abruptly opened a drawer and pulled out a black button-down shirt, flinging it at her. "Cover yourself."

Confused, she pulled the long dress shirt over her body. The material draped to her knees, and the sleeves billowed over her hands. He was a big man. The fabric smelled of rich spices and bergamot, a fragrance she now associated with him.

Every time he paced, he added to the nervous energy churning between them.

"If I did something wrong—"

"Quiet," he snapped. "I need to think."

Was he having second thoughts?

He moved like sin incarnate, his muscular, leather-clad legs eating up the distance from one wall to another. The flickering candlelight cast his sharp features in shadows, enhancing the beauty of his sun-kissed skin.

He moved to the ornate desk in the corner and removed a sheet of paper. Hunching over the surface, he jotted something down.

"Come here."

She hesitantly crossed the carpet. When she was within arm's reach, he tugged her in front of him and made her face the desk.

"Sign."

She stared down at the paper and read the jagged script.

I, Wendy Moira Angela Darling, willingly surrender my body to Captain James Hook.

X____

She stared at the simple contract. Why bother? She'd given

her verbal consent when he threatened her with the rats down below.

"I don't think—"

"I said sign." He grabbed her hand, wrapping it around the pen and forcing the tip to the slashed line he'd drawn.

Did he not realize that a contract was meaningless under duress? With a trembling hand, she scribbled her name.

"Good. It's done."

He tucked the paper back into the desk just as there was a rap at the door. Her spine stiffened, and she backed into the wall.

He unlocked the door, and several crewmen shuffled in, bearing gilded trays of food. They set the platters on the table, and the scent of roasted meats filled the chamber. The absurdity of it all—the porcelain plates, the silver forks, and the linen napkins—Wendy didn't understand the need for such formality when she was here against her will. He was getting his way whether he impressed her or not.

The men left, and her throat tightened. It was a ritual she'd never experienced, an adult dance of seduction she would undoubtedly fumble through with the awkwardness of an ignorant child.

He pulled out a chair. "Sit."

Reluctantly, she left the safety of the wall, but her feet barely moved. Each baby step only carried her an inch closer to him.

"By all means, take your time. I love to wait when I give an order."

Her halting steps forced her closer until she slowly lowered into the chair. He tucked her in, then reached over her shoulder, deliberately encroaching on her personal space to set her knife beside her plate.

"Your knife, darling."

When she hesitated to touch anything, he chuckled.

He sat in the chair across from her and served the food. She watched from under her lashes as he cut each portion with measured preciseness. He savored the first bite, chewing slowly and gracefully, appreciating every flavor as if he wished to show the utmost respect to the chef who was not present.

"It's a rude sign of privilege not to eat when a meal is offered, darling."

The food looked and smelled delicious, but she had no appetite.

When she still didn't touch her plate, he said, "Are you afraid the food is poisoned? If I wanted you dead, you'd know." He pulled her plate away, sliced her meat, and pushed it back. "Eat."

Her hand shook as she stabbed into a cut of meat and brought it to her mouth, but she tasted nothing beyond her fear.

"What do you say?"

She looked up at him, confused. Then it clicked. "Thank you, sir."

"You're welcome." His manners contradicted his cruelty, and she didn't understand where this need for decorum stemmed from.

They ate silently as he studied her, his dark emerald gaze hooded and calculating.

She looked down at her plate. "For someone so strict about manners, you seem to forget it's impolite to stare."

"I don't give a shit about manners. But I demand the respect of every single person on my ship, including you."

"Aren't manners and respect the same thing?"

"No. Manners are merely polite words. They hide a person's true motives. Respect is an ingrained form of honor."

"Well, some might say it's disrespectful to stare."

"I plan to do many disrespectful things to you tonight."

Her fork stilled.

"Don't look so terrified. Degradation can be quite liberating."

She wasn't exactly clear on what he meant by degradation, but it sounded horrible. She set down her fork to hide how her hand trembled. After wiping the corners of her mouth with the cloth napkin, she folded her hands in her lap, her gaze downcast.

He lifted his wine and leaned back, openly studying her no matter how uncomfortable his attention made her. "You'll regret not turning away my generosity. It does have limits, and you'll need your strength. I'm a hard man to satisfy, and I expect my satisfaction to be your highest priority."

Her heart raced. She knew nothing about satisfying a man, let alone an evil man. "Perhaps if you told me what you like—"

"It's simple. I like the thought of you on your knees, begging to do whatever is my pleasure. My darker desires will feel quite dehumanizing to someone of your stature—at first. But you'll learn your place quickly." He sipped his wine and continued to study her with that calculating stare. "Right now, you're thinking of all the ways you might escape your fate because this can't possibly be happening to you." He leaned forward and smirked. "But Daddy's money can't save you here. My ship is fast, and by the time anyone dares to approach, I'll have had you every way a man can." He chuckled when her eyes widened. "Don't look so frightened, little mouse. Depravity has its rewards. By dawn, you'll be preening every time I remind you that you're now my filthy little whore."

The shock of even hearing such cutting words left her staggered. No part of her could ever enjoy being called such terrible things. "I think I respond better to praise."

"I'll only praise you when you embrace that which will inevitably break you. Think of it as an experiment in willpower. Whose will is stronger, mine or yours?" He stretched out his legs and tapped his chin thoughtfully. "Or should the question be, which is safer—getting your way or giving into mine?"

Appalled, she said, "I don't have a filthy side."

"Of course you do. It's the disgusting part of yourself you hide."

"I don't—"

"Don't bore me with lies, darling. Challenge me, and I'll force you to your knees here and now to prove my point."

Her breath hitched, and her thighs clenched as a strange tingle of sensation throbbed low in her belly.

"Ah." He grinned. "I've struck a nerve. I bet your privileged life's filled your pretty head with notions of love and self-worth. But this isn't love, darling. And your worth is up to you. I'm afraid depravity is the only out you have."

Her gaze dropped to her plate, her appetite gone. "You're a monster."

"Am I? Or perhaps your perspective is confused. Too many people are motivated by praise, but that's not the world we live in. Praise is rarely genuine. And when it's not honest, it's a lie. The liars are the monsters, darling. Trust me on that."

"Genuine or not, praise feels good."

"Praise is a vehicle of manipulation. Does it feel good to

have a man lie about his feelings only to forget you the next morning?"

"I wouldn't know."

"I'll save you the pain. Praise is just a lie men tell when they want to fuck."

She scowled at such a hideous outlook. "Not all men are liars. Some love their partners."

He laughed. "I'm sure some do. I'm not one of them. I plan to fuck you. Hard. Greedily. Selfishly. For my amusement and nothing more. Your body will wear the proof of my depravity in ways you can't imagine. Praise means nothing to me. It's an empty, false sense of security. We can skip the bullshit, and I'll spoil the twist. I plan on having you every which way until I'm satisfied, ripping away any layer of artifice I find. So much so, you might be more afraid of yourself than me in the end." He took a sip of wine. "Then…we'll see if I still have use for you."

"I've already accepted what's going to happen to me, so you can stop trying to scare me." If his goal was to dehumanize her, she planned to hide her emotions as much as possible.

"*Am I* scaring you?"

She met his stare. "No."

"Liar."

"I'm only scared because I don't know what's going to happen."

"Are you saying you'd rather get on with it?"

If her fate was inevitable, she saw no reason to prolong things. "Yes."

CHAPTER 12

BLOOD AND LIES

He chuckled at her bravado. "You're a fascinating creature, darling." Steepling his fingers beneath his chin, his dark eyes narrowed on her. "I wonder if removing your choice has made this easier for you."

Wendy scoffed at such absurdity. "I beg your pardon?"

The side of his mouth kicked up in a half grin. "You pretend you're a good girl, but I sense something darker under the surface. For instance, if I told you—in detail—all the terrible things I planned to do to you tonight, I bet that little virgin pussy of yours would clench and pulse with anticipation."

He set his glass down and leaned forward. Lowering his deep voice, he looked at her and promised, "I'm going to objectify you, darling. I plan to fuck every tight little hole you have. Then I'll leave you dripping, claimed, and marked in such a way you'll never forget every disgraceful thing you've done. And in the end, you're going to thank me."

Every shallow breath became more challenging as her legs clenched tight under the table.

"Your cheeks are flushed, and I'd bet my right hand that virgin pussy's wet. Admit it, you're pulsing for my cock, like a slut who gets off on the thought of being used. Is your precious little clit starting to throb? I bet you'd come if I gave it a slap."

Everything he said was true. Her body responded to every word. "Did you put something in the food?"

He laughed. "No, I didn't poison your food."

She didn't mean poison. "I don't feel right."

"What do you feel?"

She swallowed. Her body was thrumming with strange energy. "I don't know. I feel trapped in my own skin." She fidgeted, unsure why his words were having such an effect on her.

"But you've felt this before, haven't you? I can picture it —you lying on some ruffled bed surrounded by opulence you did nothing to earn. Did it feel good, sliding your fingers through your wet folds, knowing at any moment someone could have walked in and caught you? Did you enjoy the thrill of possibly being caught, darling? I bet you bit your fist when you started to moan, only to discover you liked a hint of pain."

She couldn't breathe. How did he know so much? Had he been watching her?

"You tried so hard to bring yourself relief, didn't you? Did you shut your eyes and imagine someone else's hands on you?"

Again, he was right, and her startled look likely confirmed his suspicions. She'd tried and tried, but she couldn't get there. The closest she came was when she wrapped a hand around her throat, pretending she couldn't get away.

"Tell me, darling, was the hand you imagined that of your sweet friend Peter Pangbourne?"

"What? No."

"Then who?"

He was right. She had touched herself. But she never imagined Peter. It was always someone darker, someone without a face. "I don't see Peter that way."

"But you see yourself that way, don't you?"

She licked her dry lips and met his stare.

"Tell me the truth. Tell me you act like a dirty little slut when you're all alone, desperately wishing someone would treat you like one."

She couldn't deny it. He read her too well. "How...?"

The side of his mouth curved up. "You reek of secrets. I can smell them through your pretty manners as much as I can smell the arousal seeping down your thighs. And, because I'm so certain you're *not* the good girl you pretend to be, I bet you're wishing I'd put my fingers back inside of you right now. Shall we check my theories and bring you some relief?"

No one had ever read her so flawlessly. He was right—about all of it.

"So you see, darling, I won't treat you like a princess, or an heiress, or whatever you think you deserve, because I don't care about society's expectations for you. I only care about my expectations, and you're going to meet every last one. You're my new personal toy, and I'll show you exactly how men like to play with their toys. We're destructive, and we love exercising power over others."

She couldn't look at him, let alone draw a full breath. "Not all men are mean."

"Speak up."

"I said, not all men are mean."

He laughed. "There's a lie. Men are mean by nature, which is why they're refined from birth."

"You obviously weren't."

"No, but they tried. At least with me, you get honesty, unlike those gentlemen you're used to, the high society ones who act civilized but secretly mistreat their wives and blame life's little pressures for making them snap."

Leaning forward, he possessively glided a hand over her knee, and she stiffened. He applied no pressure or force but gave her a commanding look. Her knees parted slowly.

He chuckled. "See how easy that was? The least you could do is be honest with yourself and admit you're interested to learn what I can teach you."

She was intrigued, but deep-rooted shame prevented her from admitting such truths, even to herself. She thought about Peter's duality and how he performed so easily for society. Then she thought of how disappointed she was when his true selfishness came out.

"I can admit I'm curious."

"How refreshing." He leaned forward, his thick hair spilling like ink on a page as his honeyed voice dropped another degree. "Some men try to trap and hide their shadow-self. I embrace mine by letting the darkness run free. Wouldn't you prefer to feel what it's like to free all that trapped wickedness inside you?"

A hot flush burned her cheeks as he pulled back his chair. He stood in one fluid motion and went to the dresser.

"You don't have to pretend you're a good girl for me."

She watched as he methodically removed the leather belt. Stripping away his weapons made him no less intimidating. At his core, he was a primal force, now unencumbered and perpetually untamed.

He was so fluent in her body's responses that he didn't need to look at her. "Your heart's beating faster now, isn't it, darling?"

"Yes." So fast it nearly shook her words.

"Good. That's your adrenaline. It heightens the senses, so there's more pleasure, more fear. More everything."

Seconds shortened to the span of her palpitating heartbeats, and the walls tightened around her.

He turned and finally met her stare, his smile nothing short of predatory. He was savoring the suspense and using it to make her more agreeable. Returning to her side, he caressed her jaw, and she closed her eyes, ashamed that she'd succumbed so easily.

"Do you know what I want, darling?"

"No," she whispered, thinking she once had an idea what men wanted, but now he convinced her she knew absolutely nothing about such things.

His hand slid over her shoulder and between her breasts to flatten over her pounding heart. "I want your darkness," he whispered in her ear, his voice a velvet rasp that sent shivers dancing down her spine. "I want the parts you hide from everyone else, including yourself. I want the jagged pieces of your soul that scare you most. That's what I'll steal from you tonight, piece by piece, until there's nowhere left to hide."

"You're depraved," she rasped, refusing to meet his gaze.

"Perhaps we all are." He slowly withdrew his hand. "Including you."

Something came over her, and she tried to bolt from the chair, but he slammed her back down, his lips smashing hard over hers as he forced his tongue into her mouth. She bit at his lips and dragged her nails down his face, forcing him to draw back when he tasted blood.

He dabbed his lip and looked at his fingertips, then chuckled. "That wasn't very civilized."

Her mind was a whirlwind of fear, fury, and wild curiosity. She couldn't willingly give herself to him, yet she wanted him to take her. She wanted him to take everything—her pain, her frustration, and even her choice—until she was free of culpability and nothing more than a raw nerve of sensation incapable of shame.

"Shall we try that again?"

He didn't wait for an answer. This time, when he sealed his mouth to hers, he held her hair in an unbreakable grip, anticipating her attack and capturing her arms before she laid a hand on him. He forced his kiss on her with punishing possessiveness, and she whimpered, softening under his command.

He didn't kiss like Peter. He kissed like he wanted to own her soul, like she was the fountain of life, and he wanted to breathe in the very essence of her existence until nothing was left. She moaned as she found his rhythm and accepted his possession willingly. It was more pleasant if she didn't challenge him.

"That's a good little slut."

There was no escaping his claim. Her back pressed into the seat as he drove his tongue deeper, taking what he wanted.

He released her hair and held her by the throat. Her nails dug into his arms, but that only egged him on. "Show me your greedy side, darling."

Disappointed in herself, she tried to turn away, but he caught her jaw.

"I can tell a filthy little slut when I taste one. Are you going to be a frightened little mouse forever?"

Something awakened inside of her, and she stopped

retreating. Animal-like aggression tore through her, and she lunged forward, shoving her fingers into his thick, dark hair and becoming the aggressor.

He wrenched her head back, and she gasped. "You want to touch me?"

"Yes." She not only wanted to touch him, she wanted to break him with the same intent he planned to break her.

"Beg."

"Pardon?"

"Beg."

"I don't—"

"Don't play refined with me. I see you for exactly what you are. Here, you're just flesh and blood like everyone else. Beg me to touch you, and I will. Beg me for any depraved thing you want, and I'll gladly deliver you into darkness. But first, you have to ask—and you better make it pretty."

He wanted to humiliate her. And he might have if she wasn't so drunk on temptation and lust. He'd triggered her competitive nature, which was the first step in stripping away her inhibitions.

If she wanted him to give in to her, she must first surrender something to him. The game had to start somewhere. "Please?"

"Please, what?"

"Please..." Was she honestly going to ask him for the things he promised? Perhaps this was the start of the depravity he threatened. She couldn't think about how others might judge her. She could only think of her survival. Beyond these walls, no one would ever know what she said to him in private. "Please, kiss me some more."

He growled and took her mouth again, ripping open her shirt and sending buttons pinging across the floor. Cool air teased her skin, and she gasped when his hot palm cupped her breast possessively.

"Open your legs." His knee wedged between hers, forcing her legs to open wider. His fingers groped and fondled, learning her at a pace she couldn't fully follow.

A wave built on the horizon, strengthening in power until it was all that existed inside of her. She rode his hand as he rubbed between her thighs, certain he was a force of nature that would destroy whatever stood in its path, whatever she was before, and leave nothing recognizable behind. She was going to—

"Get up."

Startled by his abruptness, a slight sound of fear escaped her throat when he ripped his hand away and yanked her out of the seat. She clumsily tripped over her feet as he turned her, planting her hands on the back of the chair for support. He yanked off the shirt she wore and licked down her spine, not stopping until he was on his knees, biting into her ass cheeks.

"Wait," she gasped when she realized what he planned to do.

"That word doesn't work here." He cupped her sex and groaned. "Just as I thought. You're soaked."

He lifted her off the chair and tossed her onto the blood-red coverlet of the dark, canopied bed. There was no time to assimilate as he roughly tugged her forward.

Then time stilled and he paused, a strange ripple of hesitation skittering across his dark features. He cursed under his breath and balled his outreached hand into a fist.

"Who are you?"

"I...told you. I'm Wendy Darling—"

"No." He wasn't asking her name. "There's something

else, something different." He stepped back from the bed, spooked by something she'd missed.

"Did I do something wrong?"

"Stop talking," he snapped, his dark eyes shifting with distrust.

She waited for him to continue, but he took another step back, putting more distance between them. Had she repulsed him in some way?

A sense of failure consumed her. That was when she acknowledged that part of her did want to please him.

What was wrong with her?

They should hate each other. She should be clawing out his eyes and cursing him to hell and back. But she needed to prove to herself that she could do this. Her need to succeed was driven by more than fear. It was driven by a dark and deeply buried seed of hope.

She wanted him to help her find this other side of herself. He might have intended his intentions as a threat, but the more he spoke about depravity, the more his words struck like a delicious promise.

Was that why he stopped? Did he sense her eagerness? Did that spoil his plans to torment her?

She wanted to pull him closer. She wanted to break herself on all his hard edges until she was so thoroughly shattered there was no salvageable part left of who she was. Only a truly damaged woman would crave such things, but no one else had ever made such an exhilarating promise to her before, and she was curious about what she'd find on the other side.

"Turn around. On your belly. Face down."

She did as he said and waited, flinching when he finally traced a delicate knuckle down her spine. She braved a glance over her shoulder.

"I said turn around."

She returned her gaze to the blankets and frowned. That gentle touch was more disarming than all his forcefulness. She preferred the chaos. It made it harder to think. The stillness left nowhere to run away. She had to bear the truth and acknowledge that she was allowing this not because he removed her choice but because she liked his hands on her.

The bed dipped as he pushed her thighs open. Warm breath moved over her as he leaned closer. She waited silently as he regained control, glad his little scare hadn't spoiled his plans.

"Like a delicate flower." He traced a finger along her slit, rimming her soft, pink folds without actually penetrating. "I wonder, what kind of woman responds this way to having her choice stripped away."

She closed her eyes, wondering the same thing.

His stroking fingers moved so lightly over her skin her body rose to meet his touch. "I don't even have to take it. You're giving yourself to me."

She could feel him in every cell of her body despite him barely touching her. He was in her veins, pulsing in places she couldn't name, as if her heart pounded out his name, *Hook, Hook, Hook, Hook*...

"I can see you clenching. That's your body begging for me."

Anticipation stretched and consumed her. He seemed to be dragging it out on purpose—a new way of tormenting her and forcing her to see what she really was.

She gasped. Perhaps he was right. Maybe she was a whore.

His fingers trailed over her, steadily tracing her most

private parts, then teasing every ridge of her spine. He was all she could feel, and it became a game to lay still for him.

"Nothing will ever feel as good as losing to me, little darling." His finger slipped between her folds. "But first, we must clear the way."

"Ah…" His finger pushed deeper with ease, gliding into her with a sense of ownership that deliberately forced her to face this new intimacy. He stopped when he reached the proof of her virginity.

"Imagine how tight you'll feel stretched around my cock. I'll own your innocence then, the way no other man could ever claim any piece of you."

She shivered as his whispered words breathed across her spine, his finger making shallow dips in and out of her. Turning his hand, he teased her clit.

She might be his prisoner, but she wasn't suffering. It only hurt when the shame came in. Because he was right. What kind of woman is aroused by having her choice stripped away?

He climbed over her, blanketing her body with his weight as he fingered her pussy and whispered in her ear. "I bet you taste like innocence when you come."

He was fully clothed, but she felt the weight of his erection pressing into her back. He changed the position of his arm, reaching under her and between her legs to finger her from the front as he ground into her from behind. The pressure built and rubbed faster. Then, her body was overcome by sensation. Her mouth opened in a silent cry as ripples of energy flowed over every muscle, bursting outward from the tiny storm he created inside of her.

"What a filthy little slut you are, coming all over my hand." He laughed and bit her ear. "You hate how much you want me to take everything from you, don't you? But there's no denying that you love being set free. It feels good when we're not so refined, doesn't it, darling?"

She closed her eyes as the shameful truth became harder to deny.

He flipped her to her back and smashed her breasts together, holding them in the combined grip of both his hands. "I asked you a question."

"Yes." Her brow pinched. She couldn't look at him. He was destroying her values and making her want things that were inherently wrong. He was a tyrant in the body of a god. If only he looked more like the criminal he actually was.

His hair trailed over her sensitized flesh as he bent to suckle her breasts. Wet heat engulfed her nipple in an unbearable tight pull she hadn't expected. She gasped and shoved at his shoulders, unprepared for the sharp sting, but he only sucked harder, capturing her arm and slamming it down. The more pressure he pinned her with, the more she wanted him to take from her.

How did he know her body could switch like that? It didn't make sense that fear and pain could so easily convert to pleasure and desire.

Her body reflexively arched into him, and he released a growl of satisfaction. "Look at you." He pinned her other arm above her head. "You're starving for a hard fuck, aren't you?"

She gave up the internal battle to lie and, instead, sobbed in defeat, "Yes!"

He'd ruined any sense of modesty she had left, so what was the point in denying what he could so clearly see?

"You've already given in. I didn't even have to use force. I think we both know what that makes you, don't we, darling?"

She closed her eyes, turning her face away to disassociate,

but he caught her chin and forced her to acknowledge the truth.

"Open your fucking eyes. You're not a child. Stop hiding like one."

She compelled herself to meet his dark stare. He was right. She was hiding from the truth. Years of grooming and refinement shackled her in an emotional straightjacket, and he was untethering the most depraved parts of her, the parts she dreaded others seeing.

"Tell me what you're thinking right now."

She liked being his possession, and she might even be enjoying this more than any stable person should, but she still couldn't form the words.

"Say it. I won't judge you."

All of her life, she'd put herself second to meet everyone else's expectations first. Giving in to her darkest desires felt too much like she was disappointing everyone who mattered.

"Don't think of anyone else. Only yourself. Only of your promise to please me. That's all that matters right now. Throw everything else away and admit the kind of woman you actually are."

Tears welled in her eyes. "Please..." she begged, on the edge of corruption. "I can't make myself say it."

"You can. You can say whatever the fuck you want." He pulled her legs apart, pressing two fingers inside of her, stretching her. "Tell me you're mine, and I'll make you a woman once and for all." He pressed deeper, showing her how close they'd come to irrevocably changing everything. "Say it, and it'll be done."

"I can't!" she yelled, as frustrated with her inability to communicate as she was with her need to please everyone before pleasing herself.

His fingers disappeared, and then he was holding her down and glaring into her eyes, nose to nose, as he pinned her hands over her head.

"A cage is still a cage, darling, no matter how big or lavish or invisible the walls. Silence won't make your darkest desires any less true. Neither does conformity. You're only lying to yourself, and you're doing so because you're afraid the world won't like what's hidden inside."

He was right. She was scared. He was awakening parts of her she could never admit to hiding. She lived in the real world, where polite conversations and modesty still mattered. Who would she become if she unchained herself from society's reins? What would her value be if she were no longer the woman her mother and father raised her to become?

He was asking for authenticity, but that level of truth terrified her. She feared rejection, her parents' disapproval, and her reputation burning like a bridge until all she'd worked toward was nothing but soot and ash on the wind.

The thought left her mute. It wasn't by choice or stubbornness. Her silence was truly a result of fear. Fear that once she admitted such things, the words could never be unsaid. The thought paralyzed her.

He dragged his lips to hers and kissed her slowly. "I can taste it on your tongue. You have so much inside you want to say. Whisper it to me, and the cage will fall. Speak your desires, and I'll make them yours."

"I need…"

He hung on her silence, his eyes alert and his desire to free her clear, but her words were trapped, and she couldn't get them out.

"Say it. Tell me, and we'll demolish the cage together so you're finally free."

Her gaze snapped to his, her enemy shifting into a dangerous enabler who could destroy her but also liberate her from the crushing weight that came with aligning with polite society. She couldn't be a part of her destruction, but she didn't want it to stop.

"Say it."

It was there, lodged in her throat like a poison she couldn't get out. "I want..." she swallowed, but the truth stayed wedged in her throat. "I like it when you..."

"When I what?"

She didn't know the words. Mortification choked her. She needed him to be the big, bad wolf, to take all the choices and responsibility away.

Her eyes closed. "I can't say it."

His hand closed around her throat. "Is it here?" His grip tightened, and she nodded, tears of frustration stinging her eyes. "Do you need me to force it out of you?"

Her lashes lifted, and she met his stare. What did he mean?

"I can, you know. I can make you do all the horrible things you're too embarrassed to say. It'll be easy because you want to. And the moment you stop hating yourself for wanting such sinful things, all that resistance will disappear." He leaned down, his breath teasing the shell of her ear as he whispered, "Whose approval do you want most, darling? Theirs, or mine?"

Her heart raced wildly. It was a horrible betrayal.

He was her enemy who planned to vanquish her, not her hero. She needed to keep sight of who and what he was and not romanticize this into something it wasn't.

But the paradox was pulling her in. In relinquishing power, she was liberated from the weight of decision, from the endless labyrinth of choice and consequence. Submission offered an escape hatch, a space where her mind could unlatch and her body could simply *be*.

How had he stripped her so bare so quickly? He'd narrowed her focus to the immediacy of sensation, the rhythm of command and response. It was uncomplicated art, simplistic and raw. And she craved feeling so untethered, wondering what it was that he did to anchor her so completely in the present moment.

A tear seeped from the corner of her eyes as she looked up at him—a dark and dangerous stranger with his hand cuffed around her throat. His was the only approval that mattered at that moment.

"Yours, sir. I want yours."

His victorious smile was slow and wicked. "There it is, the truth you were so afraid to admit." He rocked his hips forward, grinding his arousal into her thigh as his finger pumped shallow dips in and out of her. "There's so much I'm going to teach you."

His kiss was a devastating show of promise and desire that further pulled her under. She feared she might never see her family again. What if he changed her so much that she lost her sense of connection to the girl she was? What if she forgot where she came from and no part of her life fit her anymore?

It was more than surrender. This ship, this place, this man...they were reshaping her into something she couldn't fully envision, but she knew she would never be the same once this was over.

"A symbol of broken resistance." He sank his fingers deep, and she gasped when he fully penetrated her. It was quick and complete, the physical barrier of her innocence gone.

His long fingers dragged down her stomach, leaving a pale smear of pink. "Crocodile tears won't help you now, little mouse." He softly caressed her breasts. "Though you are beautiful when you cry."

She was glad to be rid of one hurdle, though she never expected it happening this way. "Thank you, sir."

His mouth twitched as he sensed her genuine gratitude. Then he slowly admitted, "It was my pleasure."

She weakly smiled. Yes, it was. But the relief of being rid of such a barrier was hers.

He gave her a choice, and she chose to surrender.

Power was ceded, and now she must make him her greatest priority, as he commanded. "I'm glad you're pleased."

He cocked his head as if trying to decipher any motive behind her words. "You're as dangerous as a siren, aren't you?" He caught her by the back of the neck and pulled her into a possessive kiss.

Once more, awakening something inside of her. Should she ever get off this ship, she wasn't sure she'd ever go back to being the proper, well-mannered, conforming woman she'd been groomed to be.

The longer he kissed her, the more unhinged her desire to have him grew. She clung to his shoulders as he pressed another finger inside of her, stretching her more than before. He countered every ounce of pressure with pacifying pleasure, stroking and kissing her breasts, nibbling her ear, and delicately licking her lips. He used pleasure-pain to build her tolerance for more, and the duality of his touch showed her just how far her body could be pushed.

Sensations built and transcended into an overwhelming unknown as he mastered her like a fine instrument. Soon, she was digging her nails into his flesh and tugging at his clothes, searching for purchase as the mounting pleasure spiked.

"That's it," he coaxed, stroking those long fingers deeper. "Take it like a good girl."

The tension burst inside of her like a collapsing star rushing through the galaxy. Her toes pointed, and her muscles locked as pleasure poured from her, slickening his fingers so he could slide deeper still. She moaned and writhed, but he kept going, hooking his fingers inside of her, probing and rubbing until she lost control of her responses, and he took full command of her body.

"Beautiful." He kissed her possessively, her thighs wet with her climax, the proof of her arousal covering his skin.

Tears wet her face, but she had no memory of crying. It was too much, too fast to catalog every little sensation and emotion. She lost sight of where she ended and he began. A scary thought that tugged a jagged breath from her lungs and caused her to sob in shame.

His lips dragged over her features with entitled possession. "Hush, darling, Daddy has you now."

His tongue stole into her mouth, tender and protective, a complete contrast to the rough way he had handled her before. She stared through her damp lashes, wondering how many women actually knew pleasure like this could exist. He spoke of degradation, which might possibly be what this was, but she didn't feel destroyed. On the contrary, she felt taken apart and set free.

She was never meant to enjoy it, but she had. And while she should be sick with shame, she felt too good to feel anything other than liberated, even as his captive.

"I hate you," she rasped, unable to hide her internal struggle from him.

He chuckled and kissed her throat. "Does such a lie bring you comfort?"

"Yes."

"Then I'll allow it."

She relied on such a lie because facing her emotions at the moment was too confusing. She'd barely fought him. And he was right. She wanted to thank him.

"You're twisted."

His hand stilled for a split second, then he continued stroking her. "Imagine your gratitude when I fully break you. This is only the beginning, little darling."

She shivered and closed her eyes, unable to imagine feeling more transformed than she already felt. He'd opened her mind to untold pleasure, and somehow, she was still a virgin.

She'd imagined how it would be and had a thousand different fantasies, but her mind was so limited. She never imagined anything this all-consuming. It was no wonder people found sex addicting. But she hadn't even had sex yet.

He was right. This was only the beginning.

He slipped out of the bed, and his absence hit like palpable pain. "Where are you going?"

"Rest. I'll only be a moment." He moved to the table and took a sip of wine.

She couldn't rest because she feared if she closed her eyes, she'd wake up, and this would all be a dream. Tracking him like an addict tracks their next fix, she monitored his every step.

He moved with inhuman agility. Every natural gesture was an erotic glimpse into his private world. She liked it when he casually tucked his hair behind his ear or scratched an itch. He was poetry in motion. Incredibly powerful, yet those glimpses of ordinary motions brought him closer to her level and made him relatable. Perhaps even attainable.

It was then she acknowledged that she could see this evolving into something more. He could probably leave the door wide open at this point, and she wouldn't run.

"I think you've domesticated me."

He chuckled. "That's an interesting way to put it. You were rather feral a few minutes ago when you came all over my hand."

She hid her smile in the pillows, certain her cheeks were flushing pink. With a content sigh, she lounged back and stared at the amber shadows that glowed and flickered overhead. "If I've gone feral, it's because you made me so."

"One might say you have an issue with accountability."

She snickered. "One might say you're a savage."

"Right on both accounts."

He was as unruly as the flickering flames. Powerful and unpredictable. Her earlier opposition had been wasted on him. He claimed he'd get everything he wanted, and now she was convinced he would.

Twirling her hair around her finger, she stared at the canopy, wondering what would become of her. Would he keep her as some sort of ship slave, tied to his bed by day and taken hard by night? Grinning at the thought, she silently laughed. There was definitely something twisted and wrong inside of her.

She should be questioning how much time she had left. Reality beckoned as the fleeting thought of her home life crept in. This was a dangerous place, and he was obviously a dangerous man, yet she felt secure in the fact that he clearly coveted her. Was she safe enough to ask what his plans were?

She rolled to her side, angling her elbow to rest her head on her hand. "Do you plan to kill me?"

He stilled from unbuttoning his shirt as if her blunt curiosity caught him off guard. "Ah, to die would be a great adventure."

Her smile faltered. "Is that a yes, then?"

He glanced at her through narrow eyes. "I'm afraid you're much more useful to me alive."

Her smile returned. "Because of all the things you're going to do with my body?"

"That, and other reasons."

Other reasons? The sense of security she'd been luxuriating in vanished, and she frowned again. "What does that mean?"

The air chilled when he pinned her with a sharp glare. "Don't question me." Malevolence flashed in his eyes, and she drew back. His unreadable expression clarified nothing aside from the fact that they were not on the same side. The sense of closeness was gone, as if he'd stripped off a mask and his true nature returned.

What a fool she'd been to think this was something other than a game to him. Seconds ago, she felt more connected to him than anyone else in the world. Now, she just felt stupid and alone.

How could she be so dumb? He was a criminal. A pirate. And she gave herself to him.

Her skin chilled as she sat up, pulling the covers to her chest.

She was a gullible idiot, desperately painting pretty pictures of her dishonor to somehow romanticize captivity. She could not have made it easier for him. He called her a slut because she conceded like one.

She could still fight him. She could escape the next time they docked. No one needed to know what happened here. She could bury it like a secret for the rest of her life.

"Would you like some wine before we continue?"

Her panicked stare met his. They weren't finished. How was she going to stomach more now that she realized she meant absolutely nothing to him?

Or did she? She needed to know his reasons for taking her. She couldn't believe anyone could be that detached and, at the same time, that intimate. There had to be something real between them.

Or was she thinking like a fanciful child again?

"There were at least fifty other women at that lagoon."

He glanced over his shoulder and cocked a brow in question. "And?"

"Why did you only take me?"

He crossed the room slowly, not stopping until he leaned over her, forcing her to angle back as he caged her in and stared directly into her eyes. "Careful, darling. You're trespassing on private territory."

"Why won't you tell me?"

"Because it's not your business."

"But you said—"

He caught her chin and dragged his thumb over her lips, silencing her. "There are better uses for your mouth. This is the last time I'll warn you. Don't question me again."

If she did, would he punish her?

He said there would only be truth between them, but that was a lie. He was holding something back from her, something he never planned to share.

"Was I a target? Did you intentionally send Jukes to—" Her words cut off as he flung her to her back, pushing her onto the bed as his hand closed around her throat in warning.

He didn't need to apply pressure. The warning was in his eyes. "Hush now."

He abruptly released her, and she panted, unsure how much more she could push him without truly regretting her words. Only when he sensed she understood how truly serious he was did he return to the table.

She watched his back as he finished the glass of wine in two long swallows and then stripped off his shirt. The flash of tanned flesh distracted her. Muscles bulged about his shoulders, ropes of sinew twisting down his arms.

White marks formed long, thin scars across his sun-kissed skin, every single one a secret he refused to share, yet she wanted all of them. Such beauty made it too easy to forget he had the body and the mind of a killer.

When he finally faced her again, his expression was unreadable. The engorged head of his cock peeked past the waistline of his black leather pants. It was the first time she'd ever actually seen a man's body like that.

"It's time we finish what we started."

Uncertainty spiraled inside of her. She scooted back, her inner turmoil spinning into fear.

He no longer felt like someone she could trust—a foolish misapprehension if there ever were one. But that illusion of safety had helped her, and she wished she could have it back now.

Crawling further into the pillows, she tried to hide, but there was nowhere to go. She couldn't do this. She couldn't give herself to a man like him.

"Look at me." His words penetrated her panic, creating a false sense of intimacy between them.

She liked his hands on her, and now she hated herself for allowing him to touch her. She was losing her mind. "You tricked me."

"I've been nothing but honest with you."

That wasn't true. He was hiding his motive. Until she understood why he chose her, there would be lies between them.

"What's gotten into you?"

As if he knew her well enough to even ask such a thing. "Nothing."

"That's a lie. You're upset."

"How would you know?" The gall of him to call her a liar when he was the one hiding his motives.

His frown deepened. "I think we've established that I can read you like a book."

"I'm not as transparent as you think."

His eyes narrowed. "Don't push me, darling. I've been more than gracious with you—"

"You kidnapped me!"

His jaw ticked. Keeping his voice dangerously low, he warned, "I suggest you get over whatever fixation put you in this mood. My patience is expiring."

"Mine already has."

He grabbed her ankle and yanked her forward, making it unmistakably clear who had the final say. "Do you think I care?"

"You're hateful!"

She tried to get away from him, but he pulled her back and snarled, "That may be true, but you signed yourself over to me knowing exactly what I was."

They faced off in a moment of truth. He was a tower of secrets, and she was as transparent as glass. He saw through her and never lost the upper hand. When she took a swing at him, he caught her arm in an unbreakable grip.

"Careful, darling." He watched her with the eyes of a depraved man. "Fight, and I'll enjoy it just as much. Yield, and you won't get hurt."

She'd promised her surrender, and he intended to make good on that promise, no matter what.

Jagged breaths sawed in and out of her as he waited for her resistance to fade. There was no getting out of this. She was defeated and outmatched without a fight.

Closing her eyes, she turned her face away, letting go of all the tension in her body.

He eased back and frowned. "What is this?"

What did it matter? He won.

She lay limp before him until he fisted her hair, forcing her to look at him. "Answer me."

"I don't know what you want me to say!"

"Why are you acting differently?" His eyes searched hers, misleading her to believe, once again, that he cared.

"I'm acting like myself."

"This isn't you."

"Maybe it is. Maybe I'm not as transparent as you thought."

His eyes narrowed, and the energy between them chilled. "You think this attitude of yours will stop me?"

"No."

"Then why not enjoy yourself."

"Will that make it easier for you?" She met his stare with cold, hard truth. "If you're the self-proclaimed monster you say you are, what does it matter how I feel?"

"I suppose it doesn't." He seethed, shoving his pants off. Somehow, her words offended him but did not deter his plans.

"I told you before, good manners are wasted in carnal matters." Jerking her forward, he pried open her legs. "Fight, cry, scream. Your fate is inevitable."

He stroked himself as he leaned over her. His touch was cold, nothing like before.

The blunt tip of his erection nudged her opening, and she reflexively pulled back. Panic welled in her eyes. She always knew this part would hurt, but she feared him wanting to cause her more pain than necessary.

"Please," she begged. "I'm scared." Without the mask of affection, she couldn't get there. He'd destroyed her flimsy illusion, and she needed it back.

The tension in his shoulders loosened, and he gentled his hold. Something merciful shifted in his eyes. "Relax. Life is full of pain, but we're much stronger than you realize."

He traced his fingers over her, easing his way, but the pressure consumed her. He was stretching parts of her that had never felt strain.

"Tensing will only make things harder on yourself." His swollen cock breached her opening, and she gasped.

He was too big. It was never going to work. Frantically, she dug her nails into his shoulders, but he lowered his weight so she couldn't escape.

"Look at me." He framed her face, holding himself in a way that stretched her without penetrating her. "It has to happen."

"I know."

She never wanted to stay a virgin this long, but she also didn't know what drove him to take her virginity from her. She'd always assumed it would feel more meaningful and less like she was a means to an end.

Accepting her fate, she took a deep breath and said, "Do it."

"As you wish." He thrust, burying himself to the hilt.

The breath left her lungs in a whoosh. It was done. She'd never felt so possessed or detained. Startled, she gasped when his lips brushed softly over hers, an absolute contrast to the strange sensation of being impaled.

Dragging his lips to her ear, he made soft, shushing sounds as he held her tight. "Hush now, little darling. Let the pain in, and it will pass."

Her eyes closed, and a jagged breath skipped past her lips, hardly reaching her chest.

He waited, seated deep inside of her, for her to adjust to the intrusion. "Take a deep breath."

She did as she was told, feeling him in her core.

"No longer an innocent, now, are you?"

The pain was a double-edged sword. As the physical ache faded, the emotional hurt grew in palpability. She wanted to feel connected to him, but logically, she knew better.

She once again wondered if she could break down his walls and build a sense of intimacy between them. Maybe then the impersonal parts would hurt a little less? She needed to try, because she needed that false sense of connection back or she was going to die like this in his arms.

Lifting her face to him, she softly kissed his lips. For a moment, he froze, seemingly startled by her initiative enough to allow it, but when she wreathed her arms around his neck, he growled and shoved her down to the mattress, pinning her there and studying her suspiciously.

"I just wanted to kiss you."

"No one touches me without my permission."

What a hypocrite. "I'll be gentle." She tried to stroke his arm, but he captured her hand. Forcing her submission with no hint of leniency.

He flexed his hips in warning, reminding her that she was at his mercy. "Don't push me."

She gasped but made no objection as the ache in her core shifted to something sensual they both seemed to feel. Their eyes locked, and he appeared as startled by the jolt of pleasure as she.

"I could break you," he reminded, watching her through narrow, distrustful eyes.

"I think you already have."

He scoffed. "What a naive thing to say." He grabbed her breast in a punishing hold and fiercely claimed her mouth.

She met every hard, demanding stroke of his tongue with submission, giving him whatever he wanted, but that only seemed to frustrate him.

He ripped his mouth away and scowled. "You think you can manipulate me?"

"I'm not trying to."

He shoved his hips forward. "Is this what you want, to see how cruel I can get? Do you think you're safe now because you've given in?"

She gasped, and he did it again, rutted into her with demanding strokes so that she had no choice but to suffer his dominance. But it wasn't the punishing force he hoped for. Instead, he shocked her with unforeseen pleasure every time he bent her to his will.

She felt him in her stomach, on her skin, and in every tired muscle. He embedded himself so deeply into the hidden parts of her that she doubted she'd ever fully get him out.

Her cries of pleasure destroyed the silence as he thrust faster, forcing moans out of her with each hard flex of his hips. When she slid across the bedding, he tugged her back with greedy need.

"I'm not a fucking game you play." He arranged her body, and she became his malleable puppet. His fist knotted in her hair as he ground his hips into her, working hard to get a reaction other than pleasure from her, but she was lost in a haze of sensation. It was so much more encompassing than she'd ever imagined.

"God damn you." He crushed his lips to hers in a brutal, unyielding kiss that left no room for escape, purposely using his mass and strength to weigh her down as he fucked her hard, but she didn't make a sound.

Time slowed and the kiss gentled. Her heart raced as she panted against his lips. Drawing back, he looked down at her in confusion and cursed, *"Fuck!"*

He sprung off the bed.

Startled by his abrupt withdrawal, she sat up, the ache in her stomach making it palpably clear she was no longer a virgin. The soreness was already setting in. "Is something wrong?"

"Quiet." He paced the carpet, raking his fingers through his hair as an aching void took shape inside of her.

The sense that she'd somehow bested him should have left her feeling empowered, but she only felt abandoned and confused by his mercurial shifts.

"James?"

He froze, tension noticeably twitching down the muscled back. His voice dropped dangerously low. "I told you not to use my name."

Gideon also warned her, but without a reason, their warnings seemed pointless. "Why can't I?"

"Because I fucking said so!" He was on top of her before

she saw him move. "Say it again. I dare you. See what happens."

She wanted to. She wanted to look him in the eyes and call him by name so he knew she wasn't afraid of him. But that was a lie. She was terrified.

Instead, she bravely caressed his cheek and flinched when he caught her wrist in an unbreakable grip and growled. "Don't."

"I only wanted to touch you."

He flung her touch away and sprang from the bed, leaving her naked and trembling. Snatching up his clothes, he left without dressing and slammed the door.

She gaped at the empty room, confused by what just happened. Dropping her face into her hands, she collapsed onto the pillows and stomped her foot in frustration. "Damn it."

THE SHADOW NEVER LEAVES

The door slammed behind James as he angrily shoved his legs into his pants. What the hell just happened? Tucking himself away, he froze at the sight of her innocence smeared on his still-swollen flesh.

He needed air and rushed for the surface like a drowning man, unable to catch his breath he rushed past Gideon as he came from the opposite end of the corridor.

"Cap'n—"

"Not now," he snarled as he stormed up the steps.

The moon hung low on the horizon, painting silver shadows on the deck as dawn softened the sky with a deep purple haze. Standing at the prow, James clenched the cold wood of the railing as he stared out at the endless expanse of black water.

The memory of her confused gaze haunted him. Could she actually trust him? Why? He'd done nothing but torment and threaten her.

He couldn't think of her tears. Women cried. She'd been innocent. He might have been too rough.

But he knew that wasn't it. She was upset, yes, but not for the right reasons. She should have hated him the moment he laid a hand on her, but she didn't. Somehow, she accepted his authority and found the strength to surrender to it.

The only thing she wanted was a sense of connection, which was the one thing he couldn't give. This was never about her. It was about his brother and taking revenge. It only worked if she hated him.

His hand balled into a fist as he glared at the black ripples and clenched his teeth in frustration. He closed his eyes and pictured her look of panic when he practically ran from her.

She was never meant to surrender this easily. Nor was she meant to crave closeness from him.

It had to be a trap. But if she were merely trying to manipulate him, why did she seem so genuinely betrayed by his enforced boundaries?

Cutting off all tenderness hurt her on a deeper level, not because she couldn't handle the physical, but because she relied on the emotional. She desperately craved a sense of intimacy he could not fabricate—for her or anyone.

That was why she wanted to use his name and why he could not allow it. But disappointing her in the wake of such stunning submission was somehow worse than causing her physical pain. Her look of bewildered confusion manifested in his own discomfort, and that was never part of the plan.

She called him James, a name no one had used since he was a boy. The man he'd become could not reconcile with the child he'd been. The atrocities he'd done…

His eyes closed as he recalled her questions. She wanted to know why he'd brought her here. And damn him for wanting to tell her. He knew better than to share such vulnerability. He trusted no one.

Damn him for wondering what it might be like to share his deepest secrets with a woman like her. She was a sheltered, pampered thing who would never understand why he did the things he did. She knew nothing of hardship or true survival. She was a privileged little rich girl who had daddy issues for days.

She was a temporary means to an end, not a long-term investment. He didn't need that sort of responsibility in his life. Nor did he trust that she'd actually want such things, but she made it damn hard to believe she couldn't want those things when she fit him so perfectly, matching his selfishness with untapped desperation of her own.

Perhaps it was better that she enjoyed it. That had never been his expectation, but it would make it easier to live with his actions in the end.

Or was it all an act to steal the upper hand? He honestly couldn't tell anymore.

She was pure light but also darkness. Those two qualities rarely accompanied each other, but when they did shadows formed, and that was where he thrived.

Damn her for luring him into her sweet innocence, for making him want to comfort her the way he comforted no one. He was a fucking pirate, not a goddamn protector. Who the hell was she to get under his skin?

His eyes opened on a hard exhale as he stared over the waves.

Last night, when he saw her on the cliffs, standing like a goddess draped in a blood-red symbol of his past, his life flashed before his eyes. Recognizing his coat on her shoulders, his heart punched through his chest with territorial need.

That was when he knew it had to be her. If Peter gave her the coat, she must hold some importance to him.

His foolish brother had risked his life coming onto his ship in the dead of night. For weeks, James tried to interpret the meaning behind his thievery. In the end, he decided it was a threat.

Peter did not want his past to disrupt his future. Breaking into his private chambers and stealing something personal sent a clear message that he wanted him to leave the Isles of Kassel. He obviously wanted James as far away from his life as possible.

For twenty years, James had held out hope that they might reconcile, which was what brought him to the Never Lands in the first place. Now, it was clear the brother he knew and loved was gone. The stolen coat severed any remaining illusion of loyalty between them.

Peter took the coat as a warning, which only provoked James to get closer, making it clear that he took orders from no one. He planned to haunt Peter's present life until he apologized for the past.

When he spotted Wendy standing like an ethereal angel on the cliffs, something dark and sinister came over him, and he vengefully formed a plan to not only reclaim his coat, but to steal the woman wearing it as well.

His selfish brother never showered women with gifts of value. Even his rumored fiancée was without a ring. And that tiny blonde woman they called Belle, she never got more than a night from Peter. But Wendy got the coat, so she obviously meant something to him.

As the ship approached the lagoon, James' instincts burned with singular, unyielding focus. Peter had stolen from him, and now he would steal something irreplaceable in return.

Like the pelts and skulls surrounding Peter's home, his

brother needed all his little trophies and treasures to remind the world how brave and fearless Peter Pangbourne was. What a lie. His brother was a coward. He was for Peter and only Peter. And he would betray anyone to save himself. James had learned that firsthand.

But, like all self-serving narcissists, Peter hated losing, especially in front of others. Stealing Wendy would be a public affront, and his brother's oversized ego would leave him no choice but to retaliate, which would inevitably lead to James having the face-to-face that he wanted.

Yes. That was the plan. He needed to stay focused on the end goal. He wouldn't be satisfied until he confronted his brother once and for all. Then, he would have the sweet satisfaction of informing him of all he'd stolen.

James' mouth curved as he anticipated how rewarding that moment of revenge would be. Some things were far more valuable once lost forever. Now, he had three treasures his brother coveted—his coat, the girl, and her virginity.

It was done.

His conquest was a monumental success. So why didn't he feel victorious?

"Cap'n, is everything alright?"

He glanced over his shoulder at his rigging officer. "Everything's fine."

"The cageling?"

"She's fine." She wasn't, but his crew didn't need that information.

Perhaps he should order her another bath. She was undoubtedly sore after he rutted into her like a goddamn animal. Why had he been so damn rough? The plan was to punish Peter, but once he had her in his bed, he realized how different Peter's life truly was.

Women like Wendy did not associate with men like him, but they flocked to duplicitous liars like Peter. Where was the justice in that?

"Sir?"

"Goddamn it, Smee, can't you see I'm thinking?"

"Yes, Cap'n. Apologies for disturbing you," he sputtered, backing away.

She claimed Peter meant nothing to her, but it would have only been a matter of time before his slimy brother took her virginity and tossed her away like yesterday's rubbish. Now, that couldn't happen.

James shut his eyes, blocking out the regret that tried to seep in. "Wait," he called to Smee.

"Yes, sir."

"Go check on her. See if she needs anything—a fresh bath or perhaps some tea." Women liked tea, didn't they? "And knock before you enter."

"Of course, sir."

Once again, alone with his thoughts, he stalked the length of the deck.

The plan was simple. He intended to defile her and send her back to Peter ruined.

Mission one accomplished. Now, he only needed to wait for his brother to arrive. There was no need for him to do more.

But if he wanted more, the option was there, waiting on his bed. A dangerous temptation if there ever was one.

Nowhere in the plan was he supposed to covet what he never meant to keep. Yet, he wanted her with ruthless entitlement, the way he desired various treasures stolen throughout the years. But keeping her was not the plan and he needed to stick to his strategy.

Capture. Debauch. Confront. Crow.

Getting emotionally attached was never wise.

What was it about her that made her so special anyway? Women never occupied his thoughts longer than a quick fuck.

Perhaps it truly was her innocence. The more he broke down her barriers, the more she looked to him for guidance. So trusting. So pure. No one had looked at him like that in years.

It softened him.

Thank God he regained his senses and left her there. He knew better than to trust a woman.

His mother was a whore.

Sister Nagina was a monster.

He would be a fool to think Wendy might be any different. They were all cold and calculating, and he needed to remember that as much as she needed to remember her place.

She was a means to an end, nothing more. And he was taking his fucking coat back.

He rarely thought about the orphanage, but he forced himself to face those horrific memories now, needing them to ground him in his resolute purpose so he would not waver when he returned to his chambers.

He pictured Sister Nagina's scaly skin. Could still feel the weight of her leather sap baton slapping down on his flesh as his youthful screams cried out for mercy.

The heavy leather pouch was her favorite toy. It concealed a twelve-inch steel rod that was dense enough to break bones. She called it Blackjack. Ironically, that was the name strangers also often used for him.

She was a vicious dictator. For a larger woman, she carried herself silently like a true predator, a sharp-toothed crocodile who devoured little boys. They often heard the snap of the metal clicker she kept in her hand long before they saw her coming.

Click...Click...Click...

The echo of that subtle click still haunted him.

Once was a warning.

Twice was a penalty.

Three meant he wouldn't sit comfortably for days.

She was a villain cloaked in hero's clothes. Saint Mercy's Home For Orphaned Boys was nothing more than a prison for lost souls.

Glancing down at his hand, he stretched his fingers as a reminder that any damage she'd done had long ago healed. It was the internal scars that lingered the longest.

Back then, his sole focus had been protecting Peter. He had a plan—a perfect plan—but everything fell through the moment James let emotion override his gut instincts. Had he proceeded with single-minded determination, they would have escaped.

He and Peter would have stuck together. They would have stayed as close as brothers could possibly be. Instead, his plan went to hell the moment he allowed softer feelings to get involved.

Peter had fallen ill with the flu. As he waited for his brother to heal, the weather turned and they were trapped by one blizzard after another. Then came the outbreak of chicken pox that spring. By the time that first summer came around, it was too late. Peter was gone.

Adopted by a family that only needed one boy and taken away before James ever got the chance to say goodbye. James waited for his brother to call, write, or visit, but he never did.

Nagina, the crocodile, mocked his pain, taunting him for being an unwanted, unlovable soul. Then, as the other boys disappeared, her focus tightened on James. She became an inescapable tyrant he survived day after miserable day.

Seasons turned without any word. And with every passing year, it became more certain James would never get an adopted family of his own.

He didn't know where to find his brother or what Peter's new name might be. And his worry for Peter's safety haunted him. But in the end, the abuse became too much and he had to leave.

Fuck that orphanage. And Fuck Peter.

James learned to rely only on himself. He appreciated his crew but needed no one, including some inexperienced woman who hoped to get past his boundaries with tenderness when he knew perfectly well it was impossible not to hate him after all he'd done to her.

That prissy act of hers might fool others, but he knew firsthand how much depravity loved to hide under polished surfaces. The upper class was the most twisted of all.

Two fingers, and he had her writhing for more. Why? Because some part of her knew she couldn't get away with such whorish behavior anywhere else. She was using him as much as he was using her.

What an act she put on, pretending she could possibly care about him. She might think she could match his darkness, but she had no idea how dark he could go. They didn't call him Black Jack for nothing.

Meeting his cruelty with tenderness was a tactic. A smart one. One that could have crushed him had he stayed a second longer in her presence.

No one had ever tried to nurture or hold him. Not his mother. Not the whores at port. And certainly not the men on his crew.

Those soft lips and the way she caressed his cheek. Did she have no self-preservation? He was a goddamn bastard, purposely showing her how rough and uncaring he could be. What the fuck was wrong with her? Why couldn't she hate him? He needed her to hate him or he would never gladly let her go. And she needed to go. Women like Wendy had no place on his ship.

He recalled how she looked up at him like some sort of protector, and his jaw tightened. He'd threatened to degrade her because he wanted to taunt her. He never expected her to accept her fate so easily.

His grip tightened on the rail as he breathed in the briny sea air. This was the church he prayed to. The wide-open isolation always had a way of bringing clarity, and he slowly came to realize everything he needed to do.

It was time to finish what he'd started. He was determined to see this through before the black sky fully faded with the encroaching dawn. He needed to be done. With all of them.

Attachment was dangerous. The sooner he cut ties, the better.

He lived only for himself because that was the surest way to survive.

She didn't belong here. She had a life and a family, a home, and a function in society. Any impression she gave that he could possibly fit into her world was a lie, a taunt to punish him the way he threatened to punish her.

He'd underestimated her. Now that he'd cleared his head, it was apparent she was only trying to use her body to manipulate him and gain the upper hand. It was a psychological game for sure, but he at least had the common sense to realize he was being played.

She thought she could outwit him by using his name? He

would punish her every time it crossed her lips until she learned.

James... Never before had his name sounded like such a whispered caress.

James... He'd warned her not to use it, but she went ahead and disobeyed him anyway.

James... He wanted her to breathe it against his ear, over and over again, as he buried himself in the sanctuary of her body.

"Fuck!" She was not his fucking sanctuary! What was wrong with him?

China rattled at his back, and he spun on Gentleman Starr, holding a tray of steaming coffee. The man nearly spilled the entire thing when James growled at him.

"What do you want?"

The entire crew would be up and moving soon, and whispers about the woman in his cabin would turn to speculation he didn't need.

"Just bringing your morning coffee, sir."

He hadn't slept. Coffee was a good idea. It would help him focus on his objective. He considered how little she'd eaten last night. "Have another tray sent to—"

"Already done, sir. Or—at least—I tried. She turned me away."

"I beg your pardon?"

Gentleman Starr fidgeted under his moth-eaten dress coat. "I personally delivered a tray—some fruit and eggs, a little tea to soothe any soreness." He cleared his throat. "She ordered me to take it away."

"She *ordered* you?"

"Yes, sir."

He ground his molars. "Who's the fucking prisoner here?

Take the tray back to her and command her to eat. Tell her I demand it."

"Sir, I told her you'd be disappointed."

"And?"

"She, uh… Well…"

"Spit it out!"

"She said, *'good*.'"

James had to laugh. The little bitch was pushing her luck.

"Go tell her if she doesn't eat some fucking breakfast, I'm going to come down there and shove something far worse down her throat."

Gideon's eyes widened. "Yes, Cap'n." He set the steaming tray aside and scuttled off to follow orders.

The longer James contemplated her defiance, the harder his cock grew. Was she hoping he'd punish her? Was that what she wanted?

This wasn't about pleasing her, but the desire to do so was undeniable. No one should have that sort of power over him. Who was the master manipulator here, her or him?

He'd shown her too much leniency, and it was fucking with his head. She needed to learn who was in charge. Then he would send her back ruined as promised, and Peter would learn never to fuck with him or his property ever again.

His knuckles whitened, the railing groaning beneath his grip as his cold façade slid back into place. Turning abruptly, he set his thinking to selfish. She was his toy, his captive. Her feelings should not come into play.

His heavy footfalls thudded against the deck as he proceeded with absolute purpose. He planned to destroy her, and he was sticking to the plan.

The wind whipped at the black sails billowing above, reminding him exactly who he was. He was a black-hearted sea captain who relied on no one but himself. A cold, loner of the seas, perfectly content to make his own rules.

When he thought of her delicate, silky skin, he fantasized about letting his darkness rub off on her, marking her with his mouth, hands, and seed. He allowed no room for regret. Regret was a festering weakness. He only needed confidence. This was his ship, and he had complete authority over everything on board—including her.

Bursting into his quarters, he startled her back from the table, where she nibbled the fucking food he'd ordered. He slammed the door, irritated by her audacity to first send food away without knowing when her next meal might come. A show of privilege if there ever was one.

Detecting his dangerous mood, she had the good sense to scurry onto the bed. "I didn't think—"

"Quiet." He wanted no words to pass between them. No chance of her softening his resolve.

"Y-you seem upset." She darted to the far side of the bed.

"I said no talking." His cock hardened as he grabbed her ankle and hauled her back to him.

"Wait!" She tried to slip his grip, but he caught her and bent her over the mattress, showing her who was in command.

"You will learn to take orders without question while on my ship."

She drove her elbow into his ribs and he grunted, forcing her to her belly and kicking her ankles apart. "Yield."

She struggled as she panted beneath him, but he kept her restrained.

"You signed yourself over to me, darling, and I'm far from satisfied. Yield, or it's down to the barracks you go."

She gentled immediately, which only enhanced his anger. Yes, he wanted her to surrender, but he also wanted her to fight. Her self-control infuriated him for reasons he couldn't understand.

She should have clawed and kicked and bit him. Instead, she submitted. Why? Did she do so out of fear or was this one more way she hoped to influence him?

It seemed sacrilegious to cause such a fierce woman to cower, but he had no choice. She had to bend to his authority like everyone else on his ship.

Just as his crew had signed contracts, so had she. The end.

He wouldn't actually send her down to the barracks where his men slept. And he'd never force anyone to live off rats in captivity. But he needed her to believe he could go that far if challenged, or she would continue to defy him to the very end.

He truly was a monster.

But there was no going back now.

"You will not confuse me with heroes from your storybooks. Do you hear me, darling? I'm not someone you can save. Any thoughts of redemption are wasted on me, so keep your gentle caresses and give up any hopes that you could soften me by use of my name. I'm not your fucking friend. I'm the enemy." A truth both of them needed to see. "And that contract you signed says your body belongs to me."

"I wasn't fighting you. I was only doing what came naturally to me."

Bullshit. She wanted to disarm him with kindness to turn the tables on him.

"Maybe you should have fought. At least then I'd believe your sincerity."

Fisting her hair, he aligned his body with hers and offered no warning as he shoved into her, asserting his total authority with a satisfied groan. She gasped, rising on her tippy toes as he buried himself to the hilt, but then she leaned into him and moaned.

He covered her mouth, not wanting to hear such sweet sounds of pleasure. Every time he expected her to hate him, she somehow had the opposite response.

"Your body fits mine like a glove," he growled into her ear. She moaned against his hand and he flexed his hips, grinding himself deeper into her heat. He needed her this one last time. Enough to get her out of his system so he could give her back and move on.

Why did she feel different from every other woman he'd had? What was it about her? Perhaps he needed to fuck her out of his system. Maybe that was the only way to get her out of his head and think logically again.

Gripping her by the hips, purposefully leaving marks on her flawless skin, he tugged her closer, fucking her hard, selfishly, intending to bury his release so deep inside of her he'd be embedded in her for days.

She would remember his possession long after the ache in her body faded. Traces of his possession would drip down her thighs so she could see the monster he was. A cruel, unbending, villainous wretch who cared nothing for redemption and could not be saved.

Tugging her hair, he forced her body to arch into him. "Do you see how little I care for your comfort? I'm not your friend, darling. I'm your captor, and you are my filthy little slave." He shoved her forward, thrusting deep as he forcefully came inside of her.

His muscles jerked, and his spine twitched. Never before had he had such a brutal release.

Gripping her flesh, he spread her thighs wide. His cock slid slowly from her wet pussy, and his mouth curved with a wicked grin when the proof of his claim seeped from her swollen folds.

There, he thought, as her body pulsed in his absence. "Not so virginal anymore, are you?"

When she didn't move, he frowned and cocked his head. Her arms were trapped beneath her chest, and her dark ebony waves hid her face. He swept the strands away. Her feathered lashes cast shadows on her porcelain skin.

Was she hurt? How was she so still?

"Open your eyes."

She blinked and looked back at him with that crystal blue stare. No tears.

"Is there something you wish to say?"

She licked her lips, then rasped, "Thank you, sir."

His heart stopped as he staggered back. He'd been the one to order her gratitude but now regretted such an order. Forcing her appreciation only embedded lies between them, and he much preferred her raw truth.

"I don't believe you." They locked stares, and he challenged her to speak the truth. "If you don't hate me by now, I've clearly been too soft."

He was a mind fuck son of a bitch, purposely trapping her so she couldn't win whatever game they played. She either admitted she hated him and faced the consequences or embraced his depravity and opened a door for far worse. Either way, she was at his mercy. Who was the master manipulator now?

Her labored breathing was as wild as her eyes as she licked her lips again. "But, sir, I liked the way you are with me."

He stilled.

She was lying.

She had to be.

He'd stolen her choice and been more than rough with her despite knowing she was innocent and inexperienced. He was growing tired of her duplicity.

"I order you to speak the truth."

She panted softly, her body still recovering from his use. "I am."

Fury erupted inside him, tempting something all too alluring he had no right to imagine. She could not be so proper and hide that much darkness inside her. She was one of them. Nothing like the cheap women at port or the men on his crew. This was a game she played. Nothing more. And she was going to lose.

"Is that the kind of filthy little slut you are? You like being used hard and put away wet?"

"I guess I do, sir."

What had he awakened in her? If she was telling the truth, this behavior would not stop after he let her go. Who else would touch her like that in the years to come?

Furious at the thought of anyone else laying a hand on her, he delivered a punishing threat. "If you enjoy being used so much, perhaps I'll call my crew in, let each one of them have a shot—"

The breath knocked out of him as he doubled over, catching himself on the bed where she had just been. Searing pain slashed at his side. Turning his hand from his torso, he found traces of blood.

"You little bitch."

She was fast. Faster than he thought possible and far more dangerous than he realized. Glancing down at the gash in his side, he laughed. He deserved that and more for making such a groundless threat. The disgusting thought of letting any man lay a filthy hand on her should have cost him his tongue. And he was proud of her for fighting back. But she was going to pay.

It was far from a lethal wound, but it could have been deadly had she known how to hold a knife properly. And how fucked was he for wanting to teach her?

The knife, which she'd dropped in her escape, clattered to the floor. He kicked it aside. "Not very refined of you, darling."

Her eyes were wild as she watched him from the other side of the bed. He had the pleasure of seeing the exact moment realization set in and she understood there would be consequence for her actions. A big one.

"I'm sorry."

A truth or a lie?

He cocked a brow, amused by the riddle she posed but still bleeding all the same. "It's wise to be afraid."

She mirrored his steps, backing up every time he strode closer.

"There's nowhere you can run that I won't follow now."

She bolted for the door, but he got there first, slamming it shut before she opened it a crack.

"No!" she screamed and kicked as he dragged her back to his chest.

His hand closed around her throat, his bloodied fingers pressing down on her racing pulse. "Who taught you how to hold a knife?"

"No one."

"That's obvious."

She slammed her elbow into his ribs, and he grunted but didn't let her go. He dragged her down to the rug, where she fought and scratched like a feral cat.

"What did you think would happen?" Yanking the chains, he pulled her up by her wrist. "When you pull a knife on an enemy, you better be prepared to finish the job."

"No!" She jerked her arm back before he could lock the cuff.

"Stay still!"

"No! Get off me!"

He thought he wanted her submission, but this fire in her eyes was worth far more. Somehow, he managed to get the chains onto her wrists and locked. "You have only yourself to blame!" He was covered in scratches and blood. "I trusted you, and look how you repay that trust."

She jerked her trapped hands and growled, "You're incapable of trust!"

"Enough!" he barked, disturbed by her statement's accuracy.

She seethed and glared at him.

"I gave you a choice, and you surrendered. I'm not interested in your regrets or second thoughts. Is that clear?"

"Crystal," she said through gritted teeth.

"Strike me again, and I really will move you below deck."

Her eyes were wild, and her hair was a mess.

"This is my ship. No one raises a hand to me, let alone gets away with stabbing me." It didn't matter that he'd had mosquito bites that bled more. She'd tried to purposely injure him, and that needed to be addressed.

"You deserved it! You were going to give me away to your crew."

"Quiet." Hearing it from her mouth sounded even worse.

"You be quiet!"

He towered over her, and she bent back, finally shutting

her mouth. "You want to challenge me? Open your mouth again and see what happens."

Her lips pressed tight, and she shook her head. "Fuck you," she growled through clenched teeth.

"Fuck me?"

"Yes. Fuck you," she repeated, her voice shaking.

"Very well." He went to the wall to turn the crank. Slowly, the slack on the chains tightened.

Her wild eyes looked up at the ceiling where the metal clinked through the iron hook. She had no choice but to clamber to her feet, and soon she was teetering on her toes, her arms stretched far overhead as the muscles in her stomach contracted and her breasts flattened from the pose.

He dragged a wingback chair to the carpet and set it aside. "I've been too lenient with you." Moving behind her, he gripped her breast with punishing possessiveness and whispered into her ear, "I'm going to punish you for what you did, darling. And by the time I'm finished with you, no resistance will be left."

His hand trailed down her stomach, and he pressed his fingers inside of her, swirling traces of his release with her arousal, getting his fingers nice and wet. When she moaned, he yanked her head back and shoved his fingers down her throat, making her gag.

"Savor that, darling. It's what complete ownership tastes like."

Her garbled outrage made him laugh as he held her jaw, forcing her to adapt to the panic and learn how to breathe.

"Better get used to it. Soon, it'll be my cock sliding down your throat as I fuck that pretty little scowl off your face."

"*Huck hou*," she garbled.

"Filthy words for a filthy slut." He wedged his fingers into her mouth, stretching her lips and forcing her silence. "Right about now, your gag reflex is starting to spasm, but there's nothing you can do. Your eyes are starting to tear from strain as much as outrage because now you realize I'm coming for that precious self-control of yours, and I don't plan on leaving anything behind." Withdrawing his hand, he slapped her ass hard, and a startled squeak escaped her throat. "When you learn to savor such loss of control, all the tension disappears." He gave her hair a tug and whispered in her ear, "I might be incapable of trust, but for you, my dear, trust is all you have. How much can you trust a man to take care of you after you try to kill him? It's a delicate balance, you see, and darling, you've just rocked the boat."

He slapped her ass again, and her eyes dilated. The tension in her arms eased ever so slightly. She tried to look up to avoid his gaze, but he saw right through her.

"You like it when I punish you because it gives you a form of penance you can process. You want to be punished, don't you? Because you feel horrible about cutting me with that knife." He loosened the chains, providing enough slack to push her hand over the gash on his side. "You want to match my darkness, darling? Match my pain?"

He swung his hand again, cinching the chains tight once more and deepening the red handprint that already showed on her lush flesh.

She cried out, lips parted, eyes hooded, and whispered, "I'm sorry, sir."

"Have you had enough? Are we even now?" His nails scraped slowly over her sensitized flesh.

She shook her head. "No. I deserve more."

"Deserve or want?"

"Both."

His cock was rock hard as she teetered before him, arms restrained overhead, and her lush ass puffy and ready for the taking. "Beg me."

"Please, punish me for what I did. I want to be a good girl again."

He slapped her ass several more times until she was reduced to a panting mess. Groping his swollen cock, he stroked it against her bare thigh. "And what should we do about that dirty mouth of yours?"

She bit her lip and looked at him repentantly.

He chuckled. "Suddenly quiet as a mouse." She met his stare but remained silent. "Good girls do as they're told." He stepped back and looked down at the gash in his side. Her gaze followed his. "Tell me why you did it. The truth, now."

Her lips pursed as her eyes squeezed shut.

"Are we back to acting childish? You know I can see you when you close your eyes. You don't actually disappear."

Her chest lifted with each labored breath.

"Tell me why you wanted to hurt me." She had a hundred valid reasons, but he needed to hear her motive. He wanted to understand what finally provoked her to rebel after relinquishing so much.

"You left me here all alone!" she finally snapped. "You took everything I had, then left!"

"I was coming back."

"How was I to know that? You sent Gideon—"

"*Gideon?*" He scoffed. "You use his first name as if you're old friends."

"He's more a friend to me than anyone else on this ship."

"Careful, darling. Any kindness Gentleman Starr has shown you has been at my command. Let's stay on topic. You were upset I left…"

Her eyes glazed. "That's it."

"That's it? I left, so you tried to stab me?"

"Yes!"

"Not because I fucked you or called you names."

"No. I did everything you asked, but you punished me anyway."

He frowned. His taking some air was not meant to punish her. It was meant to bring clarity about her purpose here. And why was he suddenly justifying his choices? She was lucky she didn't nick an artery or hit his kidney.

"The only thing your outburst proved is that you can't be trusted alone. That's going to complicate matters for you."

Her lips formed a firm line, and she shook her head. Did she regret not doing more damage now that her predicament had changed?

He pushed her, letting her twirl on her toes while he thought about what to do with her next. "I took exactly what you offered."

She scowled, but pain hid in the depths of her stare. Pain he put there by not fully considering her feelings.

His memory flashed to a time when he'd been left utterly alone in a frightening place, his family and comforts long gone. The recollection knocked the wind out of him. He remembered crying—not because of his lashings or empty stomach but because he didn't understand why his mother or Sister Nagina couldn't love him. Their neglect was never their fault. He'd always internalized it and made it his own.

Was that how he made her feel? Abandoned and undeserving. He'd threatened to break her, but never in that way.

He lowered the chain, taking the strain off her arms. "Take a deep breath."

As much as she might hate him, she still obeyed and took

a long breath. He could hear her dismay through the jagged way the air entered her lungs.

"Let it out slowly." Her brow softened as she looked up at him. There was so much longing in her eyes that he found it hard to deny her anything in that moment.

Tracing his fingers over her cheek, he lowered his voice. "Good girl."

It was the praise he vowed not to offer, but she *was* a good girl, doing exactly as she was told, accepting that he was in total command, and she deserved a reward more than she deserved any punishment.

Her lashes lowered, and she nuzzled into his hand, soft and utterly trusting.

For a split second, he imagined what it would feel like to have her there by choice. He quickly shoved the insane thought away. She would have never stolen that knife if she wanted to be here.

"Let me make it all better." Slipping into the chair, he caught her hips and positioned her knees on the upholstered arms, forcing her to use her core muscles so she didn't fall. He caught her hips and dragged her to his face, sliding his tongue through her slit.

Her breath quickened, and she panicked when he licked her again. "Wait—"

"Not a chance. Daddy's hungry." He swirled his tongue around her clit. "Mmm… You taste sweet, like innocence and privilege, yet salty with my claim."

"You can't—"

"Hush." He dove in and didn't let up until she learned those words didn't work on him. "There's a good girl." Closing his lips around her swollen clit he sucked hard, using his tongue to tease her to climax.

A deep red flush covered her breast as he stripped away whatever sense of modesty she had left. As soon as she came, he pushed her toward another climax, never giving her a chance to come down. Pleasure built to an intensity that bordered on pain, and he watched the moment she succumbed to surrender, losing herself in a place of bliss and torment where she no longer had to think. She only had to feel.

"That's it. Look how your body responds to me." He fed his fingers into her, pumping quickly as she lost control to another orgasm. His chest was soaked, but he still wanted more. He wanted every drop of her pleasure and the final say over her pain.

"Please, it's too much."

"Take it like a good girl." Hooking his fingers inside of her, he teased the spot that made her cry out. He drank every drop that spilled from her. "Beautiful."

She folded forward, weak and tired, but he was far from done.

He stroked her spine, giving her a small reprieve. "Just relax and let Daddy take care of you."

He lowered her into the chair and dropped to his knees, devouring her softly. A single touch jolted her like an electric shock, but she made no objection as he ate his fill of her pretty, pink pussy.

He lifted her back onto his lap once he'd had his fill. "See how much you gain when you truly let go?"

Cradling her close, he stroked the swollen lips of her sex. She shivered in the aftershock of so many orgasms. He petted her softly, hoping to soothe any aches that already set in.

She sighed as if enjoying his touch, resting her head against his chest, eyes closed and her face a serene work of art.

"Unfortunately, my cock's rock hard. Which means I'll probably fuck you like an animal at least one more time before you get to sleep."

A quiet sound of distress left her throat.

"If you're too sore, there's another option." He traced his finger back and pressed lightly against her virgin hole. "I won't be satisfied until I claim all of you."

Her dark lashes lifted as she met him with that penetrating blue stare. He watched as curiosity battled caution.

"Imagine how my cock will feel when it stretches you here. Tight. Intense. Full. Until the mind goes numb, and all you can do is feel my possession. In you. Over you. Total ownership." He needed to get back inside of her. "Does the thought scare you?"

She nestled closer and sighed. "Not if you promise to hold me."

He stilled from stroking her. Fuck. In the end, she'd gotten her way. Perhaps they both had. Now, he wasn't so sure her actions were as calculated as they first seemed.

"I'll hold you," he said, realizing he had no desire to let go.

She smiled against his chest. "Then I'm all yours."

There had to be a limit to the depravity she'd allow. He needed to find it. The darkness inside of him would not be satisfied until she was fully his. He stilled. Could it be that simple? Was his ownership all she wanted? The sense that she truly belonged to him and could not be disowned?

"It is a little slut then, isn't it?" He pressed his finger into her back entrance, and she gasped. "Is this what you want? You want me to break you here, as well, and fully make you mine?"

His painfully engorged cock pulsed as he sank his fingers

deeper into her tight little hole, but rather than cry or beg for mercy, she made a stunning sound of pure intrigue as if she truly wanted more.

His knuckle wedged snugly against the muscle, but she didn't fight it. "If you don't hate me by now, you're about to." Withdrawing his finger, he stood and unlocked the chains, carrying her to the bed.

Snatching the bath oils from the table by the tub, he positioned her over the edge of the bed. "Hold yourself open for me." He showed her how to grip her cheeks, and she did so without protest, giving him a clear view of both holes.

He dropped to his knees and smeared the oil over her skin. When he sank a larger finger into her tight little virgin hole, she broke her silence and pressed up on her toes.

"Ah! *Sir...*"

"Don't try to escape it."

Watching her regain control of her panic was breathtaking. Her breathing leveled, and she flattened to her feet.

He rewarded her with a soft kiss on the spine. "Good girl. Now, let's try again."

She gasped as he stretched her quickly, forcing one then two fingers inside of her so as not to prolong the shock. He rewarded her with a few strokes over her swollen clit, to balance the pain with pleasure.

"Beautiful."

Her moans hit a crescendo when he plunged his other fingers into her pussy, the dual penetration driving her to new levels of pleasure as she fell into another subspace.

"That's a good little slut. You trust Daddy to take good care of you and take everything he gives you."

Her moans grew louder, edged on by his depraved words

of praise as he fucked his fingers into her. Hooking his fingers, he teased her clit, and she went off like a geyser.

"What did I tell you?" He smeared her release over her thighs and pussy. "No resistance left. Only need."

He watched in awe as her body gaped for more. Gripping his swollen cock, he kissed the base of her spine.

"You're ready for me."

He helped her further onto the bed and aligned their bodies. Guiding her shoulders down, he put her in a position that would hopefully ease any unnecessary pain. She was small, and he was bound to stretch her.

Spreading additional oil over her hole, he made sure she was ready. He pressed the slick, blunt head of his cock against the tight knot of her ass, and she gasped, lunging forward on instinct.

He placed a staying hand on her shoulder. "Almost there, baby. Show me how good you take my cock. Make Daddy proud."

"I'm trying." She fisted the bedding and pushed back, angling herself so that he could sink fully inside of her. A guttural moan left her throat as he fully seated himself.

Dear God, she was stunning.

He groaned as her body fisted him. "What a good girl you are, such a brave little slut." He stroked her spine, giving her a chance to adapt to the overwhelming pressure. The tension in her hands loosened as she exhaled a jagged breath.

She responded to the praise, and he was beginning to understand why. He liked it, too. He enjoyed sharing with her how much she pleased him, and how a single compliment motivated her to take things further.

"Are you a good girl, darling?"

Her breath was labored. "Sometimes."

"What about now?"

"No, Daddy."

"No? Why not?"

"Because right now, I'd rather be your good little slut."

He nearly spilled his nut. "Then my good little slut you'll be." He thrust his hips and grunted, relishing her sweet words. "Whose body is this?"

"Yours."

"That's right." He slid as deep as he could fit, purposely holding her by the back of her neck to demonstrate his dominance.

Her lips parted as heat engulfed him. Then she glanced over her shoulder and their eyes met. Something inside of him shifted into fear. She was looking at him in that way that left him too exposed.

"Lower your gaze."

A divot of confusion formed in her brow.

"Do it."

Reluctantly, she turned her head and looked away.

It was a look that would haunt him forever, a look that made him believe her feelings were real. A look that would later destroy him when she left because no matter what passed between them now, they both knew exactly how this would end.

He thrust harder, shoving back the sense that anyone could leave him so exposed. He took from her with total entitlement, unable to bear the way she seemed to see into his soul. No one else had ever looked at him like that. And never before had he wanted to possess a woman so completely.

"Such a good girl," he said, not wanting to make his issues hers. He reached for her swollen clit. "You take direction so well."

In only a few rubs, she was coming on his fingers again. His cock pulsed as her body clenched around him, and then he was pumping his release into her.

Slowly withdrawing his cock, he watched his cum seep from her pulsing hole. "Perfect." He lowered her to her stomach and kissed her temple. "Wait there."

He poured warm water from the kettle into the wash basin and dampened a soft cloth. She sighed as he carefully cleaned her body, taking extreme care with her most tender parts.

When he finished, he returned to the basin and washed himself.

She lay so still, he assumed she'd fallen asleep until she softly said, "I never meant to …"

He set aside the soapy water and returned to the bed. "What was that?"

She looked up at him with those big blue eyes. "Nothing."

He caught her chin. "No. Finish what you were going to say."

She swallowed and lowered her stare. "I never wanted to hurt you."

He'd forgotten about her little assault, but it must still be weighing on her. "I think we're even."

She met his stare. "I don't want you to share me with other men."

Her directness, in the face of his unpredictable temper, left him in awe. She was indomitable when she wanted to be.

"I won't let anyone else touch you."

Relief transformed her face. "Thank you, sir. You're the only one I want that way."

He was fucked.

Cupping her cheek, he looked into her eyes and vowed, "It

will *only* ever be me. Anyone else lays a hand on you, they'll lose it."

She smiled. Dark circles shadowed her eyes. It had been a long and trying night, and the devil only knew the last time she slept.

"You need rest." He pulled the covers over her. "After you sleep, I'll have a fresh bath drawn."

She opened her eyes. "Are you leaving?" The desperation in her voice confused him.

"I have to check on the crew."

"Stay." Her hand curled around his. "Please."

It was a simple plea, but it knocked something loose in his chest. Glancing at the soft way she held his hand, he tried to remember a time when anyone else had ever touched him so gently.

"Don't worry about me."

Her hold tightened when he tried to pull his hand away. "But someone has to. You need rest, too."

"You want to worry about me? That was a big job for anyone."

She looked up at him with those trusting blue eyes and nodded. "It wouldn't be a job. I'd take care of you if you'd let me."

It was a mistake he couldn't resist. But how was he supposed to turn down such a sweet offer?

Stretching out beside her, he folded his hands behind his head. "I'll stay for a few minutes. Then I have things to do."

She smiled, lifting the covers and cuddling close to his side. His throat went dry when her soft curves molded to his hard edges, and she rested her cheek on his chest.

Now, who was the inexperienced one?

Her fingers trailed over his abs, and his eyes went wide. She was barely touching him, yet somehow destroying him.

She lifted her head, and her hair tickled his chest. Tiny kisses peppered over his abdomen as she moved lower. His dick instantly hardened when her hand reached for him.

She didn't ask permission, and he had plenty of time to stop her, but he wanted to see where this led. Her innocence showed in the shy way she fondled him, but that didn't detract from the pleasant sensation of her hand on him.

She kissed lower and then pressed her soft lips to the engorged tip of his cock. Warm breath skated over his flesh as she hesitated. She traced her lips over the side but didn't seem to know what else to do.

He gently gathered her hair so he could see her beautiful face. "Try putting it in your mouth, darling."

She looked back at him and then returned her focus to his cock. Slowly, she parted her lips and gave the tip a wet kiss.

"More," he rasped.

She kissed the tip again, this time wrapping the head of his cock in the wet heat of her mouth.

"That's it." He cupped the back of her head, pressing her lower. "Relax your jaw."

When she did as he instructed, he flexed his hips, bumping the back of her throat, then let go of her. She looked up at him in astonishment, her full lips parted as if hungry for more.

He stroked her cheek and grinned. "We'll do more of that later. For now, you need to rest."

"But—"

"Later." He pulled her back to his chest, desiring that unfamiliar intimacy more than anything else at the moment.

He allowed himself this unique second of desire, knowing it wouldn't last forever.

He'd never slept beside anyone—save his brother—and that was before the orphanage. The novelty of sleeping beside a woman left him far from at ease, but the longer she curled into him, the more his guard came down, and he wanted to stay there, wrapped in her softness, listening to her breathe.

She nestled into his chest, her warm little body a constant source of comfort. It became hard to swallow as he stroked his hand slowly up and down her arm.

His eyes grew heavy, and he briefly thought about the unattended weapons on the dresser. He could warn her, but he didn't want to. He wanted to test the theory that he could trust her enough not to leave the bed.

Unfortunately, when he awoke, she was gone.

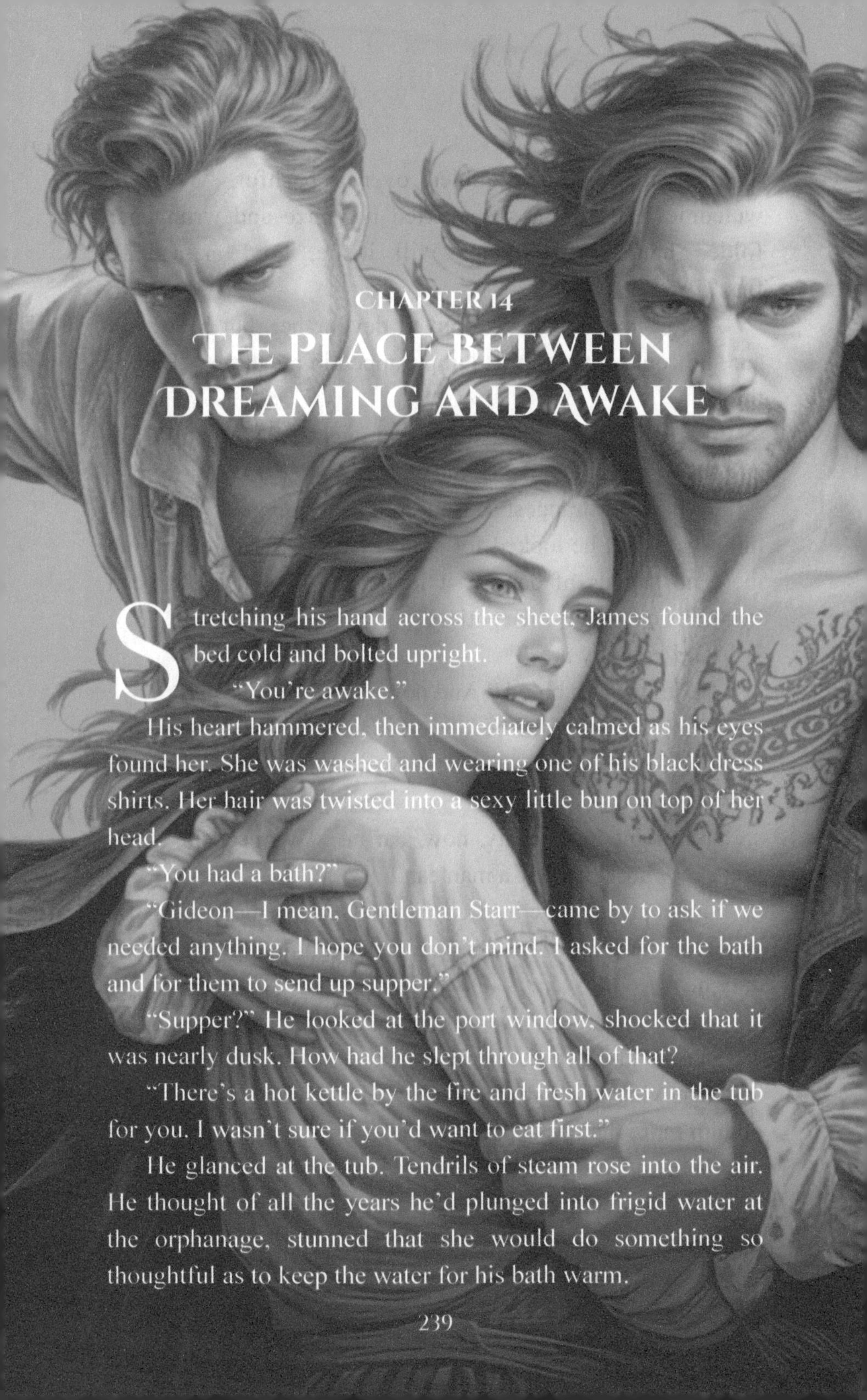

CHAPTER 14

THE PLACE BETWEEN DREAMING AND AWAKE

Stretching his hand across the sheet, James found the bed cold and bolted upright.

"You're awake."

His heart hammered, then immediately calmed as his eyes found her. She was washed and wearing one of his black dress shirts. Her hair was twisted into a sexy little bun on top of her head.

"You had a bath?"

"Gideon—I mean, Gentleman Starr—came by to ask if we needed anything. I hope you don't mind. I asked for the bath and for them to send up supper."

"Supper?" He looked at the port window, shocked that it was nearly dusk. How had he slept through all of that?

"There's a hot kettle by the fire and fresh water in the tub for you. I wasn't sure if you'd want to eat first."

He glanced at the tub. Tendrils of steam rose into the air. He thought of all the years he'd plunged into frigid water at the orphanage, stunned that she would do something so thoughtful as to keep the water for his bath warm.

"Thank you."

She smiled and stumbled over a bashful, "Y-you're welcome." Blushing, she averted her gaze and wrung her folded hands. "So, which will it be, food or a bath first?"

At the moment, he wanted to devour her, but he wasn't sure he could eat with this lump trapped in his throat. "Bath, I think."

"Perfect." She set a folded towel over the ledge of the tub and sat on a short stool. "Come on then."

He had the strangest sensation he was being set up. Scanning the room, he looked for signs of trouble. Not only were there no signals of danger, it looked as though she'd been busy. His quarters were spotless.

"Did you tidy up?"

"A little. I was bored." And now she was being shy.

Climbing out of the bed, he stretched and stilled when her eyes widened. She quickly looked down as her blush darkened.

"No point in modesty, now, darling. I've been inside of you every possible way a man can."

She kept her gaze averted, but he spotted the twitch of a smile. As he stepped into the tub, he caught her taking a peek at him.

"Look your fill. I have no shame."

Her breath hitched, and he chuckled, sliding into the water and removing his body from view. He liked having her eyes on him more than he should.

"What do you see when you look at me?"

Her gaze jumped to his. "Authority. Strength. Power."

"Scars?"

Her head tilted. "Yes. But also beauty."

That was enough of that. He eased back and closed his eyes.

"Is the water warm enough?"

The heat was divine. "Yes."

"Good." She reached over his shoulder, and he caught her wrist faster than a croc snaps up its prey. She held a washcloth in her hand. "I was only going to wet the cloth."

"Why?"

"So I could wash your back."

No one had ever bathed him that he could remember. He was a grown man. He could wash himself. But still, he released her to see if she actually would.

As she dragged that cloth over his chest, he discovered new levels of pleasure. Never before had bathing been more than a necessity. She transformed it into something luxurious and sinful. Shutting his eyes, he leaned back and rested his arms on the ledge, allowing her to carry on.

"Are you sore?"

Her hand stilled, and he took that as confirmation. "I was. Soaking in the bath helped."

"I shouldn't have been so rough with you—at least not for your first time."

"I didn't mind."

He glanced back at her. "You don't have to say that."

"But I'm fine. There's just a satisfying ache where you've been. It's nothing I can't live with."

He lifted a brow. "*Satisfying*?"

She blushed again. "Yes, very."

His cock hardened under the water. "The ache will ease in time."

"Not if you have me again before it fades."

Was she truly offering herself? Or was this another game?

She bit her lip in that sexy way she often did. "What are you thinking?"

Her shoulder lifted in a delicate shrug. "That you were right—about all of it."

"What do you mean?"

He watched her struggle to put her feelings into words. He suspected she knew what she wanted to say, but some part of her still feared the sky would fall if she said it out loud. Her gaze lowered, and she licked her lips. "The more I surrendered control, the freer I became."

She was either telling the truth, or he was a damn fool because he felt her sincerity in his gut. She was being honest. She liked his depraved darkness.

"You're a dangerous woman, Wendy Moira Angela Darling."

Looking through her lashes, she gave him a half grin. "Maybe I'm a pirate at heart."

She'd certainly stolen more than he'd willingly given. "Perhaps you are. But such a charming name would never work on a pirate. We'll have to think up something a little more threatening."

Her grin stretched. "Like what? Red-Handed Wendy?"

He thought of how she'd stolen his knife. "We'll call you Red-Handed Jill."

Her smile faltered. "Why Jill?"

"Why not?"

She shook her head, and her frown deepened. "Tell me why you chose me."

"I chose you because I wanted you."

Again, she shook her head. "I know you're purposely not telling me something. This wasn't about me. Not initially.

This was something else. Something personal. Was there a Jill?"

"No, there was no Jill."

"Then why would you call me Red-Handed Jill?"

He tsked. "My enemies call me Black Jack. When I was a child, my mother used to sing a nursery rhyme about Jack and Jill." Why was he telling her this? He only had a handful of good memories of his mother, and they were his. "I was trying to be clever. It was a stupid thought."

"No, it's not stupid. I know that nursery rhyme."

"You do?"

"Yes. *Jack and Jill went up the hill to fetch a pail of water. Jack fell down and broke his crown—*"

"And Jill came tumbling after." He smiled at the strange nostalgia a few short words could create. "Fitting, as I suppose I was your downfall."

"What if you were my savior?"

He looked away. "I'm no one's savior."

"Did you take me because you wanted to hurt Peter? Did he do something to you?"

"It's safest to leave our secrets in the shadows, darling." He craved telling her the whole truth, but feared her loyalties might lie with his brother. "Why would you think my taking you has to do with Peter?"

"It felt like revenge."

Something cold settled in the pit of his stomach. "All of it?"

"No. In the end, it was only about us. But in the beginning, it was clear you wanted to send a message."

"What if it was revenge?"

"It might have started that way, but I think you've changed your mind."

"How so?"

She shrugged. "I can't explain it. I just have this feeling that you would think it rude to use me that way."

He chuckled at her logic. "I used you all night."

"For yourself."

She was right. Initially, he'd wanted to use her to send a message. Now, he didn't even want to share the thought of her with Peter or any other man. She was his and his alone. "I'm glad he never had you."

"If you tell him what we did, he won't care. I was being honest when I told you I'm nothing to him."

"I believe you."

"You do?"

"Yes. But it will still matter to him."

"He's engaged to someone else."

"Nevertheless, he wanted you, and I got to you first."

"So I guess you won whatever game you're playing."

It didn't feel like winning.

The silence stretched between them.

"What's going to happen to me?"

He turned to fully face her. "What do you want to happen?" This was uncharted territory.

"I can't go back to who I used to be."

He didn't want her to go back. Period. "Life isn't easy at sea." She was cut out for better. They both knew it, and they needed to accept that their association had an end date. "It's draining and rough on even the hardest men."

"Do you ever go home?"

"I don't have a home. For two decades, the sea has been all I've known. I trust how absolutely unpredictable she can be, and therefore, I'm never disappointed."

"But you're more than twenty years old. Where did you live before then?"

Was he honestly allowing her to question him? "A place worse than hell."

"Saint Mercy's Home for Orphaned Boys?"

He stilled. "Where did you hear that?"

"The Lost Boys talked about the orphanage where they met Peter. Were you there too?"

He looked away, preferring not to see those memories right now. They were all lost boys, some a little more lost than others.

"Please tell me. I just want to understand you. I'd never betray your confidence."

Like a tower of bricks, he shuddered before his boundaries came tumbling down. "Peter was my brother."

Her eyes widened. "Because you were both in the same orphanage?"

"No, because we both shared the same mom. He's my blood."

"But your last name's Hook."

"Right. So was his at one time, before the Pangbournes adopted him." James kept his stare on the water, his memories flashing back to that horrible time. "Once we were separated, it took me a lifetime to find him. I didn't know his new name or where he moved."

"But you did find him."

"Yes. And when I finally crossed his path again, he looked right through me as if I truly were a ghost from his past."

"I'm sorry." She rested her hand on his.

He glanced at the hooks on the wall where she'd hung the coats side by side. "Then he stole from me."

She followed his stare. "So you kidnapped me in revenge."

"Well, you were wearing my coat."

Her shoulders lowered. "That's all I am then, revenge?"

He caught her hand when she tried to pull away. "No. Turns out you're something I didn't know could exist. But eventually, my plan will play out, and he'll try to steal you back. Regardless of my feelings, I'll revel in his envy when he learns what I've done to you because I'm that broken inside. And you'll likely go back to the place you came from, and over time, this will be nothing more than a story you tell about a vicious pirate and a boy who forgets."

"That's not how I'll tell it."

"No?"

She shook her head. "There was more than revenge between us, James. I felt it. I know you did, too."

Yes, he fucking felt it. He was still feeling it. It was, perhaps, the most terrifying thing he'd ever felt, and it left him unhinged in ways he couldn't explain.

"That's it." He leaned forward and grabbed her arms, pulling her off the stool and into the tub.

"Oh!" Water sloshed over the edge and onto the floor as he pulled her onto him. He needed to kiss her before it was too late, before he lost his chance forever. He didn't believe in captivity, but he desperately wanted to keep her with him forever.

He wanted her solely for himself because it had been an eternity since anyone looked at him like they needed him the way she did.

"What do you want?" he demanded, kissing her passionately. "Tell me and I'll give it to you."

"I...I don't know."

"Yes, you do." He peeled off her wet shirt and threw it aside. His mouth closed over her pert nipples, and he suckled them into sharp tips. "Would you stay here if I asked?"

"What choice do I have?"

"You have a choice. I'm giving it to you. What do you choose?"

"I...I don't know."

"Think. What does your gut tell you?"

"I don't think with my gut. I think with my heart." Her hands pressed into his chest as she searched his eyes. "Yours is racing."

He held her hand there. "What does that tell you?"

She tried to pull her touch away, but he held her there.

"You'll get bored of me."

"Impossible." He reached under the water and angled his hard cock so she could feel how utterly far from boring he found her. "I want you."

"For revenge?"

"No. I want to take care of you. You would want for nothing." He cupped her breasts, desperate to show her how satisfying it could be. "We could go wherever you desired—travel the world and see all the wonders."

"What about my family?"

His blood turned cold. "Right." He lifted her off of him, putting the necessary distance between them. "Of course, you'd want to be with your family."

"You're upset."

His lips formed a flat line. It wasn't fair to get upset because she was lucky enough to have people at home who loved her. "No, you should be with them. They probably miss you."

"It's not that simple."

"Why?"

"Because I disobeyed my father. Once he knows I'm safe, he'll be furious. I won't be able to simply disappear again."

"You're an adult, Wendy. How much control could they possibly have over you?"

"Asks the man who took total control from me last night."

"That's different. You surrendered."

"Under duress," she said with a laugh.

"Does that mean you regret it?"

"No. But I will regret leaving when you let me go."

"Who says I'll let you go?"

She met his stare, but behind the challenge hid sadness. "James, we both know this is too complicated for me to stay. At least for now."

He always knew this would be temporary, but the closer they came to the end, the more he hated the idea of ever letting her go.

"We still have time." He lifted her out of the tub, leaving a trail of water on the floor. "As long as you're here, you're still mine." He dried her before the hearth, then backed her into the wall with a possessive kiss.

When he pulled away, she looked up at him with unguarded trust. He traced his fingers down her cheek. Fearful he might lose his will and beg her to stay, he tossed a velvet cushion on the floor and took control. "On your knees."

She lowered to the cushion and looked up at him.

"Now, open your mouth like a good girl."

She parted her lips, and he pressed into her mouth. This was still new to her, so he took it slow.

"That's it. Relax your throat, and let me fuck that pretty mouth." His palms flattened to the wall as he slowly flexed his hips. "Suck it like a good little slut would."

The moment her lips tightened around him he groaned. He'd meant to be gentle, but it wasn't long before he was cupping the back of her head to protect her from the wall.

"Yes, that's a fucking good girl. Keep going. Don't you dare fucking stop. I own that filthy mouth, and I'm going to fuck it until I come."

She moaned as he slid deeper. Losing himself in the delicious sensation, his mind started to wander. This might be the last chance together.

The lump in his throat tightened, and his vision blurred. He didn't want to let her go. He could already sense how awful her absence would feel.

Alone again.

Abandoned.

"Fuck!"

"What's the matter?"

He turned his back on her, pacing the floor as he tried to get a hold of his emotions. "Is this real?"

"Of course, it's real."

How could she go from this back to her refined life? There were two totally different versions of her.

"Which is the real you, the one in London or the one here, kneeling on my floor?"

"Why does one have to be fake?"

"Because it does! If you stay here, you'd be giving up that life. If you leave, you'd go back to living like a modest little church mouse. Either way, you lose something."

"We all lose something. It's called growing up."

"No. You could have it all if you admitted what you actually wanted."

"I haven't figured out what I want yet."

"So you'll go back and pretend you're satisfied until you do?"

"Everyone's pretending on some level."

"I'm not."

"You're different."

"Because I'm honest. Think about what you're saying, Wendy. What does your life matter if it's filled with lies and you have to pretend you're someone else?" He pulled her to his lap. "If you stayed with me, you could be yourself."

"As long as I don't oppose you—"

"No, even if you disagreed with me, I'd accept you." He nuzzled her ear and whispered, "I'd take care of you, see to all your needs, and you could see to mine."

She clung to him. "To what end?"

"Why should there be an end? Why can't it be forever?"

"We barely know each other."

"That's part of the adventure. We'll learn each other's secrets. You could teach me things. And I could teach you."

"What do I know that you don't?"

"Plenty."

Until today, he didn't know what it felt like to be washed by a gentle set of hands. He didn't know how soundly he could sleep with her by his side. He didn't know that he wanted the things he never had until she gave him a glimpse of how such kindness could feel.

She shook her head. "You'll grow tired of me."

"No." The lump in his throat made it nearly impossible to speak. "You could teach me how to love."

"James…" She looked away, and he felt her pulling back, but he wasn't ready to let her go.

"You were right," he confessed. "I have secrets. But I'm

willing to give them all to you if you give me this one thing. I can change—"

"People don't change."

"Then love me the way I am. Is there some part of me that you could learn to love?"

"James…"

He couldn't bear more excuses, so he kissed her possessively, showing her how much he was willing to lay his soul bare to keep her here. "Stay with me."

"I—"

He needed more time to convince her. If he kept kissing her, she'd see.

"Stop! This isn't you!" She shoved him back and covered her abused lips. "You're not a man who begs."

Infuriated by her rejection, he toppled her to the carpet and held her throat. "Is this what you want? A monster?"

"You're not a monster either."

"Then why has no one ever loved me?"

The walls shook, and a loud bang rattled the ship. He was on his feet and rushing to the window.

"What was that?"

A small boat tied to the side of the ship. They were out of time.

"James, what's happening?"

He yanked her off the floor, deposited her on the bed, and rushed to the dresser, flinging a dry shirt at her as he pulled on pants. "Put this on. Don't move from that bed." He snatched his weapons from the dresser as another crash sounded from above, and the floorboards rattled.

"Tell me what's happening!"

"We're under attack. It looks like you're going home."

Her eyes went wide. "Peter's here? On the ship?"

He rushed to the bed, pressing a kiss to her lips as he slipped a key into her hand. "Lock the door behind me and don't open it for anyone, no matter what happens."

"What's going to happen?"

"Just do as I say." Swiping his *tourné* blade from the table, he rushed out the door and up to the deck.

Pistols fired, and men screamed. Bodies and barrels were thrown overboard while others raced into the fight. James froze at the sight of his brother battling with his crew on the lookout.

"Where is she?" Peter demanded, angling a nasty dagger with a golden blade at James.

"She's in my bed."

"Bastard!"

"Yes," he agreed, glad to finally witness his brother's outrage when he felt his revenge. "She's ruined, and I enjoyed every second of it…brother."

"She wasn't yours!" Peter rushed forward and then stilled, his golden brow twitching in confusion. "What did you just call me?"

"You're kidding. Do you really not know who I am?" Could he honestly forget him so completely?

"Black Jack," he said, lifting his blade. "I know exactly who you are—captain of this ship and scourge of the Seven Seas."

"Is that all I am? Look harder, Peter. What do you see?"

"I see nothing. A criminal."

"Shame on you, Peter. You should always know the full name of a man you rob."

"I don't care what your name is—"

"Hook." He grinned when Peter staggered back and lowered his dagger. "The name's Hook."

Realization dawned, and his jaw went slack. "James?"

"That's right. You probably thought I was dead—not that you ever cared to check."

Peter's brow hardened at the sharp criticism, and he raised his dagger again. "Don't blame me if your life's been nothing more than a reeking pile of driftwood and rum. It's not my fault you wasted it envying me."

James' mouth curved into an evil grin. "Is that what you think?"

"Why else would you take her from me?"

"She was never yours!" James had the curved blade of his *tourné* at Peter's throat before he even saw him move.

Peter laughed in his face. "As if abducting her somehow gives you a claim. At least, with me, she went willingly."

Metal clashed around them as the Lost Boys fought the crew. His brother's once-familiar eyes were no longer recognizable. He was a brat. His outlook on life was so skewed by money and ego, he'd forgotten how to feel for others.

"Entitlement has ruined you."

Even with a blade to his throat, Peter refused to shrink. "Do you think I care what someone like you thinks of me?"

"You should care." It was stunning how far apart they actually drifted. "We're brothers."

"I have enough brothers."

James glanced at the Lost Boys. "They're your brothers by circumstance. I'm your brother by blood."

"You're nothing!" Peter hurled him backward, and they were both on their feet, blades pointed at the ready. "Look at you. Look at the undignified life you lead. Did you honestly think we were the same? Did you think you had a shot keeping her?" He laughed. "Pathetic."

"You can't force her to leave if she wants to stay."

"*Ha!* Force her, did you say? She's going to walk off this rotted pile of jetsam willingly."

"She won't." James had doubts, but in his soul, he believed he knew her best. "She's not the woman you think she is."

Peter laughed again. "She's exactly who I know her to be. Good God, man, she's a complete priss—a daddy's girl. She'll return to her boring life in London and marry whoever her father tells her to. Then, she'll spit out half a dozen babies, ruin her figure, and accept her dull life because that's exactly what she's expected to do. And in between feedings and pregnancies, she might occasionally think of you. She might think of how, for one short moment, she played in the slums, but she'll never forgive you for what you did."

"No!"

"Why? Because you won't allow it? You have no authority outside of this ship. You don't exist to them, just like you don't exist to me. And soon, you won't exist to her."

James seethed with insurmountable rage. He wanted to slash the nose clean off his brother's face. "It won't happen because *she* won't allow it."

"Unfortunately, she's not going to have a say. Her father keeps her on a tight leash, and she'll do exactly as she's told." He tsked. "Can you imagine her getting fucked by some wealthy prick—"

The blade of his *tourné* slashed down Peter's cheek. "One more word, and I cut out your tongue."

Peter roared and charged forward, swiping his dagger fast and leaving a deep cut on James' arm as he pivoted away, deflecting his advance. Metal sparked as their blades clinked, matching each advance with another as they mirrored every swipe and dive. Only when James withdrew a longer blade did he get the upper hand and force Peter against the rails, but Peter ducked and lunged, driving James back again. Despite their differences in height and age, they were equally matched in a fight.

A female scream cut through the chaos, and James turned, recognizing Wendy's voice. His eyes widened when he spotted her on the main deck and not locked in his quarters where he'd ordered her to stay.

"Wendy, get back!" Peter's blade sliced a deep gash into his arm. "*Ah!*"

"James!" She raced from the stairs, putting herself directly in the path of danger.

"Get back inside!" Peter swiped again, shredding his pants to ribbons and lacerating his thighs.

"*Peter, don't!*" She raced forward, ignoring James' orders.

Peter lifted his blade, focusing only on cutting him down to size. James threw himself in the line of danger and yelled for her to stop. "I told you to stay inside!"

She staggered, and her eyes went wide just as blood rushed into his mouth.

"*No!*" She screamed.

Pain seared through his back, and he fell to his knees.

"*James!*"

He swayed as Peter withdrew his blade from his back, drowning in the blood flooding his lungs. He tried to speak, but only choked.

The Lost Boys rushed forward, catching Wendy by the arms. She kicked and fought like a feral queen, breaking free and running toward James. "Let go of me!"

James held out his arms to catch her, and time slowed.

"*James...*" her voice faded like a distant echo, and her mouth opened on a silent scream. Blood rushed to his ears.

For a moment, there was no pain besides that which played across Wendy's stunned face and the stab wound in his back. Then, a searing sense of vacancy cut through his bones.

"Noooo!" Wendy fell to her knees in a pool of blood.

He toppled forward, landing painfully on what was left of his arm. A dark-haired man kicked away what was left of James' right hand.

"What have you done?" Wendy's screams were all he could hear as they dragged her away.

Blood pulsed from his wrist, the violent rhythm mocking the steady beat of his still-pumping heart and the air burning his exposed bone and sinew. Looking up at his brother, he had no choice but to plead for mercy. He couldn't bear her to witness what would surely come next.

James sputtered and choked out one final request, "Take her away. Don't let her watch."

Peter glanced at his men and flicked his hand.

"No! You can't do this! James! Please!" Wendy's screams grew more and more hysterical until they finally disappeared.

The pain swallowed him whole. It was a cruel ending and one he probably deserved. His brother's black shadow fell over him, blocking out the light. He kicked the severed hand aside. "Now, you'll never lay a hand on her again."

James rolled to his back, staring up at the sky as he choked on the blood flooding his lungs. His mind raced over his regrets, but none were associated with Wendy. Knowing her had changed him in more ways than a weapon ever could, and her sweet touch would be the last thought he had.

The sound of fighting faded as his men came to his aide. "Cap'n!"

The world narrowed to a white-hot pinhole.

"Sir, stay with us!"

"He's losing too much blood!"

Shutting the concern of his crew out, he closed his eyes, imagining her hands on him again. *James... I'll never leave you...*

"Sir, stay with us."

James smiled, picturing her sweet blue eyes looking up at him.

"Sir, can you hear me?"

A white light blocked the sound as his body went numb. "Hush, darling..." He let out a long, wheezing sigh. "To die... would be...an adventure."

CHAPTER 15

THE CAGELING

Wendy closed the door to the nursery, but her father's booming voice penetrated the rafters and the walls. Whatever he initially thought of Peter, the illusion was gone.

Her walk of shame was not a discreet one. Peter brought her home in James' shirt and coat, and her parents assumed the worst. The evidence of her poor choices was still fresh on her skin. And there was no hiding the blood on their clothes. James's blood.

Peter tried to clean her up, but she flinched away from his touch, refusing to let him put a hand on her.

"*Fine, you explain it to your parents then,*" he'd snapped.

He didn't care about helping her. He only cared about not getting caught.

In the end, Peter accused James of everything, painting himself as a hero. But her father wasn't that gullible. He knew pieces to the puzzle were missing. When he demanded explanations, Peter teetered between playing the polite gentleman and showing his true colors—unaccountable and above criticism.

Wendy didn't care what he said anymore. The memory of Peter stabbing his brother in the back and Bayne cutting off James' hand would haunt Wendy forever. They left him there. Bleeding.

She fought as hard as she could to get back to him, but they drugged her in the end. If not for the clothes on her back, the scent of James on her skin, and her father screaming below, she might have believed it was only a dream.

But it wasn't a dream. And now her life had become a nightmare.

Pressing her face to the cool wood of her bedroom door, she tried to drown out her father's shouting as he took his fury out on Peter. She wondered what other lies he'd tell to skirt any blame.

The thought of lies made her think of James and how he only wanted the truth, no matter how ugly, unsavory, or raw. He might live the life of a pirate, but he was a far more honest man than his brother.

The rafters shook as her father raised his voice again. Peter responded to his shouting with some tale about how he had been by her side the entire time and done everything possible to keep her safe.

"Why not just tell the truth," she whispered, thinking about how Peter had blown her off the moment she refused to sleep with him.

What did it matter anyway? It was over. She was home. She was never going to see James again.

Staggering back from the door, she collapsed on her bed and closed her eyes, pressing a hand to her heart as she tried in vain to connect with James in some spiritual way. But she felt nothing. It was as if he'd never existed at all.

The door clicked, and all thoughts of James scattered to the wind like unspeakable secrets.

"Wendy?" She wiped her eyes as her mother entered the room carrying a tray with a glass of water and a small white pill. "My poor child."

"I'm not a child."

"You're still my daughter." She carried the tray to the bed. "Take this."

"I don't want to take anything."

"It will help with the pain."

Her eyes narrowed at her mother's insistence. "What do you know about my pain?"

She continued to hold out the pill and glass of water. "I know you survived an unspeakable trauma, and you're in need of rest."

Wendy's body only felt numb. The true pain was in her heart. "I'm not taking that." She still felt fuzzy from whatever drug they'd given her to subdue her onto the plane—a flight she had no recollection of.

Her mother set the glass aside. "Peter told us—"

"I don't care what Peter said. He's a liar and a monster."

Her mother tsked. "You're upset. Sometimes, when we're hurting, we lash out at those closest to us, the ones who are only trying to help."

"No, Mother. This isn't about me lashing out or being too naïve to understand what happened to me. I know what happened. I'm the *only one* who knows. But you don't care about the truth. All you and Father care about is how this will look when others hear."

"The Pangbournes are a high-profile family, dear. We must consider the best way to defuse the fallout."

"Fuck the Pangbournes!"

"Wendy!" She actually looked back at the door as if her greatest concern was being overheard.

"What is this obsession you and Father have with the Pangbournes? Is it really just their money? My God, can you think of anything else?"

"Your father has put a lot of work into situating you with a promising future."

"He's engaged, Mother!" She rubbed her temples, unable to conceive how someone could be so blinded by a bank account. "He's also arrogant, egotistical, and horribly entitled. Is that the type of man you and Father want to see me settled down with?"

"All men have ego, dear. Confidence is a good trait."

"No. There's ego, and then there's narcissism. When Peter's not the center of attention, he's dangerous and cruel."

"Perhaps you're being a bit harsh. He did rescue you, Wendy."

"I wasn't a prisoner. I could have left. He was going to let me leave."

Her mother gave her a look of doubt. "I understand how confusing these situations can become. You did what you had to do to survive, but you're not in danger anymore. Perhaps there's someone you could talk to. I'm sure the memories are overwhelming."

"Sure. Whatever." She wiped her nose and sniffled. No one would ever believe her that James had come around. As much as he wanted her to stay, she knew in her heart he would have let her leave. He said himself that he didn't believe in captivity and had no desire to keep her caged.

"But you shouldn't blame Peter, dear. From what I understand, he did everything in his power to help you."

She took a calming breath. This back-and-forth was useless. Her parents only heard what they wanted to hear. "I will never let that man near me again."

"You're upset."

"Yes, Mother. I'm upset. Now, please leave me alone. I just want everyone to leave me alone." She rolled to her side, turning her back on her mother as she left the bedroom.

Eventually, her father stopped yelling, and the front door slammed. Wendy closed her eyes, counting down the seconds before her peace was disrupted again.

Three...

Two—

Her father tapped the door, not waiting for an invitation to barge in. "I want you washed and downstairs in one hour. Leave those clothes for the maid. We'll see that they're incinerated."

Wendy sat up. "Father..."

He looked away with unrestrained fury. "It's too far, Wendy. Too far."

She wasn't going to make an excuse, just an apology. "I'm sorry for making you worry."

His mouth firmed into a flat line. "Sorry won't replace what you lost. You'll realize that soon enough."

She balled her hands into fists. "I didn't *lose* anything. I'm still me."

He shook his head. "People will hear about this. Your good reputation won't hold, and once it's gone, your options will dwindle."

She was tired of having her value tied to her virtue, which invalidly dictated her choices. Men made far worse decisions and saw no consequences. She was through with the double standards. "I can make my own opportunities if I have to."

"Yes," he agreed. "You'll have to. We'll discuss more on the subject after you've cleaned yourself up." With that final reminder, he shut the door.

When she changed out of her clothes, she didn't give them to Liza. Instead, she folded them into a small ball and hid them inside the window seat. They were all she had left of James, and burning his belongings was simply too painful to bear.

Sitting through her father's lecture had been an exercise in zoning out. She thought about how she used to climb trees and run around the yard barefoot with her belly out, equally as free as her brothers. Then one day, she was told to calm down, stand up straight, and suck in her stomach. She'd been holding her breath ever since.

Her image had become a reflection of others, a responsibility, and a detached part of herself. Who she pretended to be and how she carried herself in public was all that mattered. No one cared what was on the inside.

She'd been burying the *unsavory* parts of herself for so long, it was no wonder James had a hard time drawing them out. Since he'd freed her of her inhibitions, her old life no longer felt as natural as it once had because the person they molded her to be was not anywhere near the person she actually was inside.

As if trying to fit into clothes she'd long ago outgrown, coming home left her uncomfortable with her options and panicked to find other solutions. She was no longer that tame bird in a cage. She'd had a taste of freedom, enough to know she wanted more.

It took a whole week for her father to bear her presence

without turning and walking away in disgust, but even then, he refused to meet her eyes. As suspected, rumors got out about her wild night in the Never Lands, and then came the judgmental stares and indiscreet whispers.

It took a lifetime for some to be welcomed by society, but one improper move and a girl could be canceled in a blink. Forever.

By the end of the month, Wendy had moved from a respectable daughter position into total pariah territory. Strangers avoided her. Acquaintances shunned her. Exaggerated stories deformed the truth so much that her excuses were irrelevant. No one cared about the truth. Only James.

The most infuriating thing, however, was how little this impacted Peter's life. He wasn't branded a jezebel or called a criminal. No one knew the horrible things he'd done. They had their sacrificial lamb, and that was all they needed, apparently. And slaughter her reputation they did.

When school was back in session, she held no excitement for her new classes. After the first week of the semester, she decided not to return.

"Wendy, you can't simply give up," her mother cajoled, but there was no plucky, can-do attitude that would change her mind.

"I've made my decision."

"You're being hasty."

"I'm not. I know what I want and what I don't want."

University was not an experience she needed to have in order to feel like her life held value. Nor was a hymen or a husband, for that matter.

"This stubborn side of yours is not going to win people over."

"I don't care about winning people over, Mother." She

was learning to trust her instincts. "Why does every choice I make have to impact others?"

"Because it does."

"No, it doesn't."

"As long as you're in this family under this roof, it does." Her mother left in another frustrated huff.

It seemed much easier to free a bird from its cage than cajole it back inside. Her parents were growing tired of her combative attitude. But she couldn't return to being the miserable, agreeable girl she once was. Not at the expense of her happiness.

Wendy knew she was more than the sum of other people's opinions and was only interested in discovering her true self now that she'd freed her shadow. In her free time, she cleaned the nursery, throwing away old keepsakes that no longer held meaning and making space for whatever her future might be.

Ultimately, all that remained were her favorite clothes, a few pieces of jewelry, and James' coat, which she refused to burn. Sometimes, late at night, she'd put the coat on over her nightgown and stare out her window at the moon, wondering if—wherever James was—he could also see the stars.

Her worry never relented when she thought of him. She imagined him healed because the alternative was too horrible to bear.

There would have been no saving his hand—a severe loss that would have frustrated him to no end but not impacted his authority. James's influence over others came from within. He wore his confidence like armor, and he would not allow such a loss to hinder his hard-earned pride.

But who was taking care of him in private? His conceit was an obstacle that would impede others from seeing to his needs.

She only hoped men like Gideon Starr loved their fierce captain enough to see past the gripes and growls. James would be profoundly hurt after his brother's wretched betrayal and a beast to deal with for a very long time.

Late one night, when she couldn't sleep, she wandered the nursery, fluttering anxiously like a wild bird in a cage. The longer she paced from wall to wall, the more restless she became.

James believed it was a choice to be caged, and cages came in many forms.

With nowhere to go, she tried to free the buzzing energy inside her in other ways. Her fingers trailed over her chest, mimicking the entitled way he'd touched her. She ached to feel his hands on her again, to go to that place where only James could take her, the place where her inhibitions died, and pleasure was king.

She pressed her fingers between her legs, picturing James looking down at her as he pushed her outside of her comfort zone and into that divine place where only they existed.

She imagined his voice whispering close to her ear as his breath tickled the tiny hairs on her neck. *"I can set you free..."*

"Yes," she rasped, closing her eyes to envision his possessive hands on her as she slipped her fingers inside of her heat.

Her breath quickened as she slowly fingered herself, desperately trying to drive herself to the place of freedom and pleasure only he could take her.

"That's a good little slut..." Her fingers pumped faster. *"Let Daddy take care of you..."* But the pleasure receded before she got to that place where a woman sang to the stars.

Bunching her fists in defeat, on the verge of tears, she growled in frustration.

She couldn't breathe here. She was miserable. Alone. Incomplete.

Maybe James was right. Perhaps it was better to struggle than to be forced to live a life as someone you're not. This nursery, this house, this life… None of it fit anymore.

The damage was done. Living a quiet life would not erase the rumors. Those stories would follow her for the rest of her life, because some people had nothing better to do.

Let them live vicariously through her adventures, she thought, no longer caring about how they judged her. At least she had an adventure to speak of.

And who was to say that adventure had to be her last? If she wanted to get out of this cage, she only needed to flip the latch and leave. Fear was the only thing holding her there.

Rising from the bed, she went to the window and opened the glass. The wind kicked up the tails of her coat like heavy sails. If she closed her eyes, she could vaguely scent the salt air coming from the coast. And if she concentrated hard enough, she could imagine the rocking creak of a ship.

Turning to face the nursery, she looked at the room dispassionately. It was a time capsule that would prevent her from growing up as long as she stayed safely inside.

She went to the sewing kit, where she hid her money and counted her savings. It was enough to get back to the Isles of Kassel, but how far would she have to go to find James? He could be anywhere by now.

Her mind spun like a compass, whirling wildly over all the possible places he could have gone. It wouldn't take long for her to spend her savings, and then how would she survive?

A devious thought took hold. The old Wendy might be easily defeated, but she was no longer that malleable, obedient girl anymore. Even if it came to stealing, she would do what she must to find James.

Red-Handed Jill was going to see her Black Jack again.

Her heart beat wildly in her chest as she imagined falling into his arms. He said he didn't know how to love, but that wasn't true. Love was acceptance, and James accepted her without condition. He wanted all of her—the light and the shadows—and she wanted all of him.

Mind made up, she zipped her travel bag and changed into jeans. The coat she'd come to love rested comfortably on her shoulders as she looked back at the nursery one last time. There was no hesitation as she shut the door to her past and turned toward her future.

Her parents' bedroom door was closed, a dim light shining beneath the crack. Wendy would call them in the morning, not to justify her decision but to save them worry.

Tiptoeing down the stairs to not wake Nana, she quietly unlocked the door. This was it. She was finally doing what she wanted and through trying to please everyone else.

Slipping into the cold night, she shut the front door with a soft click and turned the key.

Sometimes, her mind played tricks on her, and as she turned, her blood chilled. In the shadows of the streetlamp, a figure stood, much like James, with natural authority and dispassionate ease.

"He's not real," she whispered, but the shadow moved to the gate in a way only James moved.

"Going somewhere?"

She didn't trust her eyes. Her gaze dropped to his hand. If he were really standing there, his hand would be gone, but the ruffled cuff of his jacket hid it from view.

"It's gone."

Her breath hitched. That was his voice. Only he could send chills racing down her spine like that.

"Are you really here?" she whispered, pinching herself to see if she felt the pain and gasped when the sting registered.

"I'm sure I'm the last person you want to see—"

"No," she stopped him right there, tossing the bag off her shoulder and onto the pavement as proof. "I was coming to find you."

"You're running away?" His gaze flicked from the bag back to her.

"I was running to you."

"Why?"

A shaky smile skated across her lips, and her confidence wavered. What if he didn't feel their connection as deeply as she did? "You're all I think about."

"In what way?"

She bit her lip. "Every possible way I can. You're my happy thought."

He glanced away and cursed under his breath. "Don't toy with me, darling."

"I'm not. You're all I've thought about since I left the Never Lands." Heat crawled up her neck. "At night—when I'm alone—it's intolerable."

He stepped forward, crossing the threshold into her yard, and then stilled, looking up at the dark windows.

"They're asleep."

He took another step, and her heart whipped wildly behind her ribs. "They say there's a phantom ache when you lose a limb, but my only pain's been here." He pressed his hand to his heart. "It's an unbearable agony, the emptiness I feel since you left."

"I have the same pain."

He closed the distance and gripped her coat. Moonlight glinted off the polished hook where his hand used to be.

"What they did to you…" She caressed the cold metal and searched his gaze. "You didn't deserve that."

"It's done. Of all the things they took from me that day, my hand was the least of it."

"I would have stayed—"

He smashed his mouth to hers, and her long-lost sense of balance returned. She climbed up his body, needing to be as close to him as humanly possible. His hands roamed over her with unapologetic entitlement until they finally knotted in her hair.

"I've been an insufferable tyrant since you've been gone."

"I'll never leave again. I want to see the world with you."

"My ship is at your command." His fist tightened in her hair, delivering the perfect pinch of possessive pain as he greedily took her mouth in a possessive kiss. "I could fuck you right here."

"I could let you." She moaned, grinding her body against his to get closer.

He grabbed her ass in an unmistakable claim. "I'm sorry," he whispered against her throat.

She couldn't get enough of his kisses. "Why?"

"Because now that I have you back, I'm never letting you go."

She framed his face and smiled against his lips. "Black Jack has finally found his Red-Handed Jill."

He growled against her mouth. "By far, the greatest treasure I've ever stolen."

The only thing he'd stolen was her heart. "I love you, James."

He stilled and searched her eyes. "Is that true?"

"I'd never lie to you."

He hugged her tight. "Then this truly is your end, Wendy Moira Angela Darling. By dawn, you'll be irrevocably mine and newly named Mrs. James Hook."

"I look forward to it."

And they lived happily—and wickedly—ever after...

THE END

Did you like visiting the Isles of Kassel?
If so, this is your invitation back. CLICK HERE to find out which wicked man—or should I say *men*—are up next in the Villains of Kassel series!

Want more edgy romance from Lydia Michaels?

Subscribe to her mailing list and receive 7 FREE books!
Click here to claim your freebies!

Free Books Here!

GILDED LOCKS

A Dark Reverse Harem Romance

She broke into the wrong house.
Now, three brutal men will make her pay—with her body,
her secrets, and her soul.

When runaway heiress Marigold Calder crashes into the
forbidden Isles of Kassel during a blizzard, she's desperate for
shelter. The isolated mountain lodge seems like salvation,
until she realizes it belongs to *The Bears*, three massive
Russian brothers who own the most exclusive—and
dangerous—private men's club in Kassel.

HUNTER

The violent one who takes what he wants

STONE

The cold mastermind who'll break her with a single look

ASH

The deceptively gentle one who's anything but safe

In Kassel, trespassing has a price. And once they catch her sleeping in *their* bed, eating *their* food, and wearing *their* clothes, these territorial predators decide she's theirs. Trapped by the storm and their obsession, Marigold discovers a dark connection between their families that turns their hospitality into a hunt for revenge. Now, they won't just keep her, they'll ruin her.

A scorching hot, morally grey, billionaire reverse harem featuring possessive anti-heroes, forced proximity, primal dominance, explosive chemistry, and a heroine who refuses to break. This standalone dark romance contains mature themes and explicit scenes that will leave you breathless.
Step into their den... if you dare.

CLICK HERE to PURCHASE

🔥🔥🔥🔥🔥

Reverse Harem/Why Choose • Dark Romance • Forced Proximity • Snowbound • Captive Romance • Morally Grey Heroes • Touch Her and Die • Possessive/Obsessive • Enemies to Lovers • Found Family • Russian Heroes • Private Club • Billionaire Romance • Secret Identity • Revenge Plot • High Heat

Take Me To Gilded Locks!

About the Author

To receive Lydia's Newsletter and 7 FREE Books, click HERE !

Free Books Here!

Lydia Michaels is the bestselling and award-winning author of more than fifty novels. She writes heart-clenching, unpredictable romance with dark elements and high heat. Her work is character-driven and bursting with broken heroes and badass females. With a sweet spot for overbearing, territorial types, her deeply emotional books are spicy, emotionally satisfying, and guaranteed to leave readers with many book hangovers.

Lydia is the consecutive winner of the *2018 & 2019 Author of the Year Award* from *Happenings Media* and the recipient of the *2014 Best Author Award* from the Courier Times. She has been featured by *USA Today*, *Romantic Times Magazine*, the *Women in Publishing Summit*, and more.

Michaels started her author career in 2007, becoming a recognized presence and advocate within the publishing industry. She is the CEO of LMC Consulting, a certified author coach specializing in character and plot development, and the founder of the *East Coast Author Convention*, the *Behind the Keys Author Retreat*, and www.LydiaMichaels-Books.com.

She is happily married to her childhood sweetheart. Her favorite things include cooking Italian cuisine, hosting extravagant dinner parties, sipping espresso martinis, listening to her husband play piano, and escaping to her coastal home on the Jersey Shore. She's an LGBTQ ally, a BLM supporter, a firm believer that the patriarchy must end (women's rights are human rights), and an advocate for pediatric cancer research.

L Y D I A

Follow Lydia Michaels on social media!
Facebook | Instagram | TikTok

ALSO BY LYDIA MICHAELS

BOOKS BY SERIES

Many first in series books are FREE

Grab them here!

MCCULLOUGH MOUNTAIN

Almost Priest *

Beautiful Distraction

Irish Rogue

British Professor

Broken Man

Controlled Chaos

Hard Fix

Intentional Risk

JASPER FALLS

Wake My Heart *

The Best Man

Love Me Nots

Pining For You

My Funny Valentine

Side Squeeze

CALAMITY RAYNE

Calamity Rayne Gets a Life *

Calamity Rayne Back Again

Calamity Rayne Gets Hitched

Calamity Rayne Over the Moon

Calamity Rayne Knocked Up

THE SURRENDER TRILOGY

Falling In

BreakingOut

Coming Home

Ruthless Billionaires

One Billion Secrets *

Two Billion Enemies

MASTERMIND

Blind

Untied

NEW CASTLE

First Comes Love *

If I Fall

Shattered Vows

Remember Me

ADDICTED TO YOU

Crush *

Bang

Throb

THE ORDER OF VAMPIRES

Original Sin *

Dark Exodus

Prodigal Son

Immortal Bastard

Primal Kill

Blood Moon

VILLAINS OF KASSEL

Hush Darling

Gilded Locks

Feast of the Fallen

STAND ALONES

La Vie en Rose

Simple Man

Sugar

Breaking Perfect

Hurt

Protege

FOLLOW LYDIA!

Do you follow LYDIA?
TikTok @LydiaMichaels
Instagram @lydia_michaels_books
Facebook @LydiaMichaels
Goodreads
BookBub

Show Your LOVE & Support the Book Community!
If you enjoyed this story, please tell your friends about it and/or leave a review.

THANK YOU FOR YOUR REVIEW!

*Reviews help authors so much! If you left a review for
this book, I greatly appreciate it!
Thank you,
Lydia*

Where can I leave a review?
Goodreads
BookBub
Lydia Michaels Shop
Learn More!